Not Our Summer

CASIE BAZAY

RP|TEENS
PHILADELPHIA

Running Press Teens
Hachette Book Group
1290 Avenue of the Americas,
New York, NY 10104
www.runningpress.com/rpkids
@RP_Kids

Printed in the United States of America

First Edition: May 2021

Published by Running Press Teens, an imprint of Perseus Books, LLC,
a subsidiary of Hachette Book Group, Inc. The Running Press Teens
name and logo is a trademark of the Hachette Book Group.

The Hachette Speakers Bureau provides a wide range of authors for
speaking events. To find out more, go to www.hachettespeakersbureau.com
or call (866) 376-6591.

The publisher is not responsible for websites (or their content)
that are not owned by the publisher.

Print book cover and interior design by Marissa Raybuck.

Library of Congress Cataloging-in-Publication Data has been applied for.

ISBNs: 978-0-7624-7229-1 (hardcover),
978-0-7624-7228-4 (ebook)

LSC-C

Printing 1, 2021

For Summer,
Thank you for so many years of friendship
and for believing in me

CHAPTER 1
K. J.

WHERE DOES SOMEONE EVEN GET A BRIGHT GREEN casket like that?

The question hasn't stopped rattling through my brain since Mom and I snuck into the chapel and slid into the very last pew. There are a lot more important things to be worried about at the moment, but all I can think is, *What. The. Hell?* Grandpa was a weird duck—everyone knew that—but I definitely never saw this coming. The wood creaks as Mom shifts in her seat and pushes a strand of hair behind her ear for the hundredth time. It's a nervous tic of hers, but I get it. Being here is beyond awkward for both of us.

Two rows ahead, an old lady with painted-on eyebrows turns to squint at us. She's probably trying to figure out why we're sitting in the back of the chapel instead of up front with the rest of our family.

Maybe she doesn't know *the story*. Or maybe she does and thinks my grandpa's death is reason enough to move past it, but fact is, the rift in my family has held strong for practically two decades now—since before my birth, anyway. Things won't be changing anytime soon. I give her a "whatcha gonna do old lady" look, and she turns back around.

Another hymn begins, and along with it, a chorus of off-key voices. Mom and I keep our mouths clamped shut—not that we know the words anyway. I stare at my shoes, questioning if gray Converse and black jeans were the wrong choice for today. It's not like I own anything nicer, and my closet has definitely never seen a dress.

Mom leans in close, her breath reeking of strong coffee. "As soon as they start lining up for the walk-by, we're out of here."

I give a subtle nod. I have no desire to see my grandpa inside that grasshopper-green death box. I'd rather remember him the way he was. Well, the way he was the last time I saw him, anyway. Was it really three years ago?

The music fades, soon replaced by the sounds of sniffling and Great Aunt Velda's babbling. It's really sad and all, but I have bigger worries at the moment. Right now, I just want to pay my respects and get out of here without my witchy Aunt RaeLynn or my equally horrid cousin Becka trying to start something with me and my mom. That's about the only thing that would make today worse than it's already been.

The reverend steps to the front again, and it takes everything I've got to pry my eyes away from the casket and focus on him.

"Elijah Walker was a unique man," he says with the air of someone who knew my grandpa well. I doubt they ever met. He's just repeating what someone else has told him. RaeLynn, if I had to guess. "He had a special appreciation for insects and spent countless hours on his collections. They were a sight to behold, from what I hear."

Yep, that confirms my suspicion. If he'd met my grandpa, then he definitely would have seen the bug collections. The reverend continues, telling a story from Grandpa's childhood. "Elijah got a pony for Christmas one year. He named her Penny, and she stayed at his grandparents' farm. He rode Penny every time he went to visit his grandparents."

I've never heard this story before, but then again, there's probably a lot I don't know about Grandpa. Of course, there's no mention of his condition—the one that kept him homebound for the past thirty years. He rarely ever left his eleven-acre property.

I glance at Mom, who's staring straight ahead, her poker face still on. There's no telling what's going through her brain right now. Maybe she's thinking about all the holidays we didn't spend with Grandpa. We should have gone around more. What happened with Mom and RaeLynn wasn't his fault. He just got caught in the middle of it all.

The reverend leads us in prayer and a final hymn begins. Mom's bony elbow pushes into my side. "Let's go," she whispers, and before I know it, she's practically dragging me out of the chapel and into the brightly lit foyer. A lady in a black pantsuit gives us a sympathetic smile. She probably thinks things were getting too difficult to deal with in there. She'd be right, but it has nothing to do with my grandpa.

Mom and I bolt to the parking lot and both sigh with relief once we reach the car. "Thank god that's over," she says, voicing my exact thoughts.

We made it and we didn't have to talk to a single person in there.

It's early May but blazing hot inside Mom's '98 Cutlass Sierra. The heat always brings out the nasty smell in here, too. Like old bologna. Mom swears there must be a piece crammed into some crevice we've yet to find. She puts the key in the ignition and turns it, but the car only makes a pathetic whining sound.

"Damn it!" She pounds her palm on the top of the steering wheel and tries the engine again. It clicks this time. "Damn, damn, damn." Her words match the beat of the annoying sound. "Why do you have to do this to me now?"

I don't mention the fact that her car tends to crap out every other month or so. She needs a new battery but won't fork out the money for one. "Do you have the jumper cables?" I ask instead.

She grumbles under her breath and fixes me with an annoyed look. "Who are we gonna ask to jump it, huh? Our family hates us, and it's not like we know any of these other people."

I stare toward the chapel, a bead of sweat now trickling down one side of my face. The rotten bologna smell has settled inside my nostrils, more irritating than puke-worthy now. You can get used to anything if you're around it long enough. "How'd Grandpa know all these people anyway? He never went anywhere."

Mom grasps the steering wheel with both hands, staring straight ahead. "Who knows? I think some of them might be old coworkers or students from the university." She shakes her head. "Maybe some other bug people, too."

The heat is really getting to me now, so I reach for my handle and shove the door open before I suffocate. A few funeral-goers stand outside the double doors, their voices carrying on the light breeze. I swipe the sweat away from my cheek with the back of my hand. "What about Digger?" I nod toward the middle-aged bearded guy standing outside the chapel entrance, lighting up a cigarette.

Mom huffs and opens her own door. "Looks like he's our only option."

Ten minutes later, Digger's white van is pulled up onto the grass beside us, and he's hooking up the jumper cables.

"Surprised you two showed today," he says in a husky voice.

Mom puts on a fake smile and gives an even faker laugh. "Oh, come on, Digger, it's my dad. Why wouldn't we come?"

Arms crossed, I keep my gaze focused on Digger. I'm afraid to look any other direction, lest someone make eye contact with me. His beer gut spills out from beneath the bottom of his gray T-shirt, but I try not to look at that part. Still leaning over the engine, he glances up at Mom. "You sure don't seem too tore up about it."

In a flash, her expression changes and she jabs a fist onto each hip. "Of course I'm upset." But then her scowl softens as she seems to remember that he's helping us in our time of crisis. "This is just . . . a little strange for us. I'm sure you understand. I've already done plenty of mourning in private."

This is true. Mom bawled her eyes out on Wednesday, the day she found out Grandpa had died. The fact that she'd learned about his death on Facebook didn't help matters. She's been in a funk ever since.

Digger connects the cables. "All right, go give it a try."

The starter clicks a few more times, then the engine rumbles to life. "Thanks, Digger," I say.

He looks at me as if he's just noticed I've been standing here the whole time. He coughs and spits into the grass. "So how old are you now?"

I push my hands into my pockets, self-conscious under the weight of his stare. "Uh, eighteen." Since a few weeks ago, anyway.

He studies me for a moment and grunts. Maybe he's just surprised I've managed to reach adulthood while being raised by my mom. I get it. It surprises me, too, sometimes.

I nod toward the cables. "I'll take those back if you're done."

"Yep." He unhooks them from the vehicles and hands them over.

"Thanks," I repeat. What else is there to say? "See ya later."

I hop in the car, tossing the cables onto the back seat. Semi-cool air blasts from the vents, and I adjust one to point right at my face. This car might be a piece of shit, but at least the air conditioner still works.

Mom waves at Digger as we back out of the parking spot. A line of cars moves up behind the hearse, preparing to take Grandpa to his final resting place, and a small stab of guilt pokes at my chest. I kind of hate that we're going to miss the graveside service, but it's not like going is really an option. No one wants us there.

As we drive toward the parking lot exit, I spot Aunt RaeLynn in her sleek black dress and three-inch heels. Standing beside a shiny red Jeep, she's talking with my cousin, Becka, and another woman. She looks up as we pass, and her mouth pushes into a deep frown. My guilt transforms into bitterness, and I have to resist the urge to flip her off. Because that would be totally inappropriate, of course. Becka's blond head whips around as she follows her mother's disapproving gaze, and I can actually see her eye roll from here.

To hell with being appropriate. I roll down the window and give them the bird as we drive away. Beside me, Mom lets out a loud cackle.

I have to laugh, too. "Man, that felt good."

As soon as we pull onto the roadway, Mom's laughter comes to an abrupt halt. When I look over, tears are once again spilling down her cheeks. "I hate this," she mutters. "I hate the way she makes me feel. Like she has a right to everything, and I don't."

A lump starts to form in my throat, but I force it back down. "She's a bitch, Mom. Just like you've always said. Hopefully, we'll never have to see them again." My words were intended to be reassuring, but Mom starts full-on bawling now. "Pull over. Let me drive."

Fifteen minutes later, we've crossed the Arkansas–Oklahoma border, and Mom's tears have dried, but now she looks like a half-crazed raccoon with black mascara smudged beneath her eyes and her face all splotchy and red. At least she held it together during the service. It would have only humiliated her more to let her sister see her like this.

I pull into Maple Village Mobile Home Park, stopping in front of the fourth trailer on the right. Home sweet home. Mom hurries inside before any of the neighbors can see her. I, however, still haven't shed a single tear. If I wore makeup, it would still be perfectly in place. Sitting on the top front porch step, I pull the pack of cigarettes from my hidey hole beneath the ceramic frog planter. I light up a cig, and after a couple long drags, the nicotine starts to work its magic. The funeral and my god-awful relatives fade from my mind. Signs of spring are everywhere—Grandpa's favorite season. *It's when the bugs come out to play*, he once told me. Grandpa and his bugs. Not sure I'll ever understand the fascination.

A bang comes from the trailer next door, and I nearly drop my cigarette. Someone yells, "Shut up!" and Carter comes busting out onto the back deck, cheeks flushed, and a scowl etched across his face. He stomps around for a few seconds before noticing me sitting here.

He freezes in place and shoves his hands in his jeans pockets, trying to look chill. "Oh, hey, K. J."

"You okay?"

Carter doesn't answer; he just comes to sit beside me. I hold out the pack of cigarettes and my lighter, which he takes. "It's my freakin' mom." He lights up, sucking in a drag. "I swear, sometimes I want to strangle her."

I can't help but smirk. I know the feeling, though my anger turns to pity when it comes to my mom most of the time. Life hasn't been kind to her.

"She's giving me three weeks after graduation to get moved out."
Carter turns to face me. "Can you believe that crap?" His deep green
eyes are distracting, but that long, stringy, ash-blond hair has always
been the deal breaker for me. Plus, he's practically like a brother. We've
been neighbors and friends for ten years now. He shakes his head.
"What the hell am I gonna do?"

I rub my chin, pretending to think about this for a second. "Hey, I
have an idea. Maybe you should quit playing *Call of Duty* and get a job."

"No shit, Sherlock." He smiles and takes another drag, turning to
stare off into the distance. The two new kids from across the street
hop on their bikes and take off racing along the gravel road. Carter
and I used to do that, too, when we were younger. It's a ten-minute
ride around the entire park. If you make the loop twice, it's almost
enough time to settle the sting after the kids on the school bus call you a
white trash dyke. "What about you?" Carter asks. "What are your plans
after graduation?"

I shrug. "Don't really have any."

He pushes his shoulder into mine. "You should. You're smart. You
should go to college or something."

"Yeah, right. Don't think many colleges are dying to snatch up
C students." I don't add that I've also got two Ds right now.

"That's because you never do your homework. You'd have straight
As if you did."

It's probably true. I can ace most tests without trying, and despite
what many people think, I actually do listen to my teachers. I just do it

while I'm doodling in my notebook most the time. After one last drag, I toss my cigarette onto the step below and squish it with the toe of my shoe.

"Mom can't afford to pay for college anyway. She can barely keep up with bills half the time."

Carter glances toward my front door, then back at me. He lowers his voice. "If she'd quit going to the casino, she might be able to afford it."

Something prickles at the base of my skull. "Shut up, Carter."

His brows pinch together like I've actually hurt his feelings. "It's just . . ."

I hold up a hand, quickly cutting him off. "You know how I feel about other people bad-mouthing my mom. That's *my* job."

He shakes his head. "Sorry. Don't be pissed at me, okay? I can't handle it right now."

I snort and give in to a smile. "Whatever."

"Hey, I've got to run to the store for some toilet paper." He nods toward the faded black Ford Ranger in his drive. "Wanna come with?"

"Tempting, but no thanks."

He shrugs. "Suit yourself."

Just as Carter's standing to leave, my phone buzzes in my back pocket. "Talk to you later, Cart," I say with a wave.

I don't recognize the number on my caller ID but answer anyway.

"Is this Katherine Walker?" The man's voice is deep and unfamiliar.

I almost hang up, figuring it's a telemarketer or someone wanting donations, but I'm feeling testy today. Maybe I'll give this guy a run for his money.

"Yep, it's me. What do you want?"

"Miss Walker, I'm sorry to bother you right now, but your mother hasn't answered my calls."

"Did she miss a payment or something? What do you want me to do about it?"

"No, no, this isn't about a bill, Miss Walker. My name is Jeffrey Sisco. I'm your grandfather's lawyer."

Something twitches inside my stomach, and I sit up a little straighter. "Oh . . . sorry."

"It's fine." A beat of silence passes. "Miss Walker, I need to meet with you and your mother. We have some matters to discuss. Your grandfather's will, namely. Your Aunt RaeLynn suggested meeting next Monday evening."

My jaw drops open and all the moisture evaporates from my mouth. I have to clear my throat in order to answer. "Um, we can't meet with her. I don't know if you know, but . . ."

"Ah, yes. I know all about the family dispute."

Heat crawls up my neck, making me itchy. Had Grandpa really told this man *everything*? "Then you should know it's not a possibility."

"It's what your grandfather wanted," Mr. Sisco says. "He was very specific in his requests."

"Listen, you really need to talk to my mom about this."

"Like I said, I've tried her phone. Several times actually. I left her a message, but she still hasn't returned my call."

Yeah, Mom can be bad about that sometimes. "I'll tell her to call you," I say. "Promise."

"You can tell her it involves a large sum of money."

I snort. "Yeah, right."

"I'm quite serious, Miss Walker."

I pull the phone away from my ear to stare at it for a moment. Is this some kind of sick prank call? I press the phone back to my ear. "Listen, I don't know what you think you're doing, but this isn't funny. I gotta go." I hang up and pull out another cigarette, rolling it between my fingers and wondering if the call was possibly legit. Grandpa had been somewhat secretive. But Mom should be the one to decide if Mr. Sisco is telling the truth or not. I push the cigarette back into the pack and slide it beneath the planter. The screen door slams behind me as I enter the trailer.

"Mom?" She doesn't answer, but shuffling noises carry from her bedroom down the hall. I knock on her closed door.

"Yeah? Come in."

I find her reorganizing her sock drawer—another nervous habit she's developed over the years. She cleans when she's stressed, or upset, or worried about something, which means our house is usually spotless. "Someone named Mr. Sisco called. He says he's Grandpa's lawyer."

She closes the sock drawer and perches on the side of her bed, staring up at me anxiously. The disastrous makeup is gone, but her nose is bright red and her face, still splotchy. "And?" she asks.

"He said he needs to meet with us. To discuss the will. He also said it involves a large sum of money."

Mom's eyes widen, so much so that they look like they might actually pop out of her head. "So that's the guy who's been calling me."

She nods with the realization. "I wonder why he didn't say so in his message."

"No idea. You should probably call him back, though."

"Let me use your phone." She stretches a hand my way. "Mine's on the charger."

"There's one little problem," I say, handing it over. "We have to meet with RaeLynn, too."

Mom's face pales, and she squeezes the phone in her hand. Her eyes shift to the floor as her shoulders rise and fall with a deep breath. "Well . . ." She looks thoughtful for a moment. "I guess we'll just have to suck it up, then."

I lean against the doorframe, trying to register what she just said. Because if I heard Mom correctly, hell has just frozen over.

CHAPTER 2

BECKA

"BECKA, PASS!"

I look right to see Leah is wide open. Dribbling past the Lady Hawks defender coming at me, I make a clean pass. With little effort, Leah collects the ball and shoots, sending the ball soaring past the keeper's outstretched hands and into the far corner of the net. Leah and I fist bump before jogging back toward center field.

"Nice assist, Cowles," Coach yells from the sidelines.

Yes, it was, thank you very much. Eyes focused on the opposing forward about to kick off, I get back into my game stance.

"Go Becka," someone yells from the stands, and I swear it sounds so much like my little brother, I have to turn and look.

Wham! The soccer ball smacks me hard in the chest, just above my left boob. I grit my teeth before anything can come out of my mouth.

I don't know who yelled my name, but it wasn't Ricky. Of course it wasn't Ricky. What on earth is wrong with me? Grandpa's funeral must be messing with my head.

Whitney's already covering my slack and dribbling upfield. I shake off the pain and move forward. A Hawks defender steals the ball from Whitney, pounding it all the way back to our defense. Dang it. I wheel around and run in the opposite direction just in time to see our keeper has snatched up the ball. I jog backward, preparing for the punt. It could be my ball again any second. My left pec still stings like the devil, but I try to stay focused.

Head in the game, I tell myself. *Head in the game.*

Sure enough, it soars straight to me. I trap the ball with my thigh and dribble upfield. Our forwards are covered up by Hawks defense, and two midfielders are headed my way fast. I fake right, then touch the ball left, trying to throw them off, but they're not falling for it. Number forty-seven—the tall girl—matches my stride, preparing to make a swipe for the ball. It's now or never. I make the shot, but my foot connects all wrong and the ball goes flying out of bounds, nowhere near the goal. The crowd groans and I squeeze my eyes shut. I can't believe I blew it like that.

The Hawks are setting up for a goal kick when three whistle blasts pierce the warm evening air. I blow out a breath, a certain emptiness filling up my chest instead. We won. Barely. Not that I had much to do with it.

Coach doesn't say a word about my missed shot. He knows I came straight to the game from the funeral, so apparently I get a free pass to screw up today. Too bad it doesn't keep me from being mad at myself. What a stupid mistake.

"Nice game," Maddie tells me, but I'm not sure she means it. That was the worst I've played in forever. She gives me that sympathetic look I've gotten to know so well lately. "And I'm really sorry about your grandpa."

I wave her apology away with my hand. "Thank you. I'm okay, though."

Maddie looks skeptical. "Text me if you need to talk, 'kay?"

I nod, knowing full well that I won't. At least not about my grandpa. "Sure."

After Gatorades and a talk from Coach, which I barely hear thanks to my loud, self-chastising thoughts, we all head our separate ways. Mom wraps an arm around my shoulder as we walk toward her Jeep. Neither one of us says a word.

Back at home, dinner is some kind of cheesy casserole Mom microwaves and serves up on paper plates. Someone from church has dropped food off every day since Grandpa passed.

I take a seat across from her at the kitchen table. "This one looks good. Or at least better than that meatloaf thing yesterday."

She gives me a half-hearted smile. Now that her makeup is washed off, the dark circles beneath her eyes are more prominent. She looks exhausted. Older, too. "It's Mexican lasagna, I think. That's what Mrs. Rayburn brought last time . . ."

Neither of us wants to talk about last time, though, so instead we dig into our dinner. For a while, the only sounds are those of silverware scraping on our plates and the ticking clock on the nearby wall.

"So," I say, trying to make conversation, "when's Tim coming home?"

Mom takes a sip of water and settles back into her chair. "Next Tuesday."

In some ways, my stepdad lucked out. He's been in China on business and missed this whole ordeal with Grandpa. "It's weird that they wouldn't let him fly back early for the funeral." I take another goocy bite. Only there's a jalapeño hiding inside this one, and I need to guzzle half my glass of sweet tea in order to soothe the burn on my tongue.

Mom shrugs. "It was an important deal. It would have cost too much to fly him home and then back to China again." She pokes at the casserole with her fork. "And it's okay. I handled things fine on my own."

She did, but I know she would have much rather had Tim here. At least it's all over now. I shake my head, recalling the scene with my cousin and aunt outside the chapel. "Can you believe what K. J. did today? She's such a jerk."

An odd-looking smile crosses Mom's face. "Can't say I was all that surprised. And besides, you know that apple hasn't fallen far from the tree."

"True."

"Oh, that reminds me," she says, perking up a bit. "We need to meet with Grandpa's lawyer Monday evening to go over his will."

I'm not sure why mentioning K. J. made her think of that, but I nod. "Okay." Then I can't help but laugh. "I hope he's not leaving me all his bug collections."

Mom smiles—a real smile this time. "No, I believe he's left all those to the Entomological Society."

"Thank goodness." I swipe at my forehead with pretend relief. "I didn't know where in the world I was gonna put them."

"Very funny." Mom's phone buzzes and she goes to the kitchen counter to grab it. Her face brightens as she looks at the screen, and I know it must be Tim. He's likely calling before his morning meetings in Beijing. "Hey baby!" she says in that honey-sweet voice reserved only for him. "How are things?"

Gag. They've been married a little over two years, but they're still in that mushy honeymoon phase. Even though it grosses me out most of the time, it's at least nice to see my mom happy. I just hope that, unlike the last two marriages, this one actually lasts.

While Mom curls up in the living room chair, still talking to Tim, I finish the rest of my dinner and trash our plates before heading back to my room. I fall onto my bed with a sigh, my mind drifting back to the funeral. It could have been worse, I guess. Mom was relieved people at least attended. We honestly weren't sure who would show. Grandpa knew people in the entomology world—especially from back when he was an adjunct professor at the University of Arkansas— and I think he had a few friends who came over to play cards on occasion, but it was a surprisingly good turnout for someone who'd lived with agoraphobia for so long.

Not that my grandpa and I were ever super close, but it's hard to believe he's really gone. No more Thanksgiving or Christmas dinners at his place. No more trying to act interested when he went on and on about his latest insect find. Or following him around his woods as he tried to spot a Great Crested Flycatcher. Actually, the bird-watching was interesting at one time—back when I was about ten—but it all got old after a while. Now that he's gone, it's hard to know how to feel about things. I'm sad, for sure, but not in the way I might have expected. Certainly not in the way I was when Ricky died.

I stuff in my earbuds and close my eyes, hoping the music will soothe my mind. Before long, I'm bobbing my chin to a catchy beat as the lyrics repeat a line about moving on. That is *so* what I'm ready to do.

I've had more than enough of this awful day.

After practice Monday, I rush home to shower and change since we have to be at the lawyer's office by six o'clock. Mom's especially quiet on the drive and seems distracted. Or maybe even agitated. She keeps clicking her ruby red fingernails against the steering wheel and bouncing her free foot on the floorboard.

"Is something wrong?" I glance in the visor mirror, smoothing down my barely dry ponytail and applying a coat of lip gloss.

She turns to give me a tentative smile. "No, nothing's wrong. Just not sure what to expect, is all."

"Do we have time to go through the drive-thru?" The golden arches loom in the distance, and my stomach feels like it's about to cave in on itself. I didn't have time to reheat any leftover casserole at home, and lunch feels like it was an eternity ago.

Mom eyes the clock on the dash. "I guess we've got a couple extra minutes." She puts on her blinker and turns into the McDonald's parking lot.

"I'll take a large fry and a Coke."

"Alrighty." We pull up to the menu board, and Mom places the order for me.

The fries are nice and hot, but not hot enough to keep me from scarfing them down. Mom pulls back out onto the street, and I yank a fry out of my mouth to yell out as we bump onto the center median. The Jeep bounces wildly, knocking my head from side to side, but Mom maintains control and merges into the lane like she'd meant to do that all along.

"What are you doing?" I turn to give her an incredulous look. "There's no left turn there. You have to go up to the light."

Mom grips the steering wheel, her mouth pinching around the edges. "I forgot."

A cool, wet feeling spreads across my chest, and I look down to see a large splotch of Coke all over the front of my white button-down shirt. "Mom!" I yell. "Look at me! I can't go anywhere looking like this."

She glances my way briefly before peering back at the street in front of her. "Sorry, but we don't have time to stop anywhere else."

Something is definitely going on. It's not like her to drive like this or to make me go somewhere looking like a slob. I groan. "I'll just wait in the Jeep, then. I doubt you need me anyway."

"Actually, we do. This involves you, too."

"See, I knew it. I *am* getting the bug collections."

She doesn't smile at my poor attempt at humor. Instead, she grows unusually quiet again. My suspicion continues to deepen, but apparently I'll just have to wait until we get there to find out what the deal is.

We pull into another parking lot with a row of modern, two-story office buildings, and Mom parks in front of one with a sign that reads Sisco and Browning, Attorneys at Law. The Coke stain on my chest has grown to the size of a grapefruit now, and the liquid has soaked into one side of my bra. Disgusting. I pinch the fabric, pulling it away from my skin, but there's really no way to escape without taking my clothes off. "This is going to be totally embarrassing. Don't you have a scarf or something I can use to cover it up?"

Mom lets out a snort. "Yeah, Becka. I keep all my spare scarves in the back of the Jeep. Let me grab one for you."

"Hey. It's not my fault you decided to drive like a wild woman on the way here."

She gives me her infamous "Mom" look. The one that says I better shut my mouth if I know what's good for me. So, with my arms crossed tight over my chest and head hanging, I follow her inside.

The office is small, with stark white walls and absolutely no decor. The smell of tobacco lingers in the air, and it's about ten degrees too cold in here. A receptionist who appears a few years past retirement age directs us to Mr. Sisco's office—the last one on the left—and goosebumps have cropped up on my skin by the time we step into the room. The fact that the front of my shirt is soaking wet isn't helping matters.

"Hello," a round-faced man says from behind a sturdy-looking table. He offers a faint smile as he extends a hand outward, ushering us into the seats across from him. He has a receding hairline and glasses and looks pretty much the way I expected a lawyer to look. Smart, but stuffy.

"Hi, Mr. Sisco," Mom says. Her eyes dart back toward the open doorway, like she's expecting someone else to come in.

"So how are you two ladies doing this afternoon?" he asks as we settle into our oversized, cushy office chairs.

"Fine, thank you," Mom says.

"I'm just a little chilly," I add, trying to keep my teeth from chattering.

"Oh, sorry about that." He rises to his feet and moves to the doorway. "Constance," he calls down the hallway. "Could you turn the temperature up some?"

"Sure thing," she replies.

Thank goodness.

Mr. Sisco returns to his seat and glances at his watch. "We'll wait a few more minutes to get started. Hopefully, they'll be here by then."

"Who?" I ask. Would there be more lawyers coming? I can't imagine this will be too involved, but then again, what do I know about lawyers and wills and such?

Mom gives me a rushed, sidelong glance and then smiles nervously back at the lawyer, who still hasn't answered my question. Then, from down the hallway, I hear the front door open, followed by the murmur of voices. One of them is faintly familiar, and my eyes widen. Oh no. Is that who I think it is?

I turn toward Mom, but she refuses to look my way. She still has that weird, nervous smile plastered on her face. Mr. Sisco clicks the pen on the yellow notepad in front of him. Next to it sits a large maroon folder. Grandpa's will, no doubt. My arms constrict tighter across my chest as footsteps continue to thump in our direction. I suck in a breath and risk a glance back toward the doorway.

"Hi there," my Aunt Jackie says, wearing pink lipstick much too bright for this occasion—or any other occasion, for that matter. Hands pushed into the pockets of her tattered jeans, K. J. shuffles in behind her mom. Her eyes stay glued to the floor. I didn't get a good look at her at the funeral, but wow, she looks different than I remember. Especially with her hair chopped off like that. She's all grown up, too—but then again, I guess we've both changed quite a bit since the last time we saw each other. I keep up my self-inflicted stranglehold.

Mr. Sisco invites them to sit on his side of the table, across from me and Mom. Smart move, except now I'm looking at both of them, and I'd really rather not. I realize my mouth is hanging open and promptly close it. My eyes narrow, and I glare at my aunt as all the negative emotions I've ever felt about her rise to the surface. Every few seconds, my gaze shifts to my cousin, but she refuses to look up. Not quite so bold when you're not driving away, huh?

After the longest stretch of awkward silence I've ever experienced in my life, Mr. Sisco says, "Let's proceed, shall we?"

Mom still hasn't said a word. She's been digging in her purse this whole time and finally pulls out a pen and a small notepad. She focuses on Mr. Sisco, completely ignoring the other occupants in the room. A small squeak comes from her mouth, and she gives a slight nod.

"We're ready," I tell Mr. Sisco. It looks like I might have to be the one to take charge today.

He clears his throat and opens the maroon folder. "I'm going to jump right in, I guess. I have here Elijah Walker's last will and testament, but before we get to that, I'd like to read you the first in a series of letters he left for you." He looks up, and then at each of us in turn.

"Okay," I say, while my companions remain silent and frozen. So far, I'm not too impressed with my aunt and cousin. They're far less intimidating than I've always believed them to be.

After opening an envelope with the word *One* written on it, Mr. Sisco takes out a folded, peppermint green paper with what I recognize as Grandpa's handwriting on it. Aunt Jackie leans closer to the lawyer, attempting to read the letter herself. K. J. looks up for the first time, her eyes flashing to me and then my mom. I ignore her, waiting for Mr. Sisco to start reading. In the meantime, I uncross my arms. At least it has warmed up to somewhere around comfortable by now. K. J.'s eyes move back to me, specifically to the brown stain on my chest. A smile tugs at the corners of her mouth, and I quickly cross my arms again.

"Looks like you could use some of Grandpa's fortune to go buy yourself a new shirt," she says.

Her mother nudges an elbow at her, but I narrow my eyes. "Shut up, K. J. No amount of money could buy you any class. Not that Grandpa had anything to leave us anyway."

K. J.'s eyes widen ever so slightly, but her expression quickly changes to one of pure smugness. "Actually, he did." She turns to the lawyer. "Didn't he, Mr. Sisco?"

Jackie frowns and elbows her daughter again.

"Be quiet, girls," my mom hisses, "and let him read the letter."

CHAPTER 3
ELI

Hello girls,

If you're reading this letter, it means I'm gone. I wish I could have told you in person what I plan to tell you now, but I often find it easier to write my thoughts and feelings down rather than say them aloud. So here goes . . .

I know some people have always thought me to be a strange man. I have my ways, and other people have theirs. I've always thought we, as a species, should respect that more. Other people's choices, that is. I know I've certainly tried to respect the choices my daughters have made. There were many times I wanted to step in and try to mend the divide between you two, but to be honest, I didn't know where to start. Some fissures run too deep, and throwing a little sand in them will do nothing to fill the gap. And let's face it, I could barely manage to hold myself together most the time, let alone try to fix other people's problems.

I'm sorry I didn't tell you I had cancer. But I'm telling you now.

A few months back, I realized something wasn't quite right. I didn't have my usual energy when I walked about my property, and I was tired all the time. I began to worry. You know how much I detest hospitals and how I hate riding in a car, but I actually went to the doctor. (I know, it shocked me, too.) But I needed to know if I was dying. My neighbor Sheldon took me. After some tests, the doctors confirmed my fears, diagnosing me with non-Hodgkin's lymphoma. They said it was advanced, but I could start treatment to hopefully prolong my life. I considered it. I really did. But the thought of getting in a car again and making another trip to the hospital triggered a major panic attack. I decided I would rather live out the rest of my time where I'm most comfortable—at home.

I'm sorry for not telling you girls, but I knew you'd want me to get treatment. And I just wanted to live my last few months in relative peace. It turns out the doctor's estimate was wrong. Those few months have turned into nearly half a year now, enough time for me to make some important decisions. Again, I don't tell you all this to make you sad. This was my choice, and it's one I don't regret.

But let's get to the real point of this letter: I stayed quiet on matters that bothered me more than I ever let on. I hated never being able to have my family all together at once.

Jackie, I rarely saw you and Katherine, and it saddened me greatly. I know you were uncomfortable coming around, but I love both of you very much. I want you to know that.

RaeLynn and Rebecka, I really enjoyed what little time I spent with you as well. I know things have been hard since you lost Ricky, and I loved my grandson as much as I love all of you. I wish we could have all been together as a family, just once even. Charlotte and I didn't set the best example, I'm afraid, and I'm sorry for that. I'm sorry for a lot of things.

I can't change the past, but I do have one wish for the future: that my family could finally forgive all the wrongs that they have held onto for so long now. I know what I'm asking isn't simple, but I'm offering an incentive. It will be well worth your time to do as I ask. Mr. Sisco will explain the details.

I'm sure this letter has left you with as many questions as it has answers, but don't worry, I'll be writing more letters. Each will be given to the appropriate person at the appropriate time.

Until then, sending my love,

Elijah Walker

CHAPTER 4
K. J.

I'M THE ONLY ONE IN THE ROOM WHO HASN'T TEARED up. Aside from Mr. Sisco, anyway. He's thumbing through more paperwork, waiting for everyone to dry their eyes with a tissue from the box conveniently placed in the center of the table.

My lack of water works probably makes me look like a real bitch, but I'm just too nervous about what's coming. I mean, I'm sad, too. Obviously. I had no idea Grandpa had cancer, and I feel terrible we didn't go see him more, especially since he was so sick. Mom and I figured he died of a heart attack.

Mom sniffles, dabs at her eyes with a tissue, and then levels her sister with an accusatory glare. "You should have told me he was sick."

RaeLynn bristles, pushing her shoulders back. "I didn't know! He didn't tell anyone. Just like that letter said."

"But you saw him more than we did," my mom spits. "You live closer."

"He didn't look sick the last time I saw him," RaeLynn says with a scowl. "A little thinner, sure, but not horrible. He was hiding the fact that he was ill! And besides, it's not like it was that much farther for you."

Mr. Sisco's round face puckers, but he doesn't butt in. He just gets up and closes the door.

"When was the last time you saw him?" RaeLynn continues. "You could have gone to visit him more. What was your excuse?"

I can see Mom's jaw clench as she grinds her teeth. She's trying to think of a good comeback, I'm sure. Mr. Sisco returns to his seat, but still says nothing, which surprises me. I figured lawyers were supposed to be good at getting people to calm down in tense situations like this. That's how they seem on TV.

"Don't you dare try to blame this on me," RaeLynn snaps.

"Would you stop it?" Becka hisses. "Both of you. You're acting like children."

RaeLynn looks like she'd like to lay into Becka for reprimanding her but must think better of it in front of all of us.

Mr. Sisco clears his throat again. "Can we please proceed, ladies?"

RaeLynn huffs a loud breath while my mother continues to glare at her. "Yes," my aunt says finally. She lowers her head, looking ashamed. "Sorry."

Mr. Sisco starts reading from Grandpa's will. "Elijah Walker's house and possessions will go to auction with all proceeds going to the Arkansas Entomological Society."

"What?" Mom gasps. She was probably still holding out hope that he'd leave the house to us or at least some of the land. RaeLynn gives us both a self-satisfied look. I doubt she wants the property. She has her own fancy house, or so I hear.

"But a sum of $350,494 is to be divided equally among RaeLynn Shipman, Jackie Walker, Rebecka Cowles, and Katherine Walker." Mom gasps again, but this time so does everyone else.

"Grandpa had that much money?" Becka asks. She's apparently forgotten about the stain on her shirt again as she leans forward, her hands dropping to her lap. She has full, pouty lips covered in clear lip gloss, and it makes me want to smack her for some reason. But it's also kind of hilarious seeing her looking like this. I've always thought of Becka as Little Miss Perfect, but she's not looking so perfect now.

"There are, however, several stipulations," Mr. Sisco continues. "The first one being that Rebecka and Katherine's portion of the money must first go to pay for their college tuition. Acceptance to a college or university and a 3.0 grade average are required in order to retain the inheritance. Whatever is left after that is theirs to do with as they please."

My shoulders droop. Well, shit, looks like I won't be getting anything after all. It would be a miracle if any college would accept my transcript as is, and I haven't even taken the ACT.

"My college is already paid for," Becka says, frowning. "I have a soccer scholarship at the University of Arkansas."

Oh, how nice for you. I didn't think it was possible, but my dislike for Becka multiplies. I'm also miffed at Grandpa. Why couldn't he just fork over the money without all these dumb stipulations?

Mr. Sisco peers at Becka over his glasses. "In that case, the money could be used for related costs: room and board, et cetera."

This seems to please my cousin and aunt, and I roll my eyes. If Becka only knew how easy she had it. My mom's looking pretty chipper right now, too. She's probably envisioning all the ways she can spend her part of the money. I'm sure she's seeing a new car in her future and more fun at the casino. Irritation wells up inside me and my jaw tightens. Why am I getting the shaft here? It's not my fault that getting into college is almost impossible now. If I'd have known higher education was even a possibility for me, maybe I would have tried harder.

"I still don't understand how Daddy had all this money," RaeLynn says, "but this is certainly a nice surprise."

I love how she's suddenly referring to him as *Daddy*, like they were the perfect father-daughter combo. According to that letter, RaeLynn and Becka weren't around much, either.

"Let's just say he invested well," Mr. Sisco says with the hint of a smile, "but there's more."

"Oh," Mom says quietly as she settles back into her seat.

"In order for any of the four named recipients to receive their inheritance, there are five specific tasks that must be completed."

"What do you mean?" RaeLynn asks, her eyes narrowing.

Mr. Sisco pauses, glancing her way for a second before peering back down at the paper in front of him. "These tasks must be completed by Rebecka Cowles and Katherine Walker. If the tasks are not completed, in full, then the entire sum will be withheld from the aforementioned persons and left instead to the Arkansas Amateur Entomological Association."

"What the hell does the Entomological Association need all that money for?" Mom demands.

"What are the tasks?" I ask, a mixture of curiosity and dread taking over. I honestly have no clue what to expect here.

Mr. Sisco smiles again. "I'm so glad you asked."

Mom inches closer to him, trying to read the document herself. I can't see crap from where I sit.

"The following tasks are to be completed in this specific order, and all costs pertaining to them will be covered by an additional set of funds provided by Mr. Walker."

Whatever the hell these tasks are, Grandpa sure was serious about them. Nothing should probably surprise me at this point, but my spine stiffens with nervous anticipation.

"Task number one," Mr. Sisco says, his voice becoming thick with authority. "Ride a mule on the guided trip into the Grand Canyon, stay overnight at the Phantom Ranch, and return to the South Rim the following day. The trip has already been booked, since reservations must be made at least a year in advance."

"What in the actual fuck?" I mutter.

Mom elbows me again.

Becka's face is flushed pink. "I'm not riding a mule." She fixes her blue eyes on me and frowns. "And especially not with *her*."

"Be quiet, both of you," my mom says. Well, well, look who's suddenly decided to give a shit. "What's the second thing?" she asks.

"Task two is to participate in a base camp hike at Yellowstone National Park." My eyes widen, but Mr. Sisco doesn't wait for us to respond this time. "Task three is to white water raft over the Bull Sluice on the Chattooga River. Task four will be snuba diving off the coast of Key West, Florida. And, finally, task five will be to enter one event in a local rodeo."

"Wait," I say. "What's snuba diving?"

"A combination of scuba diving and snorkeling," Mr. Sisco says. "You won't need certification for it."

"Wow!" RaeLynn says, nodding appreciatively. "It's like a bunch of little mini-vacations. Except for the rodeo."

Becka's face has gone from pink to almost magenta now, and she looks like she's about to blow. Little Miss Perfect has a temper, so it would seem.

I shake my head in confusion. "I don't get it. Why would Grandpa want us to do all these things?"

"He's trying to kill us," Becka screeches, her cool finally breaking. "I'm afraid of heights. And I don't like horses."

"He never said you had to ride a horse," I say. "Just a mule. And you could ride a bull in the rodeo." The thought makes me smile.

She pounds a hand on the table. "I don't need to do any of these things. I already have my college paid for, and my mom doesn't need this money."

Now my mom is the one to redden. "Listen here, little missy, you two might not need the money, but I don't even have a reliable car.

And this could be K. J.'s only chance to go to college." Obviously, she's not remembering my less-than-ideal grades at the moment.

"Actually, I could use the money," RaeLynn says quietly. "I could pay off the rest of my debt. We still owe quite a bit on Ricky's hospital bills."

A small knot of guilt tightens inside my stomach. I'd never even met my cousin Ricky. He died four years ago, from a bad infection after having his appendix removed. He spent almost two months in the hospital. Mom and I didn't attend his funeral. We didn't even know about it until after the fact.

RaeLynn turns to Becka, her expression hard to read. "I know these are strange requests, but look at it this way, you'll get to travel all over the country. Do things you may otherwise never get to do." She gives a slight smile. "I'm a little envious actually. I'd love to go to Key West."

"Would you love to enter a rodeo?" Becka asks flatly. "Or have to do all these things with Aunt Jackie?"

RaeLynn's smile evaporates. We all know the answer to that question.

"Why us?" I ask. I seem to be the only one who isn't angry, and just trying to comprehend all this craziness. "Why not his own daughters? They're the ones who hate each other's guts."

Mr. Sisco gives me a chiding look, like maybe I shouldn't have stated the obvious. "Your grandfather thought it might be too late to mend their broken relationship, but it seems he still had hopes that his two granddaughters might learn to be friends."

I catch Becka's eye, and we both stare at one another.

"Not gonna happen," she says.

I second that. Grandpa's tasks actually sound kind of cool, but I'd never be able to enjoy myself—not with *her* tagging along.

"I know what this is," RaeLynn says, realization dawning on her face. She folds her hands on the table and nods to no one in particular. "These are the things he always wished he'd done, but he couldn't because of his agoraphobia."

Mom gives RaeLynn a blank look. Maybe she'd never realized her dad had this adventurous side. Or wannabe adventurous side anyway.

"When are the reservations for the mule ride?" I ask.

Mr. Sisco thumbs through a few more papers and then pauses, scanning through the page. "Next weekend actually." He lets out an uncomfortable chuckle. "Mr. Walker certainly wasn't expecting to make it as long as he did."

"I can't go next weekend!" Becka practically yells. "We have another playoff game!"

RaeLynn's face falls, and she pats Becka on the back.

A smile creeps across my face. I'm feeling better about this already. "That date works just fine for me."

CHAPTER 5

BECKA

I SPEED WALK AHEAD OF EVERYONE, IGNORING THE
receptionist's pleasant farewell as I push open the front door. Mr. Sisco's
words replay in my mind, making me want to scream. This whole
ordeal makes me want to scream. Missing what might be the final game
of my senior year for this first trip with K. J.? I can't even process the
idea right now.

My goal is to escape to the Jeep so I don't have to speak another word
to my cousin or aunt, but, of course, it's locked. Luckily, Mom's not far
behind. I barely get my door shut before I let out a strangled groan of frustration. "Why?" I yell at the dash. "Why do I have to do these things?"

Mom starts the engine, then sinks back into her seat with a sigh.
"Because it's what your grandpa wanted. It's his last wish. The least you
and K. J. can do is honor it."

"Really?" I turn to glare at her. "You and Jackie can hardly stand to be in the same room together. That's the most time you've spent with her in . . . what? Forever?" Mom gives me that stop-while-you're-ahead look. But this time, I can't. This isn't fair. Any of it. "This whole thing is stupid. And all so you can pay off some bills? You and Tim have plenty of money. Can't you just pay them off yourself?"

Mom's face hardens and her a hand flies up like it has a mind of its own. Instinctively, I wince, but nothing happens. When I open my eyes, her hand is resting in her lap and she's staring straight ahead.

"You don't know anything about how the adult world works, Becka. Those bills—Ricky's bills—they're like a daily reminder of what I've lost. They've been hanging over my head for four years. Four years! Do you even know what that's like?" She sucks in her cheeks and shakes her head. "Of course you don't. You have no idea what it's like to owe money to anyone. You've never even had a job."

My insides retract into a tight ball. How could she say that to me? "You've never *let* me work, remember? You told me to focus on school and soccer instead."

She doesn't respond because she knows it's true. I wouldn't be sitting on top of a full scholarship if it weren't, but she's also acting like I don't know what it's like to lose someone I love. I lost Ricky, too. He was *my* brother. It hurt more than anything. At least Grandpa had a chance to live his life. Ricky was only nine.

Thick gray clouds hover over the skyline in the distance. It looks like another spring thunderstorm will be here soon. Mom shifts the

Jeep into reverse and then exits the parking lot. We drive in silence for a long while, and I let the sadness I feel simmer back into anger. When my mom made me go to counseling after Ricky's death, I pretended to move past the anger phase of the grief process, but the truth is, I never did. I just learned to get better at hiding it. My counselor always told me, "The only way out is through," but I didn't want out. Leaving my anger behind meant being okay with Ricky's death. And I most certainly was not.

I clench my hands in my lap. I wouldn't be in this position if it weren't for my mom and her sister and their problems. Now, my entire summer is flushed down the toilet—filled with doing these ridiculous *tasks* with K. J. "The spawn of the devil," Mom used to call her, though she hasn't used that phrase in a while. She's been different since she married Tim. Calmer, for sure. Now, she pretends like she doesn't even have a sister.

"I'm sorry," Mom says after a few minutes. "I'm sorry you're having to pay for Jackie's mistakes. But you might as well make the best of it. There's not much else we can do, right?"

I don't answer.

We pass by my old middle school and the appliance store where Ricky's dad—my former stepdad—used to work. He still might, for all I know. I haven't seen him in years.

"And it *will* be nice for you to have all that extra money," Mom continues. "You could use it to get a nice apartment after your freshman year. Or you could buy a new car? How about that?"

"The lawyer said it had to go for college stuff," I mumble.

"I bet we could work a car into that somehow. I mean you'll need transportation to drive back home from Fayetteville."

"I already have a car, Mom." I don't add that I wasn't planning on coming home all that often anyway.

"Then that money will be yours to decide what to do with."

We hit a pothole and the Jeep bounces, reminding me of our median-jumping adventure on the way here. I glance down at the stain on my shirt. I can't believe I had to sit through the entire meeting looking like this. How humiliating. Just thinking of what K. J. said makes my face burn all over again.

"I still can't figure out how Dad managed to save up all that money," Mom says, distracting me.

"He invested apparently." In what, I have no idea. "Plus, he never had to buy gas. And he never went out to eat." Someone could save a lot of money if they never went anywhere, I guess.

Mom seems to consider something. "He must have been a good money manager. Too bad he never passed any of those skills on to his daughters." She smiles, but within seconds, tears have pooled in her eyes once again. This is about the hundredth time this has happened since he died. "I just can't believe I'll never see him again."

I can't believe it, either. But I'm even more surprised by this whole plan Grandpa had been hiding up his sleeve. Three hundred and fifty thousand dollars and a list of crazy tasks. Who would have ever guessed?

We've only been home a few minutes when an email from Mr. Sisco with details for my first trip pops up on my phone. My cousin's email address, KJtheDJ16@yahoo.com, is next to mine in the recipient box. What's that supposed to mean? Wow, K. J., you're so cool because you're into music. Who isn't? Then again, beckaball19@gmail.com isn't all that original, either. I scroll down to read the rest of the message and decide I should probably get a new email address before college. Something a little more sophisticated.

The email explains that our airline tickets will arrive by mail in a few days and the details of the trip are outlined in an attached itinerary. We're told what to pack: clothes for both warm and cold weather, a hat, sturdy shoes for hiking and riding. There's also an online brochure about the Grand Canyon, which I don't bother to read. With this first task booked so soon, Grandpa really must not have expected to live as long as he did. I wonder what his last days were like. The guy who delivers his groceries every week was the one to find him, and, according to the coroner, he'd been dead for a couple of days. A shiver runs down my spine at the thought. How awful, to die all alone like that.

Guilt consumes me as I recall our last visit with him at Christmas. He was thinner, like Mom said, but I hadn't thought much about it at the time. I just assumed it was part of getting old. He'd given me the same gift he gave me every year—a box of chocolate-covered cherries and two twenty-dollar bills. "Don't spend it all at once!" he'd said with a wink. I never had the heart to tell him that even a pair of jeans or shoes cost more than forty dollars. I figured that was a lot of money for him. Boy, was I wrong.

I send the itinerary to the printer and change into my pajamas. Mom and I still haven't eaten dinner, but for once, I'm not hungry. I'm not even in the mood to listen to music like I usually do. Instead, I crawl into bed and close my eyes, praying for sleep to come.

✳ ✳ ✳ ✳

The next day at school, I'm not sure if I should tell my friends about my weekend plans or not. Part of me is still in denial, hoping it was all just a really bad dream. Another part of me knows better. Lunch trays in hand, Lexi and I make our way toward our usual table near the back of the cafeteria. It's loud in here, but then again, it's May. Everyone's ready for summer. I was too . . . until now.

In her black Adidas shorts and matching sliders, my best friend looks like she could be on the soccer team, too, but the closest Lexi's ever gotten to a team sport was two years of Color Guard, which she gave up because it was *interfering* with her AP homework load.

She steps around an apple core someone's thrown on the cafeteria floor. "So there's a new Chris Hemsworth movie coming out this weekend. He's like this hot, ancient Greek warrior. It looks really good."

Oops. I'd forgotten about the movie plans we made earlier last week. The ones that already got postponed once because of Grandpa's funeral. Guess I have no choice but to tell her now. Setting my tray on the table, I take a seat. "Actually, I can't go this weekend. I'll be out of town." My shoulders slouch as I'm forced to come to grips with my new reality all over again. I uncap my bottled water and take a sip,

hoping to wash down the bad taste last weekend left in my mouth.
No such luck.

"What do you mean you'll be out of town?" Maddie asks as she
takes her place across from us. "What about playoffs?" She unpacks
a homemade lunch in matching turquoise Tupperware. I wouldn't
be surprised if her mom still makes her lunch every morning. Not
that Maddie isn't perfectly capable of doing it—that's just how her
mom is. Mrs. Tate also regularly makes Saran-wrapped, after-game
snacks for the soccer team—things like Rice Krispie treats, brownies,
or those extra-large chocolate chip cookies.

"Yeah, I have this thing . . ." I say, my voice giving away my list-
less mood. "I'll have to miss this game, but hopefully we'll make it to
the next round."

"What *thing*?" Lexi and Maddie both ask at the same time.

I take another sip of water and let out a sigh. "My mom and I
had to meet with my grandpa's lawyer yesterday. He left us an inheritance, but I have to complete these, uh . . . *tasks*." I say for lack
of a better word. "The first one is this weekend. I have to go to the
Grand Canyon."

"The Grand Canyon?" Maddie's brow furrows in confusion.
"Why would your grandpa want you to go there?"

"We have to do these things that he always wanted to do but
never did."

Lexi's face lights up. "Oh, wow. I think that's nice."

I shake my head. "I don't think it's all that nice."

"So will you and your mom be gone all weekend?" Lexi asks, ignoring my overt lack of enthusiasm.

"My mom's not going with me, actually." And here comes the fun part. "My cousin, K. J., is."

"Wait, what?" Lexi says, mid-bite into her sub sandwich. She sets it back on her lunch tray. "The one you don't like?"

Neither Lexi nor Maddie know the whole story about K. J.; I've only told them we've never gotten along, which is already proving to be true.

"That's the one," I say. "I'm ecstatic, if you can't tell."

Lexi laughs. "Oh, wow. That should be interesting."

Understatement of the year. "Please just pray that neither of us pushes the other into the canyon."

Both of my friends seem to get a kick out of this.

They have no idea I'm being completely serious.

CHAPTER 6
K. J.

CARTER AND I GET OFF THE SCHOOL BUS AT THE mobile home park entrance, him muttering obscenities about some sophomore who still owes him ten bucks, and me hugging my books awkwardly to my chest. For the first time in recent memory, I'm putting the *home* in homework. Wish I had a backpack.

"Just drop it, why don't you," I say to Carter. "He probably doesn't have the money."

"Should've thought about that before he made a bet that I couldn't get five solo wins in *Fortnite*. Dumbass. I need gas money." Carter scoops up a rock from the gravel road and throws it hard. It bounces off a broken-down lawn mower near the end of the row with a loud clank.

"Feel better now?" I ask with a smirk.

"Yep. I do, actually." As we continue toward home, he eyes my books. "So what's with the sudden interest in school?"

The question was inevitable, I guess. "Dunno." I stare at the ground. "Just figured I'd see if I could bring my grades up before graduation. You know, show my teachers I can actually do it."

"Since when do you care what they think?" Carter says with a laugh. "You never care what *anyone* thinks."

If only that were true.

"You really think two and a half weeks is enough time to bring your grades up?" he continues.

"Guess we'll find out. I'll be doing every extra credit assignment I can get."

The kids from across the street run out of their trailer and hop on their bikes again. They must be home-schooled or something. I've never seen them waiting at the bus stop. I wave as they ride past, but they don't seem to notice us.

"You gonna have a smoke first?" Carter asks.

"No, I'm out." I'd go get some, but Mom's working the late shift at Dollar General today, and I don't feel like walking all the way to the gas station right now.

"No worries, I've got some." Carter hurries inside his trailer and reappears a few moments later. We sit on my front porch stairs as we light them.

"So have you started looking for a job yet?" I ask between drags. He's leaning back on the step below me, trying to blow a smoke ring.

Unsuccessfully, I might add. It's a talent neither one of us has been able to master.

"Not yet."

"When do you plan to start?"

"This weekend, I guess," he says. "I have no idea where, though."

"What about an auto parts store or maybe a hardware store? You like cars and fixing stuff."

"Yeah—" his shoulders rise and fall in an overly dramatic shrug "—that might work."

"Then maybe you and Dax could rent a trailer or an apartment or something."

Carter sits up and slowly twists from side to side, his spine releasing a series of cringe-worthy crackles. "We've been talking about doing that, actually." He turns around to look at me. "Hey, you could move in with us, too, if you want. We could split the rent three ways."

A flash of excitement zips through me at the thought, but it lasts all of two seconds. "I don't know about that." I'm pretty sure Carter's always thought of me as one of the guys, but honestly, I think it would be weird living with them.

"Yeah, you're right." He takes one last drag before stubbing out his cigarette on the step. "You should stay with your mom for a while. She'd probably be lonely if you left."

While this is true, it's not really the reason why I'm planning on staying put for now. For one, I'll be too busy doing Grandpa's stuff this summer to get a job, and two, I'm hoping that if I do—by some miracle—get into college, I can save money by living at home. I'd hate to spend all my inheritance in the next four years.

It's strange, suddenly having a little direction in my life. Up until now, I've felt like I've been wandering around in one of those gigantic corn mazes, never sure which way to go. The bad part is, until now, I didn't really *care* which way I went.

"Whatcha thinking about?" Carter asks.

"Nothing." I stub out my own cigarette and toss it onto the lawn before grabbing my books from beside me. "Better go get started on this shit. Might take me all night to do the essay."

Carter laughs and stands. "Yeah . . . good luck with that."

By Friday morning, my stomach is one big boiling pot of nerves. I can't pay attention in my classes even though I've been giving it my best effort this week. It's not the Grand Canyon I'm afraid of or even my sure-to-be-sucky weekend with my cousin. It's the fact that in a few hours, I'm going to be flying on a plane for the first time. Mom's supposed to pick me up at lunchtime and take me to the airport.

By the time the school secretary calls my name over the loud-speaker in English class, I feel like I'm on the verge of puking. Probably not a good sign. Mom waits in the office for me, her fingers tapping on the blue Formica counter, eyes taking in the plaques and other boring decor on the walls. She looks completely out of place here. I think it's the first time she's ever been inside my high school, as a matter of fact.

She frowns as soon as she sees me. "What's wrong? You look sick." She reaches to feel my forehead with the back of her hand, and it stirs up distant memories of her doing the same when I was little. She used to say her hand was just as good as those expensive thermometers. "You better not be coming down with something. Not right now."

I pull away from her and walk toward the exit door and she hurries to follow behind me. "You don't have a fever. What's going on?"

"God, Mom, nothing. I'm just nervous. I've never flown before."

"Oh!" She gives a little laugh. "I'll give you one of my Xanax. You'll be fine." The concern in her voice is gone now.

"Can you give it to me now?" I ask a little more aggressively than I mean to. "Please," I tack on, holding out my hand.

She digs through her purse as we cross the parking lot and finds the bottle by the time we make it to the car. I heave open the door and sink into the passenger seat, my stomach still bubbling like a cauldron full of something vile.

Mom climbs in on her side and presses the pills into my hand. "Here, you better take two, just in case." I tilt my head back and pop them into my mouth, grabbing a half-empty bottle of water from the cup holder to chase them down. "I got your bag in the back."

"Thanks." I lean my head against the seat, closing my eyes. And hoping the Xanax kicks in soon.

Thankfully, by the time we get to the airport a little less than an hour later, I'm feeling much better about things. Sleepy, but better.

"Just don't drink any alcohol," Mom says when we pull up in front of the airport. "It doesn't mix well with Xanax."

I raise an eyebrow. "Wasn't planning on it, but thanks for the tip." I grab my bag and climb out of the car, stifling a yawn. "See ya."

"Have fun!" she says, like I'm in the second grade and she's dropping me off at summer camp.

"I'll try," I mumble under my breath before closing the door. Here goes nothing.

The airport is intimidating—lots of people, signs, and hallways—but I manage to get checked in and find my gate with thirty minutes to spare. No surprise that Little Miss Perfect is already here. Wearing orange athletic shorts that show off her toned legs and a gray T-shirt that says PLAY LIKE A GIRL, she looks like she could be on the cover of that sporty women's magazine she's flipping through. Her head nods to the beat of whatever music is streaming through her earbuds. Bubblegum pop, if I had to guess. I plop down in the seat beside her, which makes her jump. She pulls out her earbuds and shoots me a nasty look.

"What's up, cuz?" I say. For some reason, this makes me laugh. I seem to find it way funnier than she does, at least.

She looks me over. "What's wrong with you? Are you high?"

I laugh again. "I sure hope not." Maybe I should have just stuck with the one Xanax, though.

She inspects my face for several seconds before shaking her head. If I wasn't feeling so mellow right now, I might actually be offended. I blow out a long breath and pull out my ticket to look at the flight time again.

"Twenty-five minutes to go," I say to no one in particular. "Glad I got here early. Not really sure how this works, with boarding and all."

Becka doesn't respond and it quickly becomes apparent she has no intention of making small talk with me. She stuffs her earbuds back in and resumes flipping through the magazine. I slump down in my seat, turning my attention to the people hurrying around the airport. It's an interesting mix: an old lady with obvious dyed-brown hair hobbling along surprisingly fast with her cane. Two forty-something ladies wearing fur coats, high heels, and sunglasses like they've mistaken northwestern Arkansas for L.A. Then there's a balding, middle-aged guy wearing a gray suit and red high-tops.

"Now boarding Group A for passengers heading to Denver," a female voice says over a loudspeaker. Oh boy, that's us. I glance at my ticket again. Group B for me.

Becka and I both stand and move toward the gate, neither one of us speaking. The voice over the intercom tells us to have our tickets ready. I yawn and shuffle along as the passengers move forward.

The plane is smaller on the inside than I expected and much less fancy. It also has a weird odor, like old plastic and Ritz crackers with a dash of BO thrown in. I find my seat, which ends up being right next to the window. This morning, I would have considered that terrifying. But with the two Xanax fully working in my system, I don't mind at all. Becka squeezes in next to me, still wearing that same disgusted expression. High-top suit guy takes the aisle seat in our row.

"Could I trade seats with you, by any chance?" Becka asks him. "I get claustrophobic sitting in the middle."

She's such a freaking liar, but hey, I'm not going to complain.

"Sure," he says.

As the plane backs away from the terminal, he leans his head back and closes his eyes. A nap sounds nice right about now, come to think of it. My stomach roils up a bit during takeoff, but after we're safely in the sky (or as safe as you can possibly be in the sky), I lean my seat back as far as it will go and zonk out. I don't wake again until the man is poking me in the arm.

"You need to put your seat up," he says. "We're about to land."

"Oh, okay." I stifle another yawn. "Wow, we're here already?"

But then I remember this isn't our destination. We have a short layover in Denver. *Crap.* I hope the Xanax keeps working for a few more hours. Mom gave me two more, but I should probably save them for the return trip.

The Denver airport is way bigger and much busier than the one in Arkansas, and after a stop at the bathroom, I lose sight of Becka. Luckily, a man in a pilot's hat notices me looking confused and helps me get to the next gate. There, I find Becka with her earbuds still in and no apparent concern for my whereabouts. I decide to do the same. Scrolling through my playlist, I choose a song by Linkin Park, crank it up loud, and find my Zen. When Becka stands to get in line, I follow behind her, and since this plane isn't full, we leave an empty seat between us. By the time we land in Flagstaff, I've made it through roughly a third of my songs and the Xanax hasn't let me down yet.

I have no idea where we're going, so I stick close to Becka after we get off the plane. It's funny, because I hadn't really noticed how short she was until now. She's maybe five-three, tops, but those short legs can sure move. She walks like she's hoping she'll lose me, but I manage to keep up.

"Do you even know where to go?" I ask when we reach a dead end in the airport and have to turn back around. She doesn't answer. I sigh and pull up the itinerary again. Grand Canyon Shuttle, that's what we need to find. "Hey, there's a sign." I point up ahead.

Becka turns like she'd known that all along, even though I'm pretty sure she didn't. When we board the shuttle, she moves toward the back, and I choose a seat near the front. Sitting next to a window again, I watch the unfamiliar scenery pass as we head west. Huge pine trees line the roadway, and the jagged outline of mountains is visible in the distance. Arizona's prettier than I would have thought, and a lot greener, but now that the Xanax is finally wearing off, excitement and nervousness play a game of tug-of-war in my gut. I've never been this far away from home before.

My stomach rumbles loudly, but I'm pretty sure it's from hunger this time. Guess I never ate lunch today. I glance at the lady next to me, but she doesn't seem to have noticed the noise. Or maybe she's just too polite to act like she did. Remembering the two bags of peanuts I'd saved from the airplane, I grab one from my pocket and tear it open, but after finishing the second bag, I'm still starving. Hopefully, there'll be something to eat at the hotel. Never been to one of those either.

Becka and I are the only two people to get off at the Maswik Lodge. By now, the sky has turned orange, and the chilly air causes goose pimples to pop up on my arms. Bags slung over our shoulders, we trudge into the office without saying a word. While Becka checks us in, I fish a gray hoodie out of my bag and pull it on. She seems to know what she's doing, so I just follow after her as she gets the key cards and starts toward our room. I did hear the lady say it has two queen beds, which I'm extremely grateful for. I'd sleep on the floor before I'd crawl in bed next to Becka.

The room is small, with southwestern style bedspreads and matching desert artwork hanging above each bed. It smells a little flowery—probably some kind of air freshener—but it looks like a pretty nice place. Mom would approve, I'm sure. A twinge of something like homesickness comes over me for a second but disappears almost as quickly because what's there to miss at home, really? I kick off my shoes and fall onto one of the beds while Becka carefully unpacks a few things from her bag.

"I'm taking a shower," she says without looking my way.

Like I care. After she disappears into the bathroom, I decide I'm going to make the best of my alone time, so I turn on the TV and flip through the channels. There's nothing interesting, and I don't really feel like watching anything anyway, so I turn it back off and pull out my phone instead. Only there's no Wi-Fi. I sigh and set it on the table beside my bed. With nothing to distract me, my empty stomach commands my attention again. Surely there's some place to eat around here. Guess I better go look. Stuffing my feet back into my shoes, I grab some money out of my bag.

"Gonna go get some food," I yell toward the bathroom. "Want anything?"

"No," Becka replies from the other side of the door. "I brought some snacks."

She doesn't even thank me for asking, but whatever.

I push the cash into my pocket and head outside into the chilly night. The lady at the front desk points the way to the food court, where the only thing still open is the pizzeria. Works for me. When I return to the room with two to-go slices of pizza and a drink, plus a Twix bar from the snack machine, I balance the food on the crook of one arm and search my pocket for the key card. Only it's not there. *Shit.* I check my other pockets just in case, dropping my candy bar in the process. Nope, definitely forgot it. I knock on the door, but all is quiet inside. I knock again.

"Becka, it's me. Let me in."

Nothing but silence.

I use the side of my fist to pound a little harder. "Hey, open up!"

The curtains move in the window of the room next door, but there's no sign of life in ours. What the hell? Is she still in the bathroom? I turn and slide my back down the door, sitting on the cold cement walkway. I'm too hungry to wait any longer, so I open up the cardboard container and shovel a piece of pizza into my mouth. I'm shivering by the time I unwrap the candy bar, and the cold drink isn't helping things.

God damn it, Becka. I slap the door hard with the palm of my hand, the resulting sting making me instantly regret the action. "Open the door!"

Still not a sound.

I grit my teeth and stand. Leaving my trash on the ground, I stomp back toward the front desk.

"Can I get another key card?" I ask the woman. "Room 103."

She looks at me like I must be the most irresponsible person on earth, but she rifles through a drawer and retrieves one. "There's an added fee if you lose any more," she informs me.

"Alrighty." Becka can just cover that fee if need be.

I take the card and hurry back toward our room, but just as I'm about to use it, the door opens. Becka stands before me, dressed in flannel pajama pants and a long-sleeved shirt.

"Oh, there you are," she says, her tone completely indifferent.

I stare back at her, wide-eyed. "Are you kidding me? What the hell have you been doing this whole time?"

"Nothing," she says with a shrug. "Just listening to music."

I shake my head and brush past her with a huff. She could still hear me, I'm sure of it.

Becka puts her earbuds back in and sits cross-legged on her bed while munching on what looks like peanut butter crackers and sipping from a bottle of Coke. Funny, I pegged her for a protein bar and Evian water type of girl. I go to the bathroom to change into my sweatpants and a T-shirt but pull my hoodie back on.

"Where are you going now?" she asks as I head back toward the door. I hold up my pack of cigarettes and she rolls her eyes. "Don't forget your card this time." The hint of a smile tugs at her pouty lips.

I glare back at her. "Don't worry, won't make that mistake again."

CHAPTER 7

BECKA

IT'S ALMOST IMPOSSIBLE TO SLEEP KNOWING K. J. is in the same room. Plus, this bed is hard as a rock and my pillow feels like it's had a few too many heads on it. I stare at the ceiling for a long while before shifting to lie on my side. The red numbers on the alarm clock show 1:24 a.m. I need sleep; otherwise, I'm going to be a zombie tomorrow. Lord knows that won't be good while I'm sitting on a mule, descending into the pits of the earth. My stomach clenches tight at the thought.

I try counting backward from one thousand—a trick my mom taught me when I was little, and one I had to use quite a bit in the months following Ricky's death—but other thoughts soon push out the numbers, and I lose track of where I'm at. K. J. lets out a snort and rolls over so she's facing me, still sound asleep. The dim moonlight peeking through the curtains shines on her face, making her look completely unfamiliar. Of course, she is unfamiliar to me. Until this trip, I'd only seen her in person three times—the lawyer's office, the funeral, and once by mistake when we were around twelve. My mom and I ran into Jackie and K. J. at a Wendy's. They were coming in as we were leaving, and I remember Mom cursing under her breath, grabbing my shoulder, and practically pushing me out the front door.

I've always known my cousin best by the grade school picture hanging in Grandpa's hallway, and she's always been somewhat of an enigma to me. My trashy aunt's tomboy daughter. Turns out she's worse than I thought. She had to have been high today on God only knows what.

I roll onto my other side, forcing K. J. from my mind and my eyes closed for the hundredth time, silently repeating, "I have to sleep . . . I have to sleep . . . I have to sleep," like a mantra. Eventually it does the trick. The words mush together, my brain grows fuzzy, and sleep finally comes.

My phone alarm awakens me much too soon. Ugh. Is it five-thirty already? I sit up but have to wait several seconds for my head to clear. I was having this weird dream about playing soccer next to a giant ravine and the only way to score was to kick an opposing player into the abyss. Completely sadistic but maybe not all that surprising considering the circumstances.

K. J. stirs in her bed and swipes at her eyes. "Shit, is it time to get up?"

I grunt in affirmation and climb out of bed, taking my clothes to the bathroom to get dressed. By the time I'm out, K. J. is fully clothed and packing a few things into a smaller duffel bag, like we've been instructed to do. She wears the same hoodie from last night with jeans and a gray sock cap that nearly covers her short hair. It makes her look even more boyish. I tear my eyes away before she can notice me looking and use the mirror and sink outside the bathroom to get ready. Ten silent minutes later, we step out into the crisp morning air.

Except for a few chattering birds and the occasional rumble from a vehicle in the distance, all is quiet. The sun isn't quite up yet, and the air has a gray, misty quality to it. I breathe in the fresh smell of pine, which makes me think of the one camping trip I went on as a kid—back when Mom was married to Ricky's dad, Billy. We'd rented a cabin in Missouri for the weekend, which was fun until Mom and Billy got in a huge fight on the second night and we went home early. I doubt this trip will be any better.

As we trudge across the parking lot, K. J. pulls a cigarette from the pocket of her hoodie and sticks it between her lips.

"Really?" I ask. "Do you have to do that now?"

She smiles, obviously enjoying my irritation. "Why not?" She lights up and takes a long drag before coughing several times. "It's just the dry air," she explains.

"Yeah, sure." I shift the bag on my shoulder and read the sign up ahead. An arrow points to Bright Angel Trailhead, but we need to find Bright Angel Lodge first. The lady from Maswik gave me a map of Grand Canyon Village last night, so I pull it out again to study. "I think it's to the right up there."

We haven't gone much farther when I notice another sign and point toward it: No Smoking.

K. J. sighs and drops the cigarette, smashing it with her boot. "That figures."

I bite my lip, attempting to hide my smile of satisfaction. We take a right and follow the sign toward Bright Angel Lodge. It's a large rock A-frame building that looks slightly fancier than our own lodge.

"You both have wide-brimmed hats, right?" the woman at the transportation desk asks us. She has the tanned, leathery-looking skin of someone who has spent most of her life outdoors. She could be forty or sixty—it's hard to tell.

We both answer yes. The itinerary was very specific in what we needed to pack.

"Perfect," she says. "And have either of you ridden before?"

I shake my head, a jittery feeling expanding in my gut. I've resigned myself to the fact that I'm stuck with K. J. for the weekend, but this whole mule thing is getting a little too real now.

"I've ridden a horse a few times," K. J. says.

Great, so I'm going to look like the total fool here.

"That should help," the lady says, "but don't worry, the wranglers will give you all the instructions you need. I'm sure you'll have a fantastic time." She hands each of us a small slip of paper with our cabin number. "Have fun!"

I must look more terrified than anything because the woman gives me a reassuring smile. "Don't worry," she adds. "The mules are very experienced. Most of them have been with us for years."

"Awesome," K. J. says. "Thanks!" She actually looks excited, which only makes me feel worse. My stomach knots and a wave of nausea rolls over me, but I can't let her know I'm scared. I'm sure she'll never let me hear the end of it if I do.

"Just check in at the mule barn by eight," the woman reminds us as we turn to leave.

"Got it," K. J. says before looking at me. "Hey, wanna eat here?"

"I guess." It looks like our only option unless we go back to our own lodge.

A hostess shows us to a small table for two and I spend my time studying the menu so I don't have to look at K. J. This is bound to be the most awkward breakfast I've ever had in my life.

After the waiter takes our orders, I glance around at the other sleepy-eyed guests in the dining area while K. J. pretends the backs of her hands are the most interesting thing in the world. I pull out my phone and start scrolling through a group text between my friends from a few days ago. Lexi's love of GIFs makes me smile, and for a moment I can forget where I am. Reality snaps back when the waiter sets down my biscuits and gravy with a side of bacon and K. J.'s plate of pancakes. Neither one of us makes eye contact or talks—we just start eating.

We must be an interesting sight, two silent girls who refuse to acknowledge each other. It reminds me of how Mom and Billy were toward the end. They used to make me and Ricky deliver their messages. Things like, "Tell RaeLynn I won't be home for dinner tonight," or "Let Billy know he needs to pick you up from practice today."

"Will you need one ticket or two?" the waiter asks upon returning. Despite my nerves and questionable appetite earlier, I'd managed to scarf my food down in record time. K. J.'s just finishing the last of her pancakes.

"Two," I tell him.

He brings our tickets, and we each hand over the prepaid debit card that arrived along with our plane tickets. Mr. Sisco said they were to be used for meals and any extra fees not included in the reservations. It's like Grandpa really did think of everything.

With nothing else to do, K. J. suggests going to the barn early. It's still cool out, but the rising sun is blinding. I slip on my sunglasses as K. J. and I stand near a wood fence enclosing the mule pen. The wranglers catch the animals and lead them to the barn, one by one.

"They seem really big for donkeys," I mutter.

"They're not donkeys. They're mules."

"Same difference, right?"

K. J. cracks a smile. "Nope, a mule is a cross between a horse and a donkey. They have sixty-three chromosomes. Donkeys only have sixty-two."

Whatever. Mule. Donkey. I couldn't care less about their chromosomes, and I don't want to ride either one.

"I hope I get that one," K. J. says, pointing to the white mule being led to the barn. It's the only one that's not brown.

I don't care which one I get as long as it's gentle. The knot in my stomach coils tighter as I realize I'll be sitting on one of those mules in less than an hour. I can't believe this is really happening. What if Grandpa were here, getting ready to go on this ride instead of us? It's hard to fathom the idea. I can't remember him going anywhere besides his own property.

One time, probably around ten years ago, the two of us were out walking the trails on his land. I asked what would happen if we went outside the gate and walked down the street. A pained look crossed his face, and he told me he wasn't sure, but he'd rather not try. I pleaded with him for several minutes, but he wouldn't budge. I finally gave up. When I told Mom about it later, she said I shouldn't ever ask him that again.

"Why?" I'd wondered aloud.

She frowned and shook her head. "Your grandpa isn't like everyone else. There are things in the outside world that scare him."

"Like what?" I'd asked.

"All sorts of things, but mostly being in cars and going where there are lots of other people."

"But there're people everywhere. The world is full of them."

"Yes, it is," Mom said. "So Grandpa prefers to stay home."

That's when I first began to understand the condition that had firmly held my grandpa in its grip for so many years. After that day, I never asked him to leave the property again.

✳ ✳ ✳ ✳

By the time we're sitting on our mules at the trailhead, I feel as if I might have a panic attack myself. I've never been a fan of heights, but the Grand Canyon is a sight unlike anything I've ever seen. The chasm is both stunningly beautiful and utterly terrifying at the same time. I've honestly never seen anything so enormous and I can't help but think about the fact that I could actually die today. If Mom were here, I'm not sure she'd be okay with this. She already lost her son, after all. When I risk a glance at K. J., I find she's peering toward the canyon's edge with more of a look of anticipation.

I'm a freakin' midfielder, I remind myself. *The best on my team. I've had girls twice my size coming at me on the field. I can do this.*

My pep talk is only a temporary fix, though. When the leader of our ride, a thirty-something cowboy named Dusty, shouts for everyone to follow him, I'm right back where I was. My heart hammers as the mules fall in line, their hooves clip-clopping on the rocky ground. We begin our perilous descent, and my hand clutches the horn on my saddle like my life depends on it. It very well could, actually. Though the great void to my right is impossible to ignore, I force myself to stay focused on the space between Geronimo's floppy ears. If he has any idea that our lives are in mortal danger, he shows no sign of it.

A ways ahead of me, K. J. yells, "Yeehaw!" as she rounds the first bend in the switchback trail. I can't even dwell on her dorkiness because soon enough I'm at the same turn. I suck in a sharp breath as Geronimo's head hangs over open space for a gut-wrenching moment, but he makes the turn easily enough and lumbers on.

Just breathe, I tell myself, and that's all I can really do. Not that I'd been looking forward to this trip at all, but it's worse than I'd feared. Why anyone would actually choose to do this is beyond me, and with each step Geronimo takes down the trail, my stomach clenches tighter. I keep hoping things will get easier or I'll get used to the scenery, but after a half hour or so, it becomes clear that isn't going to happen. By now, my whole body is betraying me. My back feels like it could give out at any second, and the muscles in my right hand ache from gripping the saddle horn so tightly. Honestly, I think my hand might be permanently molded into that shape by the time we make it to the bottom. This is the absolute worst thing ever.

Every time K. J. rounds another bend in the zigzagging trail and passes back by me, she's beaming, which sends a jolt of anger spiraling through my system. How is she enjoying this? I don't get it at all. Occasionally, she glances up at me, but I force my eyes elsewhere. Then, an idea pops into my head. When she comes into view again, I try to smile and wave like I'm having the time of my life. Only my body refuses to cooperate and a little squeal escapes my mouth as I attempt to pry my fingers from the saddle horn. By the time I regain my composure, she's already moved on, probably having a good laugh at my expense.

I just want this stupid ride to be over with. What on earth was Grandpa thinking, sending us here? There's no possible way he'd ever have done this himself. This is right up there with skydiving as far as I'm concerned.

The sun is high between the two canyon walls when we make it to our first rest stop at Indian Garden. I'm tired and hot and more uncomfortable than I've ever been in my life, not to mention, my bladder is about to burst, but I've never been so happy to see some semblance of flat land again.

"Lunchtime," Dusty calls.

My legs quiver as I climb down from the saddle, and I grimace at the ache stretching down the insides of my thighs. Riding a mule must require a whole different set of muscles than playing soccer because it's like I've just had the toughest workout of my life.

I overhear Dusty saying to another guest that we're about halfway to Phantom Ranch, and my stomach lurches. I thought for sure we were closer than that. The wranglers come around, taking our mules and tying them to the hitching posts nearby. After shedding my sweatshirt, I twist my back to the right and left and do a few quad stretches to loosen up my legs. I still feel strangely bow-legged as I set off toward the restrooms.

K. J.'s already in line, and when she turns to look at me, I pretend to be interested in the surrounding landscape. She lifts the floppy rim of her hat, rubbing at her forehead, and then eyes me with a smirk.

"Having fun?"

"Sure," I reply drily.

"I really wasn't sure what to expect, but I'm having a blast."

I have little doubt that she is. I raise my eyebrow in mock surprise but don't respond. I'm not a good enough liar to pretend I'm having a good time, too. The bathroom is available, and it's K. J.'s turn. By the time I come out, she's disappeared.

One of the wranglers is passing out our box lunches, so I find a place in the shade to eat. Several other people gather together and sit around on the ground, but I haven't actually talked to anyone yet during the ride. A middle-aged man in a straw cowboy hat takes a seat nearby "How's it going?" he asks me. Beneath the hat, he has reddish-brown hair with a beard to match and he wears old-fashioned cowboy boots, which look recently polished. He's exactly the type I would expect to see on a ride like this. In my skinny jeans and pink Under Armour T-shirt, I must look completely out of place.

I force myself to smile. "It's going okay."

"This your first time down the canyon?"

"Yeah, how about you?" I open my lunch and peer inside. A peanut butter and jelly sandwich with chips, an apple, and a pickle. Better than nothing, I guess. I pick up the sandwich and take a bite.

"This is my second, but it's my son's first time." He nods toward a skinny teenage boy walking in our direction. His son gives an awkward wave before coming to sit next to his dad. He has the same reddish hair, but no beard or boots. He's sort of cute, but I'd guess he's a little younger than me, maybe sixteen. "So who'd you come with?" the man asks.

"My cousin." I glance around for K. J. and finally spot her about twenty yards away. She's sitting beneath another patch of shade, talking with several older women.

"I see," he says, probably wondering why we aren't together. I don't offer any information on the subject but, instead, attempt to check my phone. When I click on Instagram, I get a blank page with a spinning wheel, so I pocket my phone and take another bite of my sandwich.

"Where ya from?" the man asks, and I'm guessing he feels sorry for me sitting here all by myself.

"Siloam Springs."

"Arkansas is pretty country. We're from Georgia."

"I'll be going through there, too, this summer," I say before thinking better of it.

"Where 'bouts?"

"We're supposed to run the Bull Sluice, I think. You know, white water rafting."

The man takes a sip from his water bottle and gives a chuckle. "Aren't you a daredevil! I tried to get Shane to do that with me, but he wouldn't even hear of it." He gives his son a playful jab with his elbow.

Shane's face reddens and he looks away.

I give a one-shoulder shrug as a sickening feeling rises in my stomach again. I was hoping this would be the worst of the trips in terms of adventure. "Yeah, that's me," I mumble, "a regular old daredevil." Though I'm starting to think that these trips are more like a punishment for not being good granddaughters.

"Hey," a familiar annoying voice says. Great, just who I want to see.

"Hi," I mumble, only because I don't want the man and his son to think I'm completely rude.

"Can I borrow some sunscreen?" K. J. asks. "I forgot mine." My lips pucker, but I refrain from commenting. She's probably just as irresponsible as her mother. I fish the small tube from the pocket of the hoodie tied around my waist and hand it to her.

"Thanks," she says, plopping down beside me.

"You from Arkansas too?" my new bearded friend asks her.

K. J. turns to look at him. "Who? Me?"

He grins. "Yeah, you. I've just been talking to your cousin here. We're from Georgia." He glances back at me. "Name's George, by the way. George from Georgia—that's easy enough to remember, right?"

I get the feeling he's used that line a time or two before.

"I'm from Oklahoma, but not far from the Arkansas border," K. J. says. "Near Colcord."

"I see." George takes another swig from his water bottle and sets it aside. "It's nice that you and your cousin got to come on this trip together. I was really close to a cousin of mine when I was younger. We've grown apart some now, but we used to do a lot together. Nothing like this, of course, but we did some tent camping and quite a bit of fishing."

"How fun," K. J. says in a tone that suggests that she might think otherwise.

I glance around for our ride leader. As crazy as it seems, I'd rather be back on the trail than stuck here with her. There's no telling what she'll say next.

A moment later, she proves I was right to be concerned.

An impish grin stretches across her face. "Yeah, me and Becka, we're like this." She holds a hand up, her index and middle finger twisting together. "We do practically everything together." She pastes on a ridiculous smile. "Right, Beck?"

I resist the urge to grind my teeth. "Mmm hmm."

"That's great!" George says, oblivious to her sarcasm. His son, however, is staring at us with more interest now. Teenagers are experts when it comes to this sort of thing.

K. J. scoots closer to me and wraps a lanky arm around my shoulder. It takes everything I've got not to shove her away. She smiles sweetly at George. "She's like the sister I always wanted. I love her soooo much." She pulls me toward her with a little too much force, and I nearly topple into her lap.

"Time to head out!" a voice calls in the distance.

Thank goodness. I'm not sure I can pretend to even tolerate her for one more second.

"Nice talkin' to you ladies," George says, rising to his feet. "See you at the next stop."

"See you," I say.

"Bye," K. J. says with a little wave.

Once Shane and George are out of earshot, I scramble to my feet and glare down at her. "Don't ever touch me again."

Her forehead crinkles and she pretends to look hurt. "I'm just trying to do what Grandpa wanted and make friends with you."

"That's not what you're doing, and you know it." I force myself to walk away before I get too worked up.

Maybe Grandpa thought he could change things between our families with all his *tasks*, or whatever these dumb trips are, but he was wrong. There's no way in Hades we'll ever be friends.

CHAPTER 8
K. J.

"TALLY HO!" DUSTY YELLS.

"Tally ho!" we all yell back. Don't know what the hell it means, but he seems to like the phrase because he's yelled it after every stop today.

I shift my butt backward in the saddle, trying to find a comfortable position. There really isn't one, but I'm learning to deal with it. This trip has been totally worth the discomfort so far. Who would have thought? Me. On a mule. Riding into the freaking Grand Canyon. It's been the biggest rush of my life.

I reach down to give Dixie a pat on the neck. I didn't get the white mule like I wanted, but I'm over it. Dixie's taking good care of me, and I think we're even starting to bond. One of the wranglers told me she's been doing this for eleven years.

Six mules ahead, Becka rounds a bend, and I hold in a laugh. It gives me a sick amount of pleasure seeing her face so pale and lips clamped tight. She's still scared shitless! Maybe Grandpa's little vacations won't be so bad after all. Especially, if I get the opportunity to torment Becka every chance I get.

As we head out of Indian Garden, the flat land disappears, turning into a narrow trail along the edge of the canyon again. The mules automatically fall into a single file line. Even though Dusty told us not to, I pull my phone out and take a few more pictures. I've never seen so many shades of red and brown before. The colors are all crammed together like one big-ass piece of pottery. With the bright blue sky up above, it's almost enough to take my breath away.

I wave as we pass a group of sweaty hikers with their backs pressed against the canyon side of the trail. Mules get the right-of-way here, which they totally should. A couple of the hikers give a hello nod, and one lady gives me a thumbs-up. I'm glad I'm not in their boots because I'm not sure I'd be able to make it this far on foot, and I sure as hell wouldn't want to make the hike back up.

By the time we reach the end of our ride, the sun has disappeared behind the canyon walls and everything is bathed in shadows. Every bone in my body protests as I slide off Dixie and my feet hit the ground. I may not be able to walk normal for a month after this. I stifle a yawn, but my stomach flutters with excitement just like it did when we set off this morning. How many people can actually say they've been to the bottom of the Grand Canyon?

The wranglers unsaddle the mules while the rest of us trek across a bridge that stretches over a quick-moving creek. A bunch of cacti and small shrubs and trees surround us, but in the distance, a cluster of buildings appear. Phantom Ranch, I assume. I can't wait to have a look around the place.

Becka walks ahead of me, talking with that dude and his son again, but I hang back, taking everything in. It's like there's this whole little world down here, completely separate from the one a mile above us. I pause and do a three-sixty, eyeing the rugged canyon walls all around. I can see now why Grandpa wanted to come here. This place is freaking awesome. Though I haven't been inspired to do a real piece of art in a long time, I might just have to sketch this scene when I get back home.

After wandering the rock-lined paths, taking my own personal tour of the ranch, I check the cabin number listed on the slip of paper still stuffed in my jeans pocket. Number nine. Stepping inside the small building, I find a rustic-looking room with two sets of bunk beds, a sink, and a tiny bathroom. It's not near as fancy as Maswik Lodge, but it'll definitely do. Someone's blue duffel bag sits on one of the bottom beds. I guess Becka and I won't be staying here alone, which is probably a good thing. I toss my hat, along with my bag of belongings, up on an empty top bunk before venturing back outside to explore some more.

I don't see Becka again until we all shuffle in to the canteen for dinner. Our eyes meet, and an unspoken message seems to pass between us: stay the hell away from me. So after she sits at one of the long green tables, I choose a seat across the room, next to the ladies I'd met earlier on the trail. Sheila, Mary, and some other M-name I can't remember. They're a good forty or fifty years older than me, but that doesn't matter. Just like that guy on the plane, I'd take them over Becka any day.

"Looks delicious," Mary says once we've been served plates of steak, a baked potato, green beans, and a thick slice of bread.

I hold up my glass of tea in a toast of agreement. "Amen to that." Can't remember the last time I've had steak.

Even after everyone else has left, the four of us stay in the canteen, talking and telling stories. Mainly, I'm just listening—I don't have stories anything like these ladies do. Unless you count tee-peeing houses or sneaking out at midnight to smoke and listen to music with Carter. I definitely haven't driven cross-country on Route 66 like the three of them are doing.

When a lull finally settles into the conversation, Sheila looks at me. "So why'd you decide to come on this ride?"

I'm not really prepared to answer, but luckily, I manage to come up with something that sort of resembles the truth. "Actually, my grandpa and I were supposed to come together. He booked it last year and all." I stare at the backs of my hands. "But, um, he passed away recently, so I wanted to, you know, honor his memory by still coming."

It's uncomfortably silent for several seconds, and I'm not sure if it's because they know I'm full of shit or if they're just surprised.

"Wow," Sheila finally says, "I'm so sorry to hear about your grandpa."

"You're sure a brave young lady," Mary says while the other woman pats my back.

It wasn't really my intent to get their sympathy, but it feels kind of nice all the same. I look back up, giving a little shrug. "Thanks."

"Feel free to hang out with us any time," Sheila says.

"I might take you up on that."

Mary glances at her watch. "Oh, the presentation starts in ten minutes."

"What presentation?" I ask.

"Outside at the amphitheater," Sheila says. "There are two parts, I think. The history of Phantom Ranch and canyon wildlife. You coming?"

While that does sound interesting, I've got one cigarette left and I'm thinking a smoke sounds way better. Plus, I've got this extra credit poem I need to work on for English. "I don't know. I'm thinking I might turn in early."

"Okay," Mary says with a sympathetic smile. "See you tomorrow, then."

While my three new friends set off for the amphitheater, I head back toward the mule pens, where no one's likely to be hanging around. It's dark by now, but the mostly full moon and the stars give off enough light for me to make my way along the trail. I cross back over the creek, following the sweet scent of hay. I find the mules the way we left them earlier today, dozing in groups or munching on hay. I scan the pen for Dixie, finding her in one of the dozing groups.

"Hey, Dixie!" I say. She's shorter than most of the other mules but has the biggest ears of all of them. Right now, they're flopping way out to the side. I call to her again, but she doesn't pay any attention to me. Now that I think about it, I'm probably just another human to her. Just one of the many who have sat on her back. Oh well. I turn away from the pen, finding a large rock nearby to sit on instead.

After double-checking to make sure I'm alone, I pull the cigarette and lighter from my hoodie pocket. The first drag is always the best. Scooting back on the rock, I draw up my knees and tilt my chin toward the night sky. You'd think the stars would be dimmer way down here, but it's just the opposite. They're a hundred times brighter than back home, and the Milky Way looks like a ginormous, sparkling river stretching across the blackness. A sense of peace settles inside me. It's been forever since I sat outside, just looking up at the stars.

I'm still lost in thought when I hear the quiet shuffle of footsteps in the distance. I stub out my cigarette on the rock and use the heel of my shoe to dig a hole and bury it. Scrambling back to the fence, I pretend to be watching the mules as the footsteps continue to grow closer.

"K. J.?"

I turn to face my cousin, who's stopped in her tracks about ten feet away. "What are you doing out here?" I figured she'd be all about that nature program they're having.

She shoves her hands in the pocket of her hoodie and shrugs. "Nothing. Just having a look around." She sniffs the air. "Were you smoking again?"

I don't answer. It's none of her damn business what I've been doing.

"You know there's like a really big fine for that, right? Dusty talked about it before we left this morning."

"I wasn't smoking."

"Sure you weren't." She comes to stand near the railing, taking care not to get too close to me.

Guess our unspoken agreement has ended. Pity. I study her profile, that perfectly perky ponytail and small button nose. "You think you're so much better than me, don't you?" She doesn't answer, which pretty much confirms my assumption. "You know, it's not my fault what my mom did."

Becka continues to stare out at the mules. "I never said it was."

"You didn't have to."

She turns and leans her back against the fence, her face lifting toward the sky. "Listen, neither one of us wants to be here, so let's do each other a favor and talk as little as possible. All we have to do is go to these places, do what Grandpa wanted us to do, and then we get our money."

"Speak for yourself. I plan to enjoy myself actually."

"Whatever. I'm going to the cabin." Becka pushes away from the fence, starts walking away.

As soon as she's out of sight, I head back to my rock and comb my fingers through the sandy dirt. The cigarette isn't hard to find, but a moonlit inspection finds it crumpled beyond repair. Damn it. The only thing I can do is push it back into the dirt.

* * * *

We're back in the saddle again by seven a.m. I'm physically exhausted from yesterday's ride and staying up till midnight to finish my poem might not have been the best idea, but what choice do I really have if I want to get my grades up? I yawn and stretch, pain registering in every square inch of my body. The bad thing is I know it's only going to get worse after today, but I'll just have to tough it out.

Becka's blond braid swings back and forth from beneath her straw hat as she rides three mules in front of me. I think of our conversation last night: talk as little as possible. I can definitely handle that.

We start across the suspension bridge, the river rushing a hundred feet below. Even on Dixie, I can feel it sway. The sensation makes my stomach dance, but in a good way.

"This'll be a shorter route today," Dusty explains once we've all gathered on the opposite side of the bridge. "We'll have lunch at the lodge."

"Yay!" someone says from behind me, and I have to agree. A lodge lunch does sound better than another PB&J.

Dusty clucks to his mule, but then pulls up again, turning to survey our group once more. "And just another reminder, smoking isn't allowed under any circumstances in the canyon." His eyes linger on me for an extra second, making my heart skip a beat. Becka tattled on me, apparently.

The smirk on her face leaves little room for doubt, but it's not like she can prove anything. No one can. As the mules start uphill, my lips purse and I keep my eyes trained on my cousin, trying to catch a glimpse of her face each time we turn on the zigzag trail, but if she's still scared, I can't tell. This makes the ride markedly less fun for me.

We take two short rest stops today, and each time I hang with my three new pals. I've finally remembered the other woman's name. Mona. I've also learned this is the second time they've all made this ride together. After talking with them I've decided on a new life goal: I want to be like them when I'm old. Still doing badass stuff like this.

At the rim, we say goodbye to our mules, and a bus shuttles us back to Bright Angel Lodge. A dull pang gnaws at my chest. I'm relieved to be back at the top, but that also means my first-ever vacation is coming to an end. Finding an empty table at the restaurant, I search around for my friends, hoping we can eat together one last time. Unfortunately, I don't see them anywhere. They must have taken off early. Then, to my complete surprise, Becka appears and falls into the chair beside me, flopping an envelope onto the table.

"What's this?" I pick it up and turn it over, seeing both our names listed along with the address for Bright Angel Lodge. The sender is Sisco and Browning Law Office.

"Certified mail," Becka says. "I had to sign for it at the front desk."

"Another one of Grandpa's letters?"

"You're a quick learner," she says with a snort. "The lawyer said there'd be more."

"I know, but I didn't think it'd come here." I want to smack that snide look off her face, but instead, I run my finger beneath the top flap of the envelope, peeling it open.

"May I?" I ask.

Becka crosses her arms. "Be my guest."

CHAPTER 9

ELI

My Dearest Granddaughters,

I hope you've enjoyed your trip into the Grand Canyon.
You might be thinking your old Grandpa was even crazier
than you thought, but hear me out and I'll explain a
few things.

One of my favorite memories as a kid was visiting the
Grand Canyon. I was around eight when my parents took my
sisters and me there, and it's a trip I've never forgotten. We
stayed in the campground in our camper and hiked along the
rim every day. My mother didn't care to get near the canyon's
edge, but my father took me and my sisters down into it
one day. When we saw a line of mules and riders pass on the
trail, my father said they were headed to the bottom to stay

the night at Phantom Ranch. I knew I had to do that someday, so I made up my mind right then and there that I'd be back.

Well, my father passed away when I was fourteen, then Mom sold the camper, and we stopped taking vacations for the most part. When I married your grandma, I hoped we could return to the canyon, but money was tight in those days, and riding mules wasn't exactly the kind of vacation Charlotte cared to go on. After the car wreck, when my panic attacks set in, my hopes for doing any kind of traveling at all dwindled away. But when I got the idea for you two to do some of the things I'd always wanted to do, this had to be first on the list.

I'd like to tell you a little story:

Back when I was a teaching assistant at the University of Arkansas, I was in charge of one of the science labs. I'll never forget in one entomology class, there were two girls (Lisa and Jody—funny, how I still remember their names) who got into a big argument one day just as class was beginning. I don't remember what they were arguing about, but the professor told them they would be lab partners from then on. I later found out by overhearing a conversation between two other students that Lisa and Jody had attended the same high school and evidently endured some sort of rivalry for a number of years. I thought the professor was only asking for a blow-up by putting them together. I just hoped that he knew what he was doing and that the expensive microscopes we'd just gotten in would be safe.

Well, Lisa and Jody did their work, but refused to talk to each other for the first few labs. Then one day, when we were doing a beetle dissection, I noticed the two of them were actually speaking to each other. It appeared they'd become so interested in their lab, they'd forgotten their feud with each other—at least for a little while. Strangely enough, things got better from there on out.

I don't know whatever became of those girls, but I thought of them when I began planning these trips for the two of you. Hopefully, my two granddaughters can learn to talk to one another and, in time, maybe even become friends.

Love,

Grandpa

CHAPTER 10

BECKA

K. J. HANDS THE LETTER TO ME WITHOUT SAYING A word. I could be mistaken, but she looks like she's upset—if her version of upset consists of narrowed eyes and an exaggerated scowl, anyway.

"What?" I ask.

She shakes her head, and the scowl softens. "Nothing, it's just sad. I wish Grandpa could have done the mule thing, and that last part he wrote . . . here, just read it."

For whatever reason, Grandpa's words don't have the same effect on me. Mainly, I'm filled with a sense of guilt and frustration. He wanted his "tasks" to bring us together, but he should have known it's a hopeless cause. Not only does the divide between our mothers run too deep, but K. J. and I are complete opposites in every way. If we were the only two people stuck on an island and our survival depended on us being friends, I have a feeling we'd both die.

I fold the letter up, slide it back into the envelope, and lay it on the table. K. J. stares at it for a moment and then picks it up again.

"Can I keep it?" she asks.

I shrug. "Suit yourself."

A waiter sets a plate with grilled chicken, corn, and mashed potatoes before each of us. I wasn't planning on eating at this table, but I guess I'll stay put. K. J. and I both scroll through our phones as we eat. I check all the Instagram posts I've missed during the trip into the canyon and then text a selfie of me on my mule, as well as a few pics of Phantom Ranch, to my mom and Lexi. After a while, K. J. mumbles something about going to the bathroom and disappears. She doesn't return, so I just head back toward our lodge on my own. Task number one complete and only four more to go. The thought doesn't bring me any relief at all.

Monday morning, I can barely drag myself out of bed. Between Mom's endless questioning last night, the time change, and my exhausting weekend, it's really no surprise. As I sit in first hour, trying to keep my eyes open, the thought of another two-hour practice after school is almost too much to bear. But we ended up making state championships, and Coach expects everyone to be on top of their game. There's no way I can miss practice.

By lunchtime, I've managed to perk up a little. It helps that I get to tell my friends all about my horrific weekend at the Grand Canyon. I describe the terrifying mule ride and every appalling encounter with K. J., hoping they'll feel at least a little sorry for me.

Maddie's brow wrinkles with disgust as she finishes off her apple. "She sounds like a real bitch, if you ask me."

I don't know if that's the right word for my cousin, but she's definitely rude. "She's really weird. And I'm pretty sure she was high the day we left. Probably had to get one last hit since she couldn't smuggle her drugs onto the plane."

Lexi frowns. "Wow, what a loser."

"Yeah, tell me about it," I say. "I can't believe we're actually related."

"I'm really sorry," Maddie says, offering a tentative smile, "but at least you'll be getting something from all of this. Gotta think of the positives, right?"

True, but I'd give up the money in a heartbeat if it meant not having to spend one more minute with K. J. I'm only doing it so Mom can get her share.

"So what's your aunt like?" Maddie asks as we go to dump our trash. "Since K. J. seems so awful."

Everything my mom has ever said about Jackie floods into my mind, but I consider my words carefully. "She's worse than her daughter," I say, keeping my eyes trained on the floor. "She and my mom haven't really spoken in years. Until this whole ordeal, at least."

And even then, I wouldn't exactly call it "speaking to one another." It certainly wasn't by choice. I've never told anyone the full truth about things, and Lexi has always been too polite to ask for details. My cheeks grow warm and I clear my throat. "It's a complicated situation," I explain. "I'll have to tell you about it another time."

"Oh, okay, sure," Maddie says.

I can tell I've piqued her curiosity, though.

Outside of the cafeteria, Maddie goes one way while Lexi and I head toward English, our one and only class together. Lexi doesn't say a word, and I pretend to be interested in the artwork hanging along the hallway. After a quick stop by our lockers, we continue toward class.

"So did you finish your essay?" she asks.

"Yeah, on the plane last night." A small amount of relief settles over me as I realize Lexi's not going to pry. "How about you?" The question is really just a formality. Lexi would never *not* finish an assignment.

"I didn't think I was ever going to get it done," she says with a groan. "So glad that's the last one of the year."

"No kidding. I'm all essayed out."

We enter the classroom and take our seats on opposite sides of the room. I'm fairly confident Lexi won't be a problem, but Maddie, I'm not so sure about. Looks like I'll have to avoid her at soccer practice today. But even if that proves impossible, I at least have several hours to come up with an alternative story—one which wouldn't lead someone to question if they should even be friends with me in the first place.

I'm too distracted to pay much attention to Mr. Sperry, who's already lecturing about some poem by William Yeats. I really hate my aunt for getting me into this whole mess. And since K. J.'s her daughter, I have no choice but to hate her, too.

✳ ✳ ✳ ✳

"Why are we going to Grandpa's?" I ask, glancing over at Mom. She puts on her turn signal and pulls out of our neighborhood. Tim's working late tonight, so she suggested we go out to eat. It was only after we got into the Jeep that she mentioned stopping by Grandpa's house on the way.

"Mr. Sisco said I was free to get pictures and other personal items before the auction. I've been putting it off, but I figured it was time to go."

"Did he tell Jackie the same thing?"

She nods. "He told us both."

"I wonder if she's already been there."

Mom purses her lips. "There's no telling with her."

On the far outskirts of Siloam Springs, we turn onto a gravel road, and a wave of nostalgia washes over me. We didn't come to Grandpa's often, but it makes me sad knowing I likely won't ever be coming back here again. The Jeep rolls to a stop in front of the rusted red gate, and I jump out and open it so Mom can drive through. The grass along the driveway is tall and scraggly. Grandpa didn't like to cut it. He said taller grass was a good habitat for all the insects, so he only kept the area right around his house mowed short. The small, brown clapboard house comes into view, and I swallow back the lump rising in my throat.

"How're we gonna get in?" I ask.

A grim smile tugs at Mom's lips. "I know where a spare key is."

I hope she's right; otherwise, we drove all the way out here for nothing.

She kneels beside the potted plant on the front porch and pokes her fingers into the dirt. Several seconds later, she pulls out a key and wipes it off on her jeans.

"That's a strange place to keep a key." Then again, it's exactly something my grandpa would do.

The house still has the faint smell of chicken noodle soup, and I realize it's a smell I'll forever associate with this place. Mom flips on the living room lights, and we both wander around as if this is the first time we've ever been here. A thin film of dust covers the coffee table and TV cabinet, only adding to the deserted feeling of the house. Mom moves down the narrow hallway that leads to the two bedrooms, pausing to examine the pictures on the wall. I know them all by heart. There's a prom picture with my mom and dad, and one of me from fifth grade. Another of K. J. around the same age with a weird, bowl-type haircut. A photo of Ricky in his karate uniform. Aunt Jackie's senior picture in her cap and gown, and also an old family portrait. It's the only one I've seen with my Grandma Charlotte—taken back before Grandpa developed agoraphobia and my mom and aunt were little pig-tailed girls.

"I don't think Jackie's been here yet," Mom says quietly. She disappears inside Grandpa's bedroom. I trail behind her but stop in the doorway, my hand resting against the doorframe. Mom touches the dresser and glances around the room. The bed is still unmade and dust motes dance through streams of light let in by the blinds.

"Is this where he died?"

Mom gives a solemn nod.

Something tugs hard inside my chest, seeing the last things Grandpa saw before he died. A weight settles over me as the reality of his death hits all over again. Right now, the whole Grand Canyon experience seems far away. I can't be mad at Grandpa for making me do that while standing in his room. When I look back at Mom, tears glisten in her eyes. "Is there anything you want in here?" I ask her.

She moves toward the wall, where two framed handprints hang side-by-side. She takes the slightly larger one off the wall and holds it to her chest. We return to the hallway, and Mom takes the pictures of me and Ricky, but leaves all the others. I don't have to question why she doesn't take her prom picture. She hates my dad as much as she hates her sister. I'm surprised it's managed to stay up there all these years.

While Mom goes back into the main part of the house, I step into the "Bug Room," as we always called it. It was the room Mom and Jackie shared when they were kids, but now it's filled with encased collections of insects, some hanging on the walls, others sitting on shelves or on the floor, leaning against the wall. My favorite has always been the butterfly collection, with the bright rainbow of colors and different-sized wings.

Some look too beautiful to have been real, but I know they are. I was with Grandpa when he found a few of them. He was always careful to take dead or injured insects for his collections and just observe the ones that were still alive. The Entomological Society will be lucky to get all of these. He spent years working on them.

"You ready?" Mom calls, and I follow the sound of her voice. She's back in the living room with two more items—a coffee mug she'd given Grandpa for Christmas one year and a painting my grandma made long ago. We step out onto the porch, and Mom locks the door before pushing the key back into the dry soil in the pot.

"Should we give that key to Mr. Sisco?" I ask, but she shakes her head.

"Jackie might still come."

We climb into the Jeep in silence. Tears stream down both our faces as we travel along the bumpy driveway. I stare into the woods that Grandpa loved to spend his days scouring. When we stop, I get out to open the gate again. As I'm pushing it closed, I spot a walking stick insect clinging to the top rail, only a few inches away from my hand. *Diapheromera femorata.* I'm not sure if I learned the name in biology class or from Grandpa, not that it really matters. As I'm pushing the lock into place, the insect raises one of its spindly arms, almost as if in a wave. I suppose some girls might scream or be grossed out, but I just wipe away my tears and smile. I can't think of a more fitting creature to bid me goodbye.

CHAPTER 11

K. J.

FOR THE LAST FEW YEARS, I COULDN'T HAVE CARED less about graduating, but ever since learning about Grandpa's will, I've suddenly found myself giving a shit about things, like taking the ACT—thank god the school counselor found a school the next town over offering a make-up date—and finishing every ounce of my homework. I don't think my teachers knew what to make of my last-minute change of heart, but most were pretty helpful about things. I told the counselor about the will, so it's possible she filled them in on my secret. After all the extra credit, I managed to pull every single one of my grades up a little, and now all that's left is finals.

By some miracle, Carter also gets to graduate, so to celebrate we leave campus in his truck to treat ourselves to a non-cafeteria lunch on the last day before finals. After driving to the Gas N' Go to pick up some hot box food, we head to the park to have ourselves a picnic. A few other seniors are here, too, since they're letting us leave campus for once, and options are pretty limited around Colcord.

We're about to lay claim on the last open picnic table when a low voice comes from behind. "Hey, that one's ours."

I turn to see two of the football players in their blue jerseys. They each hold an extra-large drink in one hand and a pizza box in the other. While Carter and I pause, the guys waltz right past us and plop down at the table. I open my mouth to go off on them when Carter places a hand on my shoulder and shoots me a warning look.

"Come on," he says, nodding toward a shade tree with a four-square slab beneath it. "Let's eat over there."

"Good idea," one of the football players says with a coarse laugh.

Carter walks toward the slab, but I stay put for a second, glaring down at the two jocks. I take a sip of my Dr Pepper. "Think it's time to lay the jerseys to rest, boys. Football season ended six months ago."

The bigger of the two guys scowls at me. "Shut up, K. J. Nobody asked you."

"Just saying." I shrug before turning to leave. One of them mutters something else, but it's too low for me to make out.

Carter is already sitting cross-legged on the cement, so I take a seat across from him.

"I hate those guys," he says as he unwraps a Hot Pocket.

"I know, but two more days and we're done with all these a-holes and their high school hierarchy," I remind him.

"True." He eats half the Hot Pocket in one gigantic bite. "There's a bright side to everything I guess," he says, still chewing. "So . . . what's next on your grandpa's list?"

"Yellowstone." I douse my greasy burrito in a packet of hot sauce before taking a bite.

"Do you have to pet a bear or some kinda crap like that?"

"Nope, just go for a hike. Should be a piece of cake."

"A piece of cake with shit icing though, right?" Carter laughs at his own joke.

I swipe at my mouth with a napkin and nod. "Shit icing—that's a good way to describe my cousin."

"I'm only going off your description of her since I've never met the girl myself." He reaches down to flick away a beetle crawling near his foot.

I watch it roll back onto its little legs and resume its trek across the slab, but out of reach of Carter this time. "You wouldn't like her." The thought of Carter hanging out with Becka sends a twinge of jealousy through me, which is weird. It's not like they'd ever be friends anyway.

The Hot Pocket finished off now, Carter starts in on his fries. "So when do you leave to go see Smokey the Bear?"

"In a couple weeks, I think. I need to look at the dates again."

"Cool." He gives an appreciative nod. "You're, like, turning into a badass wilderness woman now."

I can't help but grin. I think that's the nicest thing Carter's ever said to me, even if it's not exactly true. "Yeah, I even get real hiking boots and everything."

"Nice."

"Hey." I pull a folded piece of paper from my back pocket and toss it toward Carter. "Can you quiz me for U.S. government?"

"Seriously?" Carter unfolds the paper and scowls down at it. "Guess you weren't joking about all this."

"Duh. I told you I wasn't."

He gives a loud sigh and crams the last few fries in his mouth. "Fine. I'll quiz you."

We make it through the whole study guide, and I'm feeling pretty good about things, especially since I have plans to do more studying at home this evening. With finals counting for a big chunk of our grades, maybe I'll even manage to pull an A or two on this final report card. Wouldn't that be something?

✳ ✳ ✳ ✳

I've barely had time to adjust to my newfound freedom before it's time for Grandpa's second trip, but my stuff is packed and I'm ready to roll. Or fly, at least. Having already tucked one flight under my belt, I'm not nearly as nervous this time around. In fact, I tell Mom I'm going to hold off on the Xanax for now, but I keep two in my pocket, just in case.

"Take some pictures, will ya?" she asks as she's dropping me off. "I'd love to see what it looks like." I could be wrong, but there might be a hint of jealousy in her voice. Too bad, so sad, I think. Grandpa knew she and RaeLynn would never go on these trips together, so she'll just have to miss out.

I haven't seen Becka since our last trip, but it's apparent our time apart hasn't made our hearts grow any fonder. She's beat me to the gate again and gives me the stink eye as I approach. I smirk, not even bothering with a greeting. She opens her mouth like she might say something, but then stays mute. I've brought reading material of my own this time: *The Maze Runner*. Figured I should start reading again since I'll hopefully be a college girl by fall. I haven't really done much of that since my elementary school trivia book-reading days, and since there was no way I was going to read one of Mom's romance novels, I visited the library. This series looked pretty cool.

When the lady at the American Airlines desk announces they're almost ready to start boarding, I reach into my pocket, checking for the pills. I'm tempted to take one of them, but I hold out. I'm a badass wilderness woman, I remind myself, and as such, I don't need to take a pill to get on a plane.

As it turns out, I *can* handle flying, especially when I'm super interested in a book. The flight is completely uneventful, and I make it a good ways through the story by the time we land in Bozeman. As we pull into the gate, I turn and peek down the aisle to see Becka sitting near the back of the plane. Lucky us. We got seats on opposite ends this time. When she looks up, I give her a cheesy smile and a wave. She stares right through me, standing to stretch instead. Looks like we're off to another great start.

* * * *

After getting checked in to our hotel, I immediately head to the indoor pool for a swim. It's surprisingly chilly in the big room, and as I'm about to jump in, I spot a fancy hot tub in the corner, which looks a little more appealing. Mom always talks about building a back deck and putting in a hot tub with her big casino winnings, but I'm not holding my breath. Any time she does win a decent amount, she usually loses it all in the slot machines.

I'm enjoying the warm water and minding my own business when an old man with a wispy comb-over steps in and settles in on the opposite side of the hot tub.

"How are you, young lady?" he asks with a yellowed smile.

"Fine, thanks."

After a few exchanged pleasantries, I'm starting to feel pretty awkward with just the two of us sitting here, so I climb back out and return to *The Maze Runner*, which I've brought along with me. It doesn't take long to get back into the book and forget about the only other person in this big room.

"Why are you reading *that*?" I jump at the sound of Becka's voice but blame it mostly on the story since the Grievers are attacking.

"Because I want to."

Tossing a towel into the chair beside me, she makes a grunting noise as she takes a seat. I try to keep reading, but it's hard to focus with Becka sitting beside me now. "Have you read it?" I ask in an attempt at civility.

"Yeah, in, like, the sixth grade."

"Oh, it was in the teen section at the library."

She gives me a look that I interpret to mean: *You're such an idiot.*

We sit in silence for a while, me trying to read and her scrolling through her phone, but after a while, Becka peels off her T-shirt, revealing a red tankini beneath. She heads toward the pool, dives in, and starts swimming laps, because that's what athletes do, obviously. At least I'm able to continue with my book in peace now.

When I come to a good stopping point, I decide I might as well hop in the pool, too. That's what I came down here for, after all. Becka stands in the shallow end, facing away from me as she squeezes water out of her hair. An idea comes, and I stealthily move toward her, pausing when I get to the pool's edge. Bending my knees, I push off from the ledge and do the biggest cannonball I can manage without getting a running start. Water goes everywhere and washes over Becka's head in a giant whoosh.

"What are you doing?" she screeches, whirling around to face me. We're only a couple feet apart, so I back up a few steps. Out of the corner of my eye, I see the old man in the hot tub watching us with interest now.

"Just wanted to cool off," I say. "Sorry, guess I didn't notice you standing so close."

She squints her eyes at me and then shakes her head. "Real mature, K. J. Act your age, why don't you?"

"How about you lighten up a little?" I raise a brow for emphasis. "Or is that too much to ask?"

I smirk and swim away before she has a chance to respond.

CHAPTER 12

BECKA

NOW THIS IS THE KIND OF TRIP I CAN APPRECIATE.
After a nice hike up to the summit of Mount Washburn and then back
down again, we reach a place called Artist Point, getting an up close
and personal view of the so-called Grand Canyon of Yellowstone.
I much prefer this Grand Canyon over the other one. First of all, we're
not nearly as high up. Second, and best of all, I don't have to go down
into it on a mule.

The whooshing river at the canyon's base, along with conversations
of dozens of visitors, make it a little difficult to hear our guide, Johan.
I take a few steps closer, not just because I want to hear his every word,
but also because I could stare at him all day long. In fact, I've been
ogling those perfect calves of his for nearly the entire hike today.

And hallelujah, we get to spend two more glorious days with him.

"Excuse me, Miss," Johan says in his sexy Swedish accent. I follow his gaze, which stops at K. J. She's standing near the lookout rail, clutching a rock in one hand like she's about to throw it over the edge. "Please don't do that."

She turns and gives a sheepish shrug. "Oh, sorry."

I shake my head, annoyance seeping into my very core. She's so embarrassing.

Johan clears his throat and continues. "So after the caldera eruption some six hundred thousand years ago, this entire area was covered by a series of lava flows. However, scientists think the canyon was actually formed as a result of faulting, and this allowed the erosion process to continue at an accelerated rate."

"Is this canyon younger than the real Grand Canyon?" I ask. "Since it's not as deep?"

"Duh," K. J. says from behind me. I pretend I haven't heard her, keeping my eyes focused on Johan instead.

He smiles, happy to answer yet another question. "This canyon is believed to be somewhere around ten to fourteen thousand years old, while the actual Grand Canyon is millions of years old."

He jabs a thumb behind him. "But the Lower Falls, which you see over there, as well as the Upper Falls were created approximately ten thousand years ago when a large glacial ice dam in Hayden Valley burst and flooded the canyon."

"Wow," I whisper, not so much impressed with the information as I am with Johan's knowledge of it. Smart, sexy, and athletic—the perfect trifecta.

"All right," he says to our small group. "We'll take a short break here if you all want to get some pictures or take a breather before we head back."

Everyone scatters, some moving to take photos of the Lower Falls, others finding a place to sit and pull off their backpacks. There's a husband and wife pair, a fifty-something man and his son, an older lady who looks like she hikes as much as Johan does, and then K. J. and me. I opt to stick close to Johan.

"So how long have you been a tour guide here?" I ask as I pull my water bottle from my backpack. What I'm really trying to figure out is how old he is. He can't be more than twenty-three or -four, if I had to guess.

"This is my second year," he says, pushing a swath of his chin-level, gold-blond hair to the side. He takes a bite of jerky, and I try not to stare as he chews. Even his jaw muscles flex in a sexy way.

"Summer job?" Maybe he's a college student.

"Nope, I work here year-round. During the tourist season, anyway."

"Ah." I take a sip of water and gaze back at the falls. I guess this place was aptly named—it's like a picture-perfect painting with the sides of the rocky canyon framing the gigantic waterfall. The air is so fresh. I wish I could bottle some up and take it back home with me.

"So what do you do?" he asks.

I can't tell if he's genuinely interested or just trying to make conversation. "I just graduated actually. I'm going to the University of Arkansas in the fall. On a soccer scholarship."

He nods, looking impressed. "Cool. I did one year of college, but it wasn't for me. It was more to make my parents happy." He finishes off the jerky and takes a swig of water from his own bottle. "I love my job here. Couldn't ask for anything better."

"That's great." I wish I had something more intelligent to add, but nothing comes to mind. "Well," I say after several seconds of awkward silence, "I guess I should get some pictures of this place before we leave."

"For sure."

As we're starting back down the trail, the older woman, Sue, catches up with Johan, asking him something about tomorrow's hike. I slow my pace, not wanting to appear too eager to stay near him.

"You like him, don't you?" K. J. whispers near my ear.

"It's not like there's anyone else here to talk to," I mutter.

"Sure there isn't."

I turn just enough to catch sight of her sly smile. She's so freaking irritating. Sue has paused to take a photo, so I move up to reclaim my spot near the front of the line. Who cares if K. J. thinks I like him. I'm not going to let her ruin *this* trip.

By late afternoon, we've finished our day's hike, and the van takes us to the Old Faithful Inn, a humongous old log cabin with three floors and a giant rock fireplace in the center. It's pretty amazing. After we have a look around the giant foyer, Johan tells us to get checked into our rooms and then meet him in the adjoining restaurant by six for dinner.

"They have superb lamb chops here," he says, adding that charming smile of his. "I highly recommend them."

Our small group breaks up, and I check my phone. Four thirty-seven. Perfect—I'll have plenty of time to take a shower and get cleaned up.

"So what'd you think of the little Grand Canyon?" K. J. asks as we make our way up the stairs toward our room. She trails several steps behind me.

I force as much nonchalance as I can. "It was cool."

"Lots of nice views, huh?"

Something about her tone tells me she's not referring to the landscape.

"Sure." I don't intend to give her the satisfaction of knowing she's getting to me. Thankfully, she drops the subject.

Our room is rustic-style, but nice, with two log-framed queen beds, matching nightstands, and a distressed, turquoise dresser. A painting of a brown bear hangs above one bed while one with a black bear hangs above the other. We haven't seen any bears yet, thank goodness, and it wouldn't bother me if we didn't at all. Before starting on our hike this morning, Johan explained how to use our bear spray, if needed. K. J. just laughed as if it were all a big joke, but I envisioned myself making a run for it instead of confronting a bear with nothing but a can of spray.

K. J. plops down on one of the beds while I head straight for the shower. It's not like I really worked up a sweat today, but I'd like to at least wash off the woods and bug spray. By the time I'm out of the shower, K. J. is fast asleep. Perfect, now we don't have to interact.

I dry and straighten my hair and then reapply my makeup, enjoying the relative peace. After dressing in my nice jeans and a button-down denim shirt, I check the time again. We still have thirty minutes until dinner, but I might as well head down and have a look around.

The Inn's gift shop is quaint, with all sorts of Yellowstone-themed decor, T-shirts, a variety of hats, and Christmas ornaments. I've never been a souvenir kind of person, but I pick out a buffalo ornament that says YELLOWSTONE across one side and go to pay for it at the counter. As I'm waiting in line, I spot Johan in the lobby, now sporting jeans and a flannel shirt. His hair is pulled back into one of those man bun things, and, holy cow, he looks good.

I make my way out of the gift shop, pretending I haven't noticed him until I nearly bump into his side. "Oh, hey," I say, trying to sound surprised.

He smiles, and my stomach does a loop-de-loop. "Hey, Becka."

I look up into the old wooden rafters, as if hoping they'll tell me what to say next. I hadn't thought that far ahead. "This is such a cool place. It really feels like we've stepped back in time."

He nods, following my gaze. "It's one of my favorite inns here."

"I can see why." I scramble to think of something else to talk about. "So, I enjoyed the hike today."

"Good deal." He glances around the foyer before noticing the married couple, Ben and Angie, and waving them over. My heart sinks a little. So much for that.

As we wait for the rest of our group, Johan tells us a little about the history of Old Faithful Inn, which is over a hundred years old. Again, I'm interested in the information, but I mostly just like to listen to the sound of his voice. If he needed a second job, he should consider doing audiobooks. I'd buy every single one of them.

When Phillip and his son, Chris, show up a few minutes later, we all start toward the adjoining restaurant.

"Has anyone seen the other girl?" Johan asks. "It's K. J., right?"

"I haven't seen her," Sue says.

I start to answer, but then snap my mouth shut. She's a big girl with an alarm on her phone just like me. Surely, she set it and will be here soon.

The restaurant is furnished with rugged tables and chairs that match the decor of the Inn's rooms. Chandeliers made from deer antlers hang from wood beams on the ceiling, and the aroma of steak wafts through the air, making my stomach rumble. A hostess shows us to a large table, and as we settle into our seats, everyone grows quiet. It's like we're unsure of what to say now that we're sitting face-to-face. The scenery gave people plenty to talk about on the hike today, but we're all still basically strangers.

"I, for one, am having a beer," Johan announces, and everyone seems to relax.

"Me too," Phillip says.

"Me three," Chris says.

I've never had so much as a drop of alcohol, but I wish I could say, me four.

A waiter comes to take our drink orders, but there's still no sign of K. J. Ben and Angie each order a glass of wine, leaving me the only one with a nonalcoholic drink. Johan makes a joke about it, but when he winks at me right afterward, my heart skips a beat.

He glances at his watch again. "Maybe she's just running a little late."

Several people murmur their concern as the waiter returns to take our orders. I just shrug and order the lamb chops.

The alcohol seems to have a nerve-settling effect on everyone, and soon we're all talking easily. Johan tells us what's in store for tomorrow's hike, and even though I've only had lamb chops cooked in red wine, I'm starting to feel all warm and fuzzy, too. I think it's mainly because I'm sitting next to him. He's wearing some kind of musky cologne that smells better than the food, and that's saying something because the food here is outstanding.

I've completely forgotten about K. J. until we're all standing to leave. She appears in the restaurant entrance, face flushed and her short hair sticking up on one side. Doesn't the girl ever look in a mirror?

She strides toward us, moving in that gangly way of hers. Her eyes narrow in confusion or maybe annoyance. "Did you guys already eat?"

"Yah, we met at six," Johan says. "Did you forget?"

"No." Her eyes cut to mine. "I fell asleep and someone didn't bother to wake me up."

Crap. Here it comes.

"Who are you here with?" Johan asks, appearing surprised.

K. J. points a finger at me. "My lovely cousin here."

Johan looks to me and then back at her. "You two are cousins? I didn't realize you came together."

"Yep," K. J. says, her eyes shooting daggers at me.

Sue gives me a chastising look before turning to K. J. "You know what? I was thinking about ordering dessert and a coffee. I'll stay here and eat with you."

The corners of K. J.'s mouth lift ever so slightly. "Thank you, Sue. That's very considerate of you." Her eyes cut to mine again.

"Sorry," I say, a little too late. "I thought maybe I should let you sleep. You seemed really tired." It's a lame excuse, but the only one I can think of on the spot. Internally, I cringe. I know how bad this looks. These other people have no way of knowing the situation with K. J. and me.

"Okay, everyone," Johan says, turning the group's attention away from me. "See you bright and early tomorrow morning in the lobby. Seven o'clock sharp."

He glances back toward K. J. and Sue, seated at the table. K. J. gives a thumbs-up, and Sue, a nod of agreement.

"Good night," Johan says before turning to leave.

I push my hands into my back pockets, following him toward the lobby. I try to think of something to tell him, some way to let him know I'm not a horrible person, but I'm not sure I can explain the situation. Especially not to a near-stranger. As the other group members head up to their rooms, Johan pauses and turns to face me. Much to my surprise, a grin stretches across his face. "So . . . do you and your cousin have some issues?"

"Um . . ." I scratch behind my ear, avoiding his eyes. "I guess you could say that."

"I had no idea you were even related."

"It's kind of a long story."

His eyes glitter with curiosity. "Oh yah?"

"Let's just say that we didn't come on this trip by choice. It was something our grandpa asked us to do. In his will. We have a ton of drama in our family."

"I see." His smile reappears. "I guess I sort of understand, then."

My shoulders relax a little. "I'm really not a bad person, I promise."

"No worries, I didn't think you were."

I should probably still feel guilty, but as I return to my room, all I can think about is Johan and that smile of his. Never mind that chiseled face and those gorgeous legs.

I could be mistaken, but I think he might like me, too.

CHAPTER 13
K. J.

AFTER A FIFTEEN-MINUTE SHUTTLE DRIVE, WE FIND ourselves at Norris Geyser Basin, which according to Johan is "Yellowstone's hottest and most changeable thermal area." I'm not really sure what he means by that, but I guess we'll find out soon enough. Sporting a man bun again today, he hops out of the shuttle and does a few leg stretches. The dude's all right, but he seems like the type who drinks green smoothies and visits the gym every day—when he's not leading eight-mile hikes, that is. And apparently he's totally Becka's type. She's been drooling over him ever since we got here.

I glare at the back of my cousin's head as she steps out of the shuttle and pulls on her backpack. I'm still pissed she didn't bother to wake me up for dinner last night. Total dick move. Everyone else shuffles out, and I'm immediately sidetracked by the putrid smell in the air. Like rotten eggs, only worse.

"That's the sulfur coming from the thermal openings," Johan explains with that corny smile of his.

I take in the brown and barren landscape. Random plumes of steam rise from the earth for nearly as far as I can see. It's like some kind of futuristic wasteland in one of Carter's video games, totally different from yesterday's scenery, but just as intriguing. I just wish it didn't smell so bad here.

Following Johan, we cross the parking lot and start along a side-walk that leads to the dismal landscape. I'm at the back of the group, just behind Angie and Ben.

"This place is incredible," Angie says.

Her husband nods in agreement. I don't think I've heard him say more than two words on this whole trip. Johan makes up for it, though; the guy hardly ever shuts up.

"Isn't it?" he pipes up now. "This is one of the coolest spots in Yellowstone. Well, not literally of course." Another corny smile.

Ha ha, I think. I study his man bun as he continues yapping, real-izing that it probably takes him way longer to do his hair than it takes me. He looks all studly and tough, but I'd bet anything he goes to a stylist and uses expensive hair gel he prefers to call "product."

Everyone pokes along, checking out the red, cracked earth on either side of us. It looks like it hasn't rained in a hundred years, though I know that's not true. Johan's already given us the scoop on yearly rain and snowfall totals. The cement walkway turns into a raised wooden boardwalk as pools of blue and gold water replace dry ground. The rotten egg smell gets worse. A grayish stream runs beneath us, hissing like an angry cat. Everyone's starting to get into full picture mode, including me. I snap a photo of nearly everything I see. Chutes of steam, bubbling streams, giant holes in the ground—you name it.

Ahead, a crowd has gathered where the boardwalk widens into a large rectangle. I soon see why. A big pool of bright turquoise water gurgles off to the right, steam rising from its center.

"What the crap?" I whisper. I've never seen anything like it. I take several more photos, including a peace sign selfie with the pool in the background.

"The thermal pools reach temperatures of roughly four hundred and fifty-six degrees Fahrenheit," Johan says. "The water is so acidic, it can melt the skin right off a person's body."

Everyone gasps, but I give an appreciative nod. Very interesting. If I were going to dispose of Becka, this would be the perfect place to do it.

We continue along the boardwalk, and like yesterday, she stays close behind Johan, hanging on his every word. I smile and sidle up next to her. She glances my way, eyes narrowing, but keeps walking. When Johan pauses again, this time in front of a small geyser, I stand so close to Becka, our arms touch. Her lips pinch together, but she doesn't dare say anything while our guide is talking. His gaze falls on us, his brow knitting, but he continues his spiel. I swear, the guy is like a walking encyclopedia.

I stick close to Becka as we move on.

"What are you doing?" she hisses under her breath.

"Just trying to spend some quality time with my cousin. It's what Gramps wanted, remember?"

Her jawline tightens, and she shakes her head.

"Hey, Johan," I call.

"Yas?"

It's so funny to hear him say that, I'm tempted to ask him another yes or no question just to hear it again, but I need to stay focused. "Becka was wondering how old you are. She wanted me to ask you."

Becka's face flushes pink, and Johan turns around, giving me an odd, squinty look before turning back to focus on the boardwalk ahead of him. No one wants to fall off this thing.

"Twenty-two," he says.

"Oh. That might be a little too old."

Becka elbows me in the side, and I wince.

"Too old for what?" he asks.

"To date Becka. She's only eighteen, you know."

She elbows me again, harder this time.

My reaction is automatic. I shove her away, and she stumbles several steps backward.

Her eyes widen in surprise and then quickly narrow into slits. "You . . ." She doesn't finish the insult but shoves me back with an amazing amount of force for someone her size.

"Hey!" I yell. Anger flashes through me. I'm suddenly back in the sixth grade, having it out with Charlie McDonald, the bully of bus number nine. I push Becka back with everything I've got. This time, she squeals as she loses her balance and teeters close to the edge, but with cat-like reflexes, she manages to duck down and recover her balance. As she squares up at me, the look on her face is murderous. Okay, maybe I went a little too far that time. I open my mouth to apologize, but before I can say a word, she draws a fist back and throws a punch that lands just below my left eye.

"Son of a . . ." Specks of light cloud my vision, and the world around me spins. Now I'm worried I'll be the one to fall into the acid water.

"Girls!" Johan yells, and he's suddenly between us. He places a steadying hand on my shoulder. "Stop it."

I hold the injured side of my face while Becka looks half-mortified, half-triumphant. The rest of our group stands there, gawking at us like we're circus freaks. No one says a word. Guess they didn't see *that* coming.

But shit, neither did I.

※ ※ ※ ※

By day three, our last day of hiking, I'm in a mega-pissy mood. My leg muscles are achy and tight, and I have a nice greenish bruise below the eye where Becka decked me. To make matters worse, I haven't had a cigarette on this entire damn trip because I wanted to prove to myself that I could do it.

When we stop to watch a herd of bison grazing in a meadow, I complain to Johan, telling him I'm not sure I can finish today's hike.

He reassures me I can and that the view of Yellowstone Lake will be worth it. He even digs into his backpack and hands me a small packet of Icy Hot to rub on my calves. Becka gives me a smug look as I sit on a fallen tree to massage it in. I'd like to kick her right in the back of her calves, but I know how that would likely turn out.

Sue slows to walk beside me once we get going again. "Feeling any better?"

Not really. "A little, I guess." I stare down at my hiking boots, which are slightly scuffed on the toes now. I'm definitely breaking them in. "Sorry to be such a weenie."

She laughs. "Oh, don't worry about it. Not everyone's used to this sort of thing."

Since Sue's taken up with me, I've learned she's a retired botanist from Tennessee. She hikes nearly every weekend in the Smoky Mountains, near where she lives. She must feel sorry for me because of the whole Becka thing, but it's kind of strange how on both trips so far, I've made friends with the grandma types. Maybe it's because I've never had a real grandma. Or maybe it's because I'm just weird like that.

"Up ahead," Johan says, coming to a stop, "we'll see some giant boulders to our right, and if you look closely, you may see some of the yellow-bellied marmots. They're one of the largest members of the squirrel family."

"Ooh, exciting," I deadpan. "Giant squirrels."

Sue nudges me with her shoulder. "You better get your camera ready." A small group of marmots does indeed appear on a boulder as we approach. "Aren't they cute?" Sue says, lifting her camera to get a shot.

I'll admit, they are sort of adorable, like a cross between a beaver and a squirrel on steroids. I follow Sue's example and take a few pictures with my phone just for the heck of it, but what I'd really rather see is a bear.

A half hour later, the Icy Hot has worn off, and my legs are killing me again. I had no idea we'd be walking so far. Or that Yellowstone would be so freaking huge. It could practically be its own state. When the lake finally comes into view, I could cry with relief. A pointed strip of land Johan calls Storm Point juts out into the water—our destination—but I've had all the sightseeing I can handle for today. All I want to do is sit down and rest. Our small group splits up, some going left and others going right to walk along the rocky beach, but I find a large rock near the water's edge and perch myself on it. Reaching down, I dip a finger into the water, finding it ice-cold.

"Not too good for swimming," Sue says with a laugh. I hadn't heard her approaching.

"Does it ever warm up?"

"Don't think so. I think I heard Johan say the average temperature is forty-one degrees."

I must've missed that piece of information.

Sue sits beside me, taking a drink from her water bottle. "So what-cha think, kid?"

I survey the lake in front of me. It's pretty, but it's hard to appreciate things when you're tired and cranky. "I think . . . I'm ready to go home."

"I'm getting there, too, but this has been fun. Haven't been here since I was a kid."

I draw up my knees so I can massage the backs of my legs again. Becka and Johan walk toward us along the beach, engrossed in conversation, as usual. I wonder what in the world they could possibly be talking about because they *can't* have that much in common. She's probably complaining about me. Maybe along with going to a stylist and using hair product, he's also the sensitive, good-listener type.

"I can see the resemblance," Sue says.

"Huh?"

"Between you and your cousin. You look the same right through here." She sweeps her fingers across her eyes.

I glance back toward Becka. "Really? I don't see any resemblance at all."

"Maybe you two should give each other a chance."

"I don't know . . ."

"Life's short, kiddo. You've got to forgive and move on."

I stare out at the steel gray water and sigh. "Yeah, maybe so."

I feel bad for agreeing, but not bad enough to tell the truth—that there's pretty much no way in hell that's ever going to happen. There's just no coming back from where Becka and I have been.

As we make our way along the trail through the pines, I'm still mulling over what Sue said, but if anyone should forgive and move on, it's my mom and my aunt. They're the ones who put us in this situation, after all. I'm still lost in my thoughts when Johan comes to an abrupt stop and brings a finger to his lips. He points off to our left.

"Grizzly," he whispers.

I squint, trying to find the bear while grabbing for my phone. Everyone sidesteps toward Johan, as if they expect him to protect them.

Beside me, Phillip gasps. "There it is." He points through the trees, and finally I see the dark, furry form about a hundred feet away. My heart pumps faster, but it's more from excitement than fear. I zoom in to get a picture, but the bear keeps moving, making it hard to get a good shot.

"It's coming this way," Chris whispers.

Thanks, Captain Obvious.

The bear lumbers closer, growing larger by the second. My adrenaline spikes, but probably not for the normal reason. "This is so awesome," I whisper.

"Uh, should we be leaving now?" Becka asks, her voice quiet but a little higher-pitched than usual.

Johan shakes his head. "It's fine. They usually don't attack a group, and we have our bear spray."

"Usually?" Becka repeats, her voice rising another octave.

The bear raises up on its hind legs and stares straight at us. My jaw drops open and I force it back closed. "That thing is a freakin' giant!" I say under my breath, snapping another picture before it drops back down to all fours.

Becka inches closer to Johan. What a wuss.

"Everyone, get your bear spray ready," Johan instructs. "Just to be safe."

I'm not really worried, but I take out the canister clipped to my belt loop. Sue clicks another photo, but everyone else looks like they're about to crap their pants. About forty feet away now, the bear pauses and raises its massive head, sniffing the air. I get another picture.

"We really should go," Becka says, turning to eye the trail behind us.

"I agree," Angie says.

Johan holds up a hand. "Not yet."

The bear pauses for the longest time, still looking our way. It seems to be making some sort of decision.

And then, just like that, it turns and moves back in the other direction. The group heaves a collective sigh of relief, while I'm left with a sinking feeling in the pit of my stomach. Just like trekking into the Grand Canyon on Dixie, seeing that bear up close was a rush, and I'm disappointed it's over.

"Do they usually do that?" Angie asks. "Get that close to people?"

"Not often," Johan says, "but we see them quite frequently. As long as you don't do anything to provoke them, you're usually fine."

The bear-induced spike of adrenaline stays with me as we start back down the trail. I pull out my phone, scrolling through the photos I just took. The one where the bear is standing on its hind legs is the best, so I text it to Carter. I may not exactly be a badass wilderness woman, but at least I saw a bear, and I wasn't the least bit scared. That should count for something.

After lunch and another short break, I've gotten my second wind. I'm ready to finish today's hike, especially after Johan informs us we might see another grizzly on our way to Elephant Back Mountain.

Becka frowns, obviously not overly keen on that idea, but I'll be on the lookout—that's for sure.

However, other than Ben getting stung by some type of wasp, things are uneventful. I'm kneeling to re-tie my bootlace when Sue pauses beside me. She's like a mother hen, especially when it comes to me for some reason. "Still doing okay?" she asks.

I stand and dust off my knee. "Yep. Much better now. Thanks." After our conversation at the lake, I'm sort of wishing I wasn't alone with her again. I tap a hand against the side of my leg and glance around the forest, grasping for some comment to make. It's been pretty much the same scenery since we started. Trees, trees, and more trees.

"I have a granddaughter around your age," Sue says.

"Oh yeah?" I kick at a rock in the path, sending it skittering down the trail. She hasn't said a word about her family this whole time. I figured she didn't have any kids.

"Yep, and a grandson. He's twelve. They're my absolute pride and joy."

"Brother and sister?"

"Yes. I only had one child myself. A son."

"I see."

"My daughter-in-law died a few years ago. Breast cancer."

I don't like how the word *cancer* makes my stomach squirm now that I know someone who's died from it. "I'm sorry," I say, and for a moment I consider telling her about Grandpa, but that would just open the door to more stories I don't want to tell. "So your son's raising the kids by himself?"

"He is, and I'm really proud of him. I know it hasn't been easy."
She pulls out her water bottle and takes a long drink.

I do the same. Johan stresses the importance of staying hydrated at least a half-dozen times a day.

"My husband and I divorced when Toby was a teenager," Sue continues. "After that, I worried he would never want to get married . . . or wouldn't stay married if he did, but he loved Marissa. He was heartbroken when he lost her. Still is."

I stare at the scuffed toes of my hiking boots. I don't really like hearing sad stories like this. I never know what to say about them.

Sue draws in a breath and then pushes it out real slow. "That's why I say forgive and move on."

I inwardly groan. Here we go again.

"You never know what life's next turn will be," she says with a hollow laugh. "My husband and I could have learned a thing or two from Toby and Marissa's relationship. Just because you're older, it doesn't mean you're wiser, you know. That's all a farce."

Being raised by my mom, I can agree with that. She's never made what I'd call wise decisions. I look up to see that the rest of the group has stopped and are waiting for us.

"Sorry, guys," I tell them.

"It's no problem," Johan says, "but we should stick together. In case of more bears."

"Good point," I say.

It's also a good excuse not to get caught alone with Sue again

CHAPTER 14

ELI

Hello Granddaughters,

If you're reading this, you must have made it through
three days of hiking in Yellowstone. That was another one of
my dreams. You may not be aware, but the Greater Yellowstone
Ecosystem is one of the largest intact ecosystems left in
the northern temperate zone. It's an amazing place, or so I've
heard. I really wish I could be there with you. I've always
wanted to see the Rocky Mountain Parnassian butterfly
(*Parnassius smintheus*), which is native to that area.

I hope the two of you are getting to know one another
by now. You've missed an awful lot in each other's lives and
maybe this time together will allow you to catch up. Please

don't let what happened between your mothers get in the way. It had nothing to do with either one of you.

Katherine, we didn't see much of each other—especially in recent years—but I've always appreciated your unique sense of humor and your carefree attitude.

Becka, I've always loved your confidence and dedication to what you do. I regret not being able to watch you play soccer. You both are such smart girls—I know you'll do well in college.

I didn't speak about your grandma often, but I wanted to take some time to tell you a little about her now. Your mothers likely haven't had nice things to say about her, but Charlotte wasn't a horrible person. I just don't think she was cut out to be a mother. That's not an excuse, but the truth. When I started refusing to leave our property, it drove her crazy. She was a busy body—always going places and doing things. She especially loved shopping for antiques. Then, after a few years, when I was getting worse instead of better, she couldn't handle it. You've probably heard the term "wanderlust." Well, that was your grandma. I bet she's living in some other country now, maybe Spain, if I had to guess. Please don't hate her for wanting to live her own life. I never have. She had her good qualities, too. She was witty and smart as a whip—just like you girls. I wish you could meet her, but I have my doubts it will ever happen. I'm sorry for that.

There's one more thing I need to let you know. For your last two trips, you will not be flying on a plane, but driving instead. A car will be provided for you. Long Creek, South Carolina, will be your first destination, and then you'll continue down to the Florida Keys. The best part is that you'll have plenty more time to get to know one another.

Until next time, sending my love,

Grandpa

CHAPTER 15

BECKA

I SHOVE GRANDPA'S LETTER AT MY MOM. I'VE BEEN home for exactly five minutes, and the first thing I did was fling all my clothes out of the suitcase in order to find this envelope in the bottom.

"We have to drive," I nearly scream, "together!"

Mom examines the letter, her brow furrowing as she reads. Her mouth sags into a frown. "What does he mean, 'a car will be provided for you'?"

"Heck if I know." I take off my shoes and throw them one at a time toward my closet, but my aim is terrible and they bounce off the wall with successive loud thunks instead.

"I'm pretty sure you have to be twenty-five to rent a car, so I don't see how this is going to work." She shakes her head. "And this part about my mother—what a joke." She hands the letter back to me with a sigh. "I don't know why he always stuck up for her after what she did to us. He always made excuses for her."

I set the letter on my bedroom dresser as Mom moves across the room to sit on my bed. Wiping her palms on her slacks, she glances around like she hasn't been in here for ages. All trace of irritation disappears from her face, but I'm still fuming.

"So how was it?" she asks. "Did you enjoy the hiking?"

I plop down beside her and fall onto my back. "The hiking was great. Yellowstone was beautiful." A groan of frustration escapes my throat. "Until K. J. tried to ruin everything, but big surprise there." I watch the ceiling fan twirl around and around above me. "I'm telling you, that girl is a nutcase."

"What'd she do this time?" Mom's tone is apathetic, as if I'm only telling her what she expected to hear.

"For one, she did a cannonball and nearly landed on top of me at the hotel pool. Totally on purpose. And then she kept trying to embarrass me in front of our hiking guide. She acts like she's thirteen half the time." I leave out the part about us fighting and me punching her in the face. It wasn't one of my proudest moments—even if she *did* deserve it. Rolling onto my side, I prop my head up with one hand.

Mom's satiny brown hair hangs over one shoulder, and she runs her fingers through it. "Maybe she inherited some of your grandpa's strange tendencies."

"She's more than just strange. She's . . . she's awful!"

Mom doesn't respond right away; instead she turns to glance at the blue soccer uniform hanging on my wall—the one from my JV year when we were undefeated. That was the year I really started believing I had a shot at getting a scholarship.

"So . . . when's the next trip?" she finally asks.

"In two weeks." I already received an email from the lawyer. Saw it on my phone as soon as we got off the plane.

Mom rises to her feet, and my bed creaks in response. She walks to the doorway but then turns and pauses. "At least you and K. J. will get a break from each other. And just think, after these last two trips and the rodeo, you don't ever have to speak to each other again."

While this is true, it doesn't give me any comfort. "I'd rather pull out every hair on my head than ride in the car with K. J. all the way to Florida."

"I'm sorry," Mom says before leaving my room. For some reason, I don't believe she really is, though. She's probably just happy she's not having to do all this crap with her sister in order to get Grandpa's money.

✳ ✳ ✳ ✳

Since we will all be heading to separate colleges in the fall, Lexi, Maddie, and I have agreed on a new summer tradition: meeting for coffee a few times each month. Today, Lexi rode with me, and we're the first to arrive at Pour Jons, so we grab a table and gab while Eric Clapton croons in the background. I continue to fill her in on the Yellowstone trip—the parts I haven't already texted her about anyway—and describe Johan in detail. I leave out most of K. J.'s antics since I'm tired of wasting my breath on her anyway.

"He sounds gorgeous," Lexi says with a widening smile. "And Swedish? Oh my god, yum."

I can still picture the glint in Johan's baby blue eyes. Yum is exactly right.

"Hey ladies!" Maddie calls, making her way toward our table. Lexi and I both wave excitedly. She pauses upon reaching us. "Coffee is on me today. Whatcha want?"

We thank her and place our orders: a latte for me and white chocolate mocha for Lexi. When Maddie returns with our drinks, Lexi leans toward her, bringing a hand beside her mouth like she's about to divulge some big secret. "Becka found herself a Swedish hottie on her trip. His name is Johan." She draws out his name, emphasizing the "h" sound.

Maddie's eyes go wide as she homes in on me. "Ooh la la. Did you get his number?"

I offer a coy smile. "Maybe . . ."

"What?" Lexi shrieks. "You didn't tell me that. Have you texted him?"

"Not yet," I admit.

"Holy crap!" Lexi says. "I better hear all about it when you do."

"We *both* better hear about it," Maddie corrects.

"Anyway," I say, ready to take the focus off of myself and something that may or may not happen. "Tell me what you two have been up to since graduation. I feel like we haven't talked in forever."

That's all the invitation they need. Maddie fills us in on her new summer job—working at her uncle's insurance firm as well as helping to coach the kids' soccer program at the YMCA. It's the same program I helped with last summer and would have considered again if it weren't for my stupid trips. Then Lexi regales us with tales from church camp, where she worked as a counselor last week. She'll be going back for another round in July.

I'm nearly finished with my latte when the door chimes and in walks none other than K. J. My stomach seizes and I almost spit out a mouthful of my drink. What are the freaking chances? She approaches the front counter, and I slink down in my chair, praying she doesn't notice me over here. But this place isn't all that big, so after she's finished ordering and steps back to wait, her eyes roam the room and, bingo, land right on me.

Lexi and Maddie are still talking, and I'm unsure of whether I should acknowledge K. J. in some manner or not. I'm afraid she'll come over here if I don't, so with a grimace, I lift my hand in a wave. She waves back, unsmiling, but I still don't trust her. For all I know, she might try to come sit with us here in a minute. My brain kicks into overdrive, trying to come up with some way to avoid her.

"Who you waving at?" Maddie asks, turning to look toward the counter.

"Oh, no one. Hey, you guys wanna go sit outside? It's so nice out this morning." It's not exactly the best escape plan, but the only one I can think of at the moment.

"Um, sure," Lexi says, her brows pushing together a little.

My friends follow my lead as I stand and head toward the front door. K. J. doesn't say a word as we pass by, thank goodness. Outside,

I wander toward the backside of the building and find an open area on the wood bench that surrounds the perimeter. Hopefully, K. J. won't see us here and will just think we've left.

"It *is* nice out," Lexi says. "Good idea."

"Yeah," is all I can say.

Then K. J. rounds the building, a coffee in each hand, because of course she would come this way. I immediately pretend to be interested in the building across the street, but she saunters straight over to the three of us.

"Hi, Becka!" she says, her voice full of false excitement. "Fancy seeing you here."

Lexi and Maddie look up at her, confusion evident on their faces. They're probably trying—and no doubt failing—to place her. When I don't respond, K. J. proceeds to introduce herself to my friends.

"Nice to meet you," Lexi says, always the polite one. Maddie just stares at K. J., incredulous.

"I'm sure Becka's told you all about me," K. J. continues. "Since we've been spending so much time together lately."

"Not really," I lie.

K. J.'s eyes narrow. "Sure you haven't."

I shake my head, realizing this isn't going to play out well, no matter what I say. "All right," I tell K. J., "you can go now."

Both Lexi's and Maddie's brows shoot up, probably because they've never heard me speak to anyone that way. But I'm not in the mood for K. J.'s crap today. She doesn't budge but instead takes a sip from one of the coffees. A wicked smile pulls at her lips. "She's probably told you guys all about the affair, too, huh?"

My mouth drops open. Now she's going to bring it up? In front of my friends? I never dreamed she'd stoop *that* low.

"What affair?" Maddie asks, her forehead wrinkling in obvious confusion.

The wickedness spreads to K. J.'s eyes now. "You know, the one my mom had with her dad. It's why our moms hate each other." She pauses, her evil gaze shifting to me. "And it's why *we* aren't exactly the best of friends, either."

Two twenty-something girls sitting nearby are staring at K. J., too, now, no doubt having heard all that, and I can feel the heat creeping up my neck.

"Oh my god," Maddie whispers, looking horrified.

K. J. seems completely unfazed by all of our reactions. She puts on her fakest smile. "Well, catcha later, ladies. Have a good day."

I'm left speechless and staring after my cousin as she strides across the street and climbs into the passenger side of a faded black truck some long-haired boy is driving.

"I'm *so* sorry," Lexi says.

"Me too," Maddie says.

Just one look at my friends reassures me that they truly are. But the damage is done. The heat has spread to my entire face now, and I'm guessing I'm somewhere around the color of a beet. There's no hiding what happened now.

CHAPTER 16
K. J.

"HOW MANY MORE BOXES?" I ASK, TAKING ONE LAST
drag of my cigarette and putting it out with the toe of my flip-flop.

"Just a few." Carter stands on his front porch with two pillows
tucked beneath one arm and a rolled up navy blue bedspread beneath
the other. He hurries down the steps and crams the bedding into the cab
of his truck. I follow him back inside the trailer to help get the last of
his stuff. His mom is at work, and he wants to finish moving everything
before she gets home. Otherwise, it won't be pretty. He's already two
days past his deadline.

"God, what's in here?" I ask as I heave a box from the floor of what
used to be his bedroom.

Carter peers in the crack at the top. "That's all my games. And the
PS4. Want me to get it?"

"Nah, I got it," I shift the box in my arms and carry it to the front door. "Guess I didn't realize you had so many."

"I'm a man of many talents."

"Pshh, whatever."

We make our way outside, and I push the box into an empty spot in the rusted bed of the truck and head back in for another. The next one is much lighter—full of his band T-shirts and socks by the looks of it. "It's gonna be really weird not having you living here anymore."

"Yeah, I know, but you can drop by our place any time you want."

I lean back against the side of his truck. "Who am I gonna bum smokes from when I'm out?"

He sets his box on the tailgate and turns to sit down. "I'll just be a few miles away, so you can still bum smokes. And besides, it's usually me bumming smokes from you."

"True." I gaze up into the oak tree that grows on the dividing line between our lots. A half-rotted piece of plywood still sits cradled between the three main branches. Carter and I built a fort the summer after he first moved here, and we spent plenty of time up there in the years that followed. I can't remember when we got too cool for our hangout, but looking at it now makes my chest ache a little.

Carter follows my gaze but says nothing. I'm not sure he has a sentimental bone in his body, but maybe that's just guys for you. He makes one last trip inside, returning with a couple CDs and a half-empty bottle of Dr Pepper. "Wanna come with? I could drop you back by later."

I stare at my feet. "Nah, I've got some stuff to do, and I need to go down to the library to fill out my college application."

"To NorthWest Arkansas?"

I meet his eyes. "Yep. Looks like community college might be my only hope for now."

Carter gives me a thumbs-up. "I believe in you, Katherine James."

I roll my eyes, but I can't stop my smile. "Don't call me that."

"Why not?" he says, teasing. "It's your real name. You should be proud of it."

I shake my head, my smile growing bigger now. "Shut up, Carter Gilbert."

"Okay, okay, I have a sucky middle name, too." He hops into the cab of the truck and gives me a wave. "I'll see ya around."

"Yeah, see ya," I mumble.

The truck door slams shut and the engine groans to life. I pull another cigarette from my pocket and light up as he backs out of the drive. The nicotine doesn't calm me like it usually does; instead, a hollow feeling carves its way into my chest. I sit down on the top porch step with a sigh. "Fuck."

Mom always says you don't know how much you miss something until it goes away. Carter hasn't even been gone for a minute and I miss him already.

✳ ✳ ✳ ✳

"Miss Walker?" The voice on the phone is familiar, but I can't seem to place it.

I decide to play it nice in case it's someone from the community college inquiring about the online application I submitted yesterday.

"Yes? Um, speaking."

Mom peers at me over the top of her romance novel, probably wondering why I'm being so polite.

"This is Jeffrey Sisco, your grandfather's lawyer."

"Oh, yeah. Hey, Mr. Sisco." I settle back onto the couch a little.

"I trust that your trips have been going well?"

"Sure, sure. They've been great. I'm ready for the next one."

"Oh good. That's what I was calling about." He pauses as if he expects me to say something else.

"Okay," I prompt.

"So your last letter mentioned that you and Rebecka would be driving, and that's what I needed to speak with you about."

"Yeah, about that, I don't have a car, and my mom needs hers for work and stuff."

"I understand. Listen, this wasn't spelled out in the will, but your grandfather set aside some extra money for the purchase of a vehicle for this trip."

"Okay . . ."

"So I took the liberty to go ahead and purchase one. It's a Honda Accord, about ten years old, but it's tagged and ready to go. I had it temporarily insured and added both you and Rebecka as drivers."

"You did?" I glance at Mom, who's watching me with full interest now.

"I need to get the vehicle to you somehow. Would you and your mother be able to come pick it up?"

I pull the phone away from my ear for a moment, looking at Mom. "Can we go pick up a car?"

Her eyes widen. "Sure."

"Alrighty," I tell Mr. Sisco. "We can do that."

"Seven-thirty, okay? At my office?"

"That works. See you then."

After hanging up, I look back at Mom. This is unbelievable. "Grandpa and his never-ending flow of cash . . . I don't get it."

Her eyes crinkle around the edges and she gives a little laugh. "Me either." Dog-earing her book, she places it on the coffee table beside her. "So who gets to keep this car?"

"He didn't say, but it's probably just for the trip."

Mom's lips pinch up, but I can see the wheels spinning in her head, and I'd bet all of Grandpa's money that she's already trying to work out a way to keep the car for herself. She stands and then disappears down the hallway. "How about we grab something at Dee Dee's Drive-In on the way?" she calls.

This must be cause for celebration in her mind, and I'll take it. "Sounds good to me."

Roughly a half hour and two orders of perfectly greasy fries and breaded chicken tenders later, we pull in to Mr. Sisco's office, a few minutes before seven-thirty.

"That must be it," I say, pointing to a silver Honda parked a few spaces down.

Mom's eyes have gone wide again, like she's spotted a hundred-dollar bill on the ground and no one's around to claim it. "Ooh, it's really nice."

We both hop out to inspect the car. The outside is in near-perfect condition. The doors are locked, but we peek inside the windows. The interior is super clean, and a strawberry-shaped air freshener hangs from the rearview mirror.

"This looks great," Mom says. "Plus, Hondas are so reliable. It's a good choice for your trip and it probably won't break down on you like my car does all the time."

"I hope not." I move around to the other side of the car, still taking it all in. "I wonder why he called us and not Becka and RaeLynn to come get it?"

A devilish gleam shines in Mom's eyes. "I'm sure there's a good reason."

We both look up as the low rumble of another car approaches. Mr. Sisco waves from behind the wheel of a black BMW. No surprise that he'd have a car worth more than everything we own put together.

He steps out and comes to shake our hands. "So here she is, ladies. I hope you approve."

Mom grins. "Definitely, thank you for calling us."

Mr. Sisco looks slightly baffled for a moment, but then fishes a set of keys out of his pocket. "Well, it's what Mr. Walker wanted. He left instructions for the two of you to pick it up."

Mom gives me a knowing glance.

Then he hands the keys to me. "Have a look inside. The insurance papers are in the glove box, and there's a manual if you have questions about how anything works. The guy at the dealership said this car only had one owner, and it's been well taken care of as you can see."

Mom laughs. "It looks practically new!"

Mr. Sisco pushes his hands into the pockets of his tan slacks. "I hope it works well for your trip, but let me know if you have any issues with it."

Mom slides into the driver's seat, folding her hands over the steering wheel. "Thank you so much, Mr. Sisco."

I walk around to the passenger side and climb in, the scent of fake strawberries filling my nostrils. A million times better than rotten bologna. "Wow—it really is in perfect condition."

Mom pokes her head out the still-open door and looks at Mr. Sisco. "So what are the girls supposed to do with it after the trip?"

"Your father left instructions for that in another letter. It's in the glove box, too."

Mom rubs her hands together, looking positively giddy. "I knew it!"

"Have a nice evening," he says with a wave. "And call me if you need anything." Then he climbs into his car and drives away.

"Get the letter out," Mom says.

I pull open the glove box, finding the envelope right away. "It's addressed to me."

"Read it aloud, then."

"All right." I pull the two pieces of folded, mint-colored paper from the envelope and clear my throat.

CHAPTER 17

#

Katherine,

It most likely hasn't been long since you read my last letter, but this one I'm writing specifically to you. Yes, it's fine if your mom reads it, too. It wouldn't surprise me if she were reading over your shoulder right now, in fact.

I know your life hasn't been easy. You and your mother have struggled financially, and there were many times when I was overcome with guilt, knowing this, especially when I had the means to help and didn't. Well, that's not entirely true. I have helped your mother out on several occasions (just ask her), but I was trying to save my money with the hope of taking both my daughters and granddaughters on all the trips I'd dreamed about over the years. We were going to be one big, happy family again.

In time, unfortunately, I realized this was all a fantasy. Not only were my irrational fears getting worse instead of better, but I doubted I'd ever convince RaeLynn and Jackie to join me on this grand vacation. Still, I held out hope for many years. Then, when I realized it wasn't only my mind that was unwell, but also my body, a new idea hatched. I wanted this all to be a nice surprise for the four of you.

This car is intended for your trip to the Bull Sluice and Key West, but it's also for you, Katherine. You'll need a reliable vehicle to get back and forth from college.

I'm afraid the inheritances will be a little lopsided since you're receiving this car on top of the money for college, but I know you need it. Of course, I expect you and Rebecka to complete the rest of the tasks to earn your inheritance, but this car is yours to keep. I don't think RaeLynn or Rebecka will mind. So please enjoy and consider this my special gift to you.

With love,

Grandpa

CHAPTER 18
BECKA

I'M SITTING ON THE BENCH ON MY FRONT PORCH, chewing on a hangnail, when K. J. pulls into the drive. Wow, I'm surprised she actually showed up at the time Mr. Sisco suggested we leave, but just the sight of her sends a rush of anger speeding through my veins. I still can't believe she embarrassed me in front of my friends at the coffee shop like that. She honks twice even though I know she sees me sitting here. I roll my eyes, push up to my feet, and trudge toward her car, lugging my suitcase behind me. After depositing my luggage into the trunk, I plop down in the passenger seat with a sigh.

"What's up, buttercup?" she says in a fake, cheery voice.

She wears cutoff jean shorts and a baby blue tank top, which is probably the nicest thing I've seen her wear yet. I don't bother answering her question. It's not like she really meant it or cares what's up with me anyway. Instead, I text my mom to let her know we're off and that I'll check in with her later today. Time to face the thirteen hellish hours to our destination. God knows, I'm dreading every second of it.

K. J. cranes her neck forward, gawking out the windshield as she backs out of the drive. "Huh, your house is nicer than I expected."

I glance up from my phone, trying to see our place through her eyes. It's just a house to me: red brick exterior with gray wood shutters and your run-of-the-mill flower garden out front. It's the third house I've lived in, but I suppose it *is* nice compared with what she's used to. Mom told me they live in a trailer house. "Thanks," I mutter.

My phone dings with a reply from Mom. She wants to know what kind of car Grandpa bought K. J.

I text back, telling her it's a Honda. Nice, but an older model.

Mom was pissed when Mr. Sisco told us about the car, but for some reason, it didn't really phase me. I told Mom that Grandpa could have left all his money to them and I wouldn't have cared. Okay, maybe that was a lie. I would have cared, but they obviously need it more than we do.

"Just so you know," K. J. says as we turn onto the main street, "I haven't driven a whole lot. Mostly because I've never had my own car before, not because I'm bad or anything like that."

Great. My hand automatically slides down to double-check my buckle. "But I figured you could drive some," K. J. continues.

"Yeah, sure."

She turns up the radio, set to some alternative station. I recognize the song by Muse even though this isn't the kind of music I usually listen to. The first two hours of our drive are completely uneventful. We listen to the radio, avoid talking, and watch the passing scenery. I'm struck by how pretty Arkansas is outside of the city limits. If I'm being honest, it's been a while since I actually paid attention.

When my mom was between husbands, we used to drive down to Pine Bluff in the summer to see one of her high school friends. We'd usually spend a week or two there, going to yard sales, playing putt-putt golf, and swimming in their backyard pool. Then later, after husband number two, Ricky came along, too. He would chatter for most of the drive down. That was before he was old enough to argue with everything I said, which was nice. I smile to myself, recalling the way he'd count on his fingers and shout "Moo!" every time he spotted a cow along the side of the road. What I wouldn't give to have him here beside me instead of K. J.

When we stop for a bathroom break and snacks, she asks if I'm ready to drive. "I brought *The Scorch Trials*," she says, holding the book up.

I shrug. Whatever. I'm more comfortable behind the wheel than riding shotgun. Once we're back on the highway, I sip from my Coke and pop mini peanut butter crackers into my mouth while listening to the quiet hum of the tires. My weird mood lingers; I didn't expect this trip to trigger so many memories. And then there's the fact that I'm sitting next to this girl that I'm just starting to get to know, but still don't understand at all.

A billboard featuring A & B Glass Company in bold letters appears, and I'm reminded of a game Ricky and I used to play on long drives when he got older. We'd find words starting with each letter of the alphabet on passing signs. Maybe I should play the game by myself, for old time's sake.

I get stuck on *K* for the longest time, until we pass a Krispy Kreme sign in Little Rock, and then I'm on the dreaded letter *X*. For the last three letters, Ricky and I always bent the rules a little so that the word could just contain the letter, instead of begin with it. I scan every approaching sign, desperate to finish the game, like somehow I'd be dishonoring my brother's memory if I didn't.

"Oh my god," K. J. says, breaking the long stretch of silence as well as my concentration. She dog-ears her book and snaps it shut. "I *cannot* believe that just happened."

I don't take the bait but instead keep searching the landscape for signs.

She takes a sip of her Dr Pepper and cracks her window even though the AC is on. "Mind if I have a smoke?"

Incredulous, I glance her way. "Actually, yeah, I do."

"It's my car you know."

"Yeah, and these are my lungs."

"Fine," she huffs, buzzing the window back up. "Guess I'll wait till we stop again."

"You'll survive."

Before long, Little Rock fades away and we're back in the countryside again. The highway narrows to two lanes as we begin to wind our way through the hills. I still need words for *Y* and *Z* but remind myself there will be more opportunities coming up. K. J. and I are still quiet even though she's no longer reading and the radio is off. Strangely, I don't find it weird or uncomfortable anymore. This is just how things are with us now.

"So . . . were you and your brother close?" she asks after a while.

Goosebumps prickle on my arms. It's almost like she knows I've been thinking about him. "Not especially," I say because, sadly, it's the truth.

"Oh . . ."

It's obviously not the answer she was expecting. "But if you mean, do I miss him, then answer is yes, I do. He annoyed the crap out of me sometimes, but I loved him."

"I always wished I had a brother," K. J. says. "I think we'd be close. You know, if I had one."

"Yeah, well, hindsight is twenty-twenty. If I'd known my brother was going to die, I would have made more of an effort to get to know him." My stomach seems to fold in on itself as the words leave my mouth, and I wonder, *Was I ever a good sister at all?*

"True." K. J. nods thoughtfully. After another beat of silence, she asks, "Do you ever talk to your dad?"

What is this, a game of twenty questions? I almost snap at her, but then, for some reason, decide, what could it hurt? "Not much," I admit. "I see him a few times a year. Usually around holidays and stuff."

"Does your mom talk to him?"

"Nope." I tolerate my father, but I still think he's a complete jerk for what he did to my mom. Though I always thought it was odd that Mom seemed to blame her sister more than her ex-husband for the affair. They're both equally guilty in my opinion.

I glance toward K. J. "Do you ever talk to *your* dad?"

She laughs. "Heck, no, that guy's an asshat. Didn't give two shits about me. He left my mom as soon as he found out she was pregnant."

"I guess we have something in common, then," I say. "Asshat dads." I try not to, but it's impossible not to smile after I say it.

She takes another sip of her drink, the straw making that annoying sucking sound when all you have left is ice. "We're also cousins."

"Being related isn't the same as having something in common."

"Why not? Our mothers are sisters. Isn't that something we have in common?"

"Whatever, you win. I don't feel like arguing right now."

K. J. heaves a deep sigh. "It's impossible to have a conversation with you, you know."

"Oh really?" I glance over at her and put a little bite in my tone. "I could say the same about you."

Like a sulking child, she slouches down in her seat and crosses her arms; but a few moments later, she reopens her book and starts reading.

That's more than fine by me. I'll take the peace and quiet any day.

✳ ✳ ✳ ✳

We stop at an Arby's in Birmingham to get dinner, and then K. J. insists on driving the rest of the way to Atlanta, where we have reservations at a Super 8 for the night. I'd rather she didn't—I feel safer when I'm behind the wheel—but it *is* her car. Plus, it's been a long day and I'm tired, both mentally and physically.

I've lost track of how long we've been back on the road, and my eyelids are starting to grow heavy when K. J. breaks the silence again.

"Hey, sorry I blabbed about the whole affair thing to your friends."

My eyes snap open and I shift uncomfortably in my seat. I guess I wasn't expecting an apology, and I'm really not sure what to say now that I'm getting one. Finding a string on the hem of my jean shorts, I wrap it around one finger and tug, but it doesn't want to come loose.

"Yeah, they had no idea," I finally admit.

"I could tell." She glances my way, but I'm still toying with the string. "And just so you know, my mom feels really bad about everything. I mean, she doesn't ever talk about it or anything, but I know she does."

"She should feel bad." My words come out harsher than I intended, but K. J. doesn't seem to notice. "How could someone do that to their sister?"

"I don't know . . . maybe there's more to the story than we know, though."

I roll my eyes. "Oh please. Don't make excuses for her."

"I'm not! God. I hate that she did that. I just wish we could maybe talk about it without you getting your panties all in a wad."

"What's the point?" I say, finally yanking the string on my shorts free. "Your mom and my dad screwed up, and now we're the ones who have to pay for it. End of story." I turn the radio back on to effectively put an end to the conversation.

It's evening and the sky is a swirling mixture of pink and orange by the time we pull into the motel parking lot. We get checked in and settled into our room, reverting back to our familiar pattern of silence. K. J. reads and I use the free Wi-Fi to get caught up on Instagram. Mom's posted a picture of herself and Tim at a fancy restaurant. They're toasting with glasses of wine. The waiter must have taken the photo. I use my fingers to enlarge the picture. Mom's wearing her favorite dark red lipstick and a floral sundress I've never seen before. She looks so happy—they both do—which for some reason, leaves me feeling empty and sad. I can't quite pinpoint why, but maybe it's because Mom has found someone to fill part of the void that losing Ricky left.

I don't have that, and I'm not sure I ever will.

It's still dark when we set out the next morning for Long Creek. K. J. insists on driving again, and I have no choice but to let her. We have less than a two-hour drive but need to make sure we get there with plenty of time to get ready for our rafting trip. Mr. Sisco's itinerary told us we're supposed to hit the river by nine.

For most of the drive, I stare out the window, watching the sun slowly emerge over the horizon, and sip from my to-go cup of coffee. I have zero energy right now, but I blame that mostly on being tired. I didn't sleep so great again last night.

By the time it's fully light, we're surrounded by fields of white. It's strange to imagine cotton growing right off a plant, but there it is, like someone's enormous popcorn bucket has spilled over. Slowly, the farm fields give way to suburbs again and exhaustion finally claims me. I don't wake until the car comes to an abrupt stop.

"Yay! We're here," K. J. announces.

I'm not sure if she's being sarcastic or if she's genuinely excited but I yawn and get out of the car.

A large, log-cabin-style building with the name Wildwater Chattooga Adventure Center sits before us. I follow K. J. inside, where we check in at the front desk and fill out some forms. Then, along with a group of about twenty-five other adventure-seekers, we're given a safety briefing and outfitted with life vests and helmets. A white bus with blue rafts tied to the top waits outside to shuttle us to the launching location.

My head is still fuzzy with sleep and maybe other things, too, but everyone else is raring to go. Much to my annoyance, people sing and carry on loudly as we bounce along the gravel road. Fifteen minutes later, we file off the bus and find our guide for today's trip—Barry, a middle-aged, half-balding guy with a friendly smile. He's no Johan, but I guess he'll do.

K. J. and I have been grouped with a family of four—youngish-looking parents and their two kids, a boy and girl who appear to be twins around thirteen. They both have that "I'd rather be anywhere but here" expression on their faces.

I can relate.

"Now for our five-mile hike," Barry says as we start along a well-worn trail through the woods. He turns to survey our surprised faces. "What, they forgot to tell you about that back at the center?" His expression is so serious that neither K. J. nor I get that he's joking until he gives a loud chuckle. "Oh boy, you two are gonna be fun, I can already tell."

"Hey," K. J. says, looking offended. "I'm loads of fun." She inclines her head toward me. "Can't speak for her, though."

I narrow my eyes but say nothing. I couldn't care less what Barry thinks of me. I'm just ready to get this over with.

The hike is mostly downhill, and it's not long until we hear the soft whooshing of the Chattooga River. The gray-green water comes into view, not nearly as menacing as I expected. Though, to be fair, I'm sure they wouldn't have us start out at the roughest part either. Something George from Georgia said back at the Grand Canyon comes to mind: he'd called me a daredevil for planning to run the Bull Sluice, which must mean that things are only going to get worse. I'd been dreading the drive with K. J. so much, I forgot to be nervous about the rafting trip, but now that I'm here the remnants of my early morning coffee and half-eaten pastry are starting to gurgle inside my stomach.

There's more excited chatter and shouting as everyone loads into their rafts. Barry holds ours steady while the family climbs in, followed by K. J. and me. It wobbles dangerously for a few seconds as he jumps into the back, but then the raft settles onto the smooth surface of the water as the river slowly pulls us out to its center.

"Paddles ready?" Barry asks.

We all hold them out in response.

"Let's do this, crew!"

I have to give him an A for enthusiasm, at least. We begin paddling the way they showed us back at the center and, thankfully, it gives me something to do besides worry about what's coming next. For a long while, the river is unexpectedly serene, with huge trees hugging in at both sides. The other groups have spread out by now, some rafts way ahead of us, while others trail far behind. The family in our raft talks among themselves. The parents are trying—and apparently failing—to get their kids excited about our adventure.

"Bet we'll hit the rapids soon!" the dad says. He has light brown eyes that twinkle when he smiles. He's probably a good dad—not the kind that would cheat with his wife's sister.

"Oh, look," the mom says. "Did you see that fish?" She points to the water, but her kids don't even bother to look.

"You two sisters or friends?" Barry asks K. J. and me.

"Neither," I say.

He laughs, like I'm trying to be funny.

"We're just fulfilling our grandpa's wishes," K. J. says and she proceeds to explain our whole situation. I glance her way between strokes. It's not that I'm upset she's telling Barry, but up until now it felt like there was some kind of unspoken agreement between us to not fill anyone in on the entire truth. I realize the family has grown quiet, and I'm certain they're listening in, too.

"Wow," Barry says, "your grandfather sure sounds like a cool guy. That's one hell of a bucket list, if you'll pardon my French."

Bucket list. I guess that's the best way to explain all of this, and I wonder why I hadn't thought of it that way before.

"So you said this was the third trip on the list, right?" he continues. "What's next?"

"Key West," K. J. says. "Don't know much about it, but it sounds cool."

Barry whistles. "Woo-ee, you's some lucky girls. I'd love to go there."

"That's on our vacation list, too," the dad interjects. He turns to flash us a smile. "Maybe a few years down the line. Name's Luke, by the way. Guess we didn't introduce ourselves properly back on shore." He nods toward his wife and then his kids. "This is my wife, Trista, and our twins, Dillon and Delilah."

"That's cute," K. J. says. "Their names."

Delilah offers a semi-smile before giving us both a once over.

"Alrighty folks," Barry says in a tone that instantly grabs everyone's attention. "Our first set of rapids is just ahead. Everyone ready?"

Perfect, I think, my heart rate quickening.

"We're ready!" Luke shouts, a little overzealous.

I peer around Delilah, searching for signs of fast-moving water, but the river looks the same as always. Then we round a bend.

"Oh man, I see it!" Dillon says.

I see it, too.

"Okay, we're gonna stay to the right," Barry says. "Everyone help out here."

We do as he instructs, and our raft picks up speed. Soon, we're bouncing along the white-crested water. Adrenaline courses through my veins, but I'm hyper-focused on rowing as hard as I can. The water tries to pull us left, and Barry yells to keep rowing right. I let out a screech as we miss a large rock by inches, but then the water calms and so does my racing heart. We did it. We worked as a team and we did it.

"Yeehaw!" K. J. yells, lifting her paddle into the air.

I can't help but smile, too. Okay, this might actually be a little fun.

"That was dope," Dillon says, which elicits a shared smile between his parents.

"Did you like it, honey?" Luke asks Delilah. Her helmet bobs up and down as her brother reaches out to give her a high five.

And just like that, my smile fades as a familiar heaviness pushes its way back in. I'm transported back to a memory of an early morning game at the rec soccer fields. Ricky, sporting a mismatched sweat suit and uncombed hair, stands on the sidelines, waiting for me as I jog off the field. We didn't win the game, but you'd never know it by the look on my brother's face. He stretches his hand up for a high five. He always wanted to be the first to give me one after a game.

"Way to go, Becka!" he yells, loud enough for everyone to hear.

We slap palms, and then I move past him to grab a drink from the cooler, still grumbling about my missed goal. At the time, I had no way of knowing that that would be the last high five I'd ever give my little brother. Or that it would be the last soccer game he'd ever attend.

CHAPTER 19

K. J.

"WATCH OUT BELOW!" I YELL IN MY BEST CAPTAIN Jack Sparrow voice before jumping from a ginormous rock.

I resurface to find Dillon cracking up. He gives me a playful splash in the face, which, of course, I have to return. Ever since I mentioned that I landed eight bottle flips in a row one time, he's been sticking to me like glue. Poor kid, he must think I'm cool or something.

"So what do you think the Bull Sluice will be like?" he asks as we climb out of the water and onto the rock again.

"No idea. Guess we're about to find out, though."

"Guess so."

Nearby, Becka and Delilah sit on another rock, sunbathing. Dillon's twin sister appears more taken with my cousin, which isn't surprising. Most girls tend to keep their distance from me for whatever reason.

Dillon and I wait behind three other guys, water dripping from our shorts and life vests. The afternoon sun is sizzling, so I'm glad Barry is letting us stop along the way to swim. Plus, it's nice having a chance to get away from Becka some.

"I hope we crash," Dillon says with a crooked grin that reminds me a little of Carter.

"I hope Becka falls out." I glance over at her, not caring if she hears me or not, but it appears she's just out of earshot.

Dillon shakes the water out of his hair. "So you guys really hate each other, huh?"

I shrug. "It's a long and complicated story." It's finally our turn to jump, so I step up to the edge. "Hey, let's see who can make a bigger splash."

He gives me another crooked smile. "You're on."

We each make our jumps, and I tell Dillon he's the winner even though I'm pretty sure it was me.

"Delilah!" he yells. "You should come try it."

Her face pinches up and she shakes her head before turning back toward Becka.

Dillon rolls his eyes. "She's such a priss."

I agree but don't share my opinion because that's probably not my place. As Dillon and I climb out to make yet another jump, Barry whistles and waves us back over to where he and the twins' parents are standing on the opposite riverbank.

"All right, folks, no more swimming stops until after the Sluice," he informs us as we get back into the raft. "It'll be coming up here in about half an hour."

"Nice," Dillon says, and we exchange a smile of excitement. Becka and I sit up front this time, and before we set off she quickly reapplies sunscreen on her arms and legs. To my surprise, she then offers the bottle to me.

I mumble my thanks, reminding myself that she probably doesn't care if I get sunburned or not; she just doesn't want everyone to think she's rude. Even though I'd remembered my own sunscreen for this trip, I left it in the car like a dummy.

I'm still rubbing the lotion onto my legs when I spot another patch of fast-moving water in the distance. "Rapids ahead!" I yell before Barry has a chance.

"Let's keep left," he instructs, so we all paddle in that direction. The raft's speed quickens, and soon we're zigging and zagging between rocks. It's a total buzz.

"Woo hoo!" Dillon yells from behind me, and Delilah gives a squeal of delight. Guess this trip isn't so lame to them now.

"Good job, gang," Barry says as the water calms once again.

"See, this is fun, isn't it?" Trista says.

Out of the corner of my eye, I see her and Luke fist bump. They seem like the perfect couple, cute and young and sort of cool. I wonder what it would have been like to grow up with a mom and dad like that. The kind who love each other and have money to take their kids on fun vacations like this. Dillon and Delilah probably have no clue how lucky they are.

"*You* having fun?" I ask Becka, because I am and maybe I just feel like being nice for once.

Her wary look turns into a halfway smile. "Yeah, I am actually."

"Cool. This might be my favorite trip so far. I can't wait for the Sluice."

Becka's brow furrows as she seems to consider something. "I think Yellowstone is still my favorite."

Pretty sure I know why, but I don't bring that up. Instead, I try to think of something else to say, something friendly, but having a pleasant conversation is still pretty much foreign territory for us, and I'm coming up short. Becka doesn't seem all that keen on chatting, either, so maybe it's for the best.

We hear the Sluice before we see it, and my excitement multiplies ten times over, but when the "Mother of All Rapids" finally comes into view, Barry tells us to row to shore.

"How come?" I ask, because it feels a little anticlimactic to stop now.

"I want you guys to see how it's done first," he says with a wink.

We climb out, and Barry pulls the raft to shore. There are several large rocks directly across from the Sluice, and they serve as the perfect front row seats. Anticipation continues to swell inside me as we join several other people there. The rapid is nothing like I pictured it, and more like a mini-waterfall instead. Totally sick.

"Here comes one," Barry yells over the roar of the water, as if we can't already see the raft for ourselves. It slips over the steep drop-off with a splash and the people inside cheer.

"Awesome," Dillon says, nudging his shoulder into my arm. I would have to agree.

Seconds later, a kayak approaches. It wobbles but makes it over the drop unscathed. I'm starting to think this won't be so bad.

"See?" Barry yells. "Nothin' to it."

Only the next raft hits the churning water and flips end over end, sending the seven occupants flying into the river. Oh, damn. Holding a hand to my forehead, I shield my eyes from the sun and watch their helmets bob along in the current. No one seems hurt, at least.

"And if we don't make it," Barry continues with a grin, "no big deal either!"

Two more kayakers, who obviously know what they're doing, pass through without so much as a bobble, and Barry must think we've seen enough because he asks if we're ready to give it a try ourselves.

Delilah and Trista are wide-eyed, and Becka looks a little greenish, but Luke, Dillon, and I raise our fists in the air and let out a war cry.

"Remember, we're going to aim for the space between those two big rocks," Barry reminds us once we're back in the raft. "Just like most of the other boats have done."

We maneuver to the left side of the river to wait for the other groups to clear out. Then, when Barry gives the signal, we paddle as hard as we can to the right.

"Hold 'er straight!" Barry yells, but the water is already pulling us forward at an angle, and our paddling is useless against the force of the current.

How the hell did those kayakers make this look easy? I try to paddle even harder but realize we're totally going to crash. Looks like Dillon is going to get his wish after all. My side of the raft hits the drop-off first, and I let out a scream, half terror, half exhilaration. The back part of the raft soars skyward and I'm launched into the air. I land face first in the water, my heart hammering against my rib cage.

After I surface, I belt out a laugh. We freakin' made it. We ran the Sluice. Who cares if we didn't exactly do it in our raft? I turn to search for the rest of my crew. Two white helmets bob along ten feet behind me—the twins—and their parents aren't far behind. Barry's somehow already made it to shore up ahead. He tugs the raft back onto the rocks, pointing to his destination and indicating we should meet him there. I give him a thumbs-up.

"Man, that was such a rush," I say to Dillon, who has managed to catch up with me now.

"That was a massive fail!" he replies, but he's grinning from ear to ear. Delilah's smiling, too, but she's probably just relieved it's all over.

"Wait," I say, scanning the water around us, "where's Becka?"

Delilah's smile falters. "Becka?" she calls, a note of anxiousness in her voice. She turns a three-sixty in the water, calling for my cousin again.

"Oh no," I mutter as I search the shoreline ahead but still don't see her. I imagine her lifeless body floating down the river. Not too long ago, I might have even wished for that, but now the thought makes my stomach twist in fear.

"Becka!" I yell again as I swim toward shore and scan the faces of the spectators. There are probably a dozen or more of them, but no one is paying us any attention. Did no one see her go under? "Becka!" This time I yell so loud that my voice cracks a little. The sick feeling in my gut intensifies to the point where I feel like I could maybe puke. Then I hear a peal of laughter rising over the sound of the rushing water.

"Hey, over here!" Perched on a rock not far from the Sluice, with her tanned legs dangling, my cousin waves at us.

What the hell? A frown pulls at the edges of my mouth, but I can't ignore the rush of relief flooding through me.

"How'd you get up there?" Delilah yells.

"I bailed early," she yells back. "I was afraid we were going to flip."

I'm not sure how I missed that, but then again everything was happening all at once. "You suck!" I yell as I grab ahold of a rock and hoist myself up onto it.

Becka gets to her feet and starts downriver, meeting up with us.

"You scared the shit out of me, you know," I say when she's within earshot.

She gives me a skeptical look. "So you're saying you would have actually cared if I drowned?"

"Maybe." I drop my gaze before turning to help Dillon, and then Delilah, out of the water.

As the four of us make our way along the river's edge, my heartbeat manages to return to somewhere around normal. I can't believe I got so worked up, but then again, maybe that's to be expected when two people have spent as much time together as Becka and I have lately. It's hard to say.

＊ ＊ ＊ ＊

We leave South Carolina for our next stop in West Palm Beach the following day. It's strange, but I can sense a subtle shift between us. Becka's behind the wheel and I have my earbuds in, listening to music she probably wouldn't care for, but it's like I can breathe a little easier around her now. Like some of the hate between us has maybe evaporated. We're nowhere near being friends, but the urge to slap her hasn't been nearly as overwhelming today. Maybe thinking she was dead for ten seconds really did have an effect on me.

I nod my head along to the beat and stare out the window. We pass another cotton field, only this one's been harvested, with round bales of cotton wrapped up in bright pink plastic. Weird how they bale it up just like hay. A ding cuts into my song and another text from Carter appears at the top of my screen. He got a job at Reynold's Auto Parts in Siloam Springs, which is cool. I respond with a thumbs-up emoji and tell him about (almost) slaying the Sluice.

We text back and forth for several more minutes, though it's mostly him just telling me about his first day on the job. He's making nine bucks an hour, which doesn't really sound like much when I think about it. Good thing he's splitting the bills with Dax.

At one point, I notice Becka peeking at my phone, so I push it down in between my legs. *Nosy much?* She quickly focuses on the road again as I stop the music and pull out my earbuds.

"I need a bathroom break," I tell her.

"I think there's another town up here in a few miles." She raps her fingers on the steering wheel before continuing. "So . . . is that your boyfriend?"

I snort. "Um, no."

"Oh, okay. Just wondered. I saw you with a guy that day when you left the coffee shop. Thought maybe that was him."

"It is him, and he's just a friend. Carter. We're texting. Ever do that with your friends?" Sarcasm oozes from every word.

"Yes," she says, frowning. "Sorry. Guess I'll know better than to ask something like that next time."

I push out a sigh and fold my arms across my chest. "It's fine. I just get sick of people always making assumptions. It gets really old after a while, you know?"

Becka rolls her eyes. "I said I was sorry. Did you ever consider that maybe I was just trying to make conversation? I don't really care if you have a boyfriend . . . or a girlfriend for that matter."

"Okay, okay, I hear you. And I don't have either one. Maybe I shouldn't have snapped at you. It's just all this closeness." I gesture around the car. "I think it's getting to me."

She nods, seeming to understand. "I know what you mean."

"At least we haven't killed each other yet. Grandpa would probably be proud."

Becka laughs. "Probably. And speaking of Grandpa, I wonder why he didn't leave us a letter after the rafting trip."

"No idea. I'm sure we'll get another one soon, though." I point to a sign up ahead. "Hey, there's a Love's."

Becka moves over to the right lane and takes the next exit.

We park, and I hop out, making a beeline for the bathroom. Becka's not far behind me. Afterward, we browse the touristy gifts, probably because we both need a little more time to stretch our legs. I find a T-shirt that says LIFE'S A BITCH, only with BITCH crossed out and BEACH written above it. Since it seems totally fitting for the next leg of this trip, I decide to splurge on it. As we're waiting in line at the register, I show Becka the shirt, half expecting her to turn her nose up because she seems so goody-goody and all, but to my surprise, she just laughs.

"I think I want to wear it," I say once we're back in the car and I start to peel off my tank top.

"K. J.," Becka squeals, eyes flashing toward two guys walking past my window.

I continue with my shirt swap anyway. "It's just a sports bra. And it's not like we'll ever see them again."

But one guy keeps staring even after I'm fully clothed. I stick out my tongue at him, and he looks away. Becka and I are still cracking up about it as we merge back onto the highway.

CHAPTER 20

BECKA

THE KEYS AREN'T WHAT I EXPECTED, BUT IN THE very best way. With the windows rolled down, K. J. and I cruise along the two-lane highway, nothing but ocean surrounding us. The sight of so much blue is surreal, and at times, a little unnerving. But it's all good. Salt water and sunlight fill my nostrils, and right now it's the most wonderful smell in the world.

"This is so badass," K. J. says for probably the tenth time. She holds one hand out the window, fingers splayed against the rushing wind as she drives. We've left Marathon behind, and according to Google Maps, the next island will be Big Pine Key.

"How on earth did they build this highway?" I ask, awestruck.

K. J. draws her hand back inside the car, curling her fingers around the top of the steering wheel. "I'm not sure. I'm gonna have to look that up later."

"So you've really never been outside Oklahoma or Arkansas? Until these trips, anyway?"

"We went to a feed mill in Kansas on a field trip one time," she says with a shrug.

I'm not exactly a world traveler, but I feel a little guilty as I count up all the states I've traveled to for soccer tournaments or family vacations—six at least. "I think maybe Grandpa saved the best place for last," I admit, because I think we're both falling in love with the Keys already. How could we not? And snuba diving sounds like a lot of fun.

"You might be right about that," K. J. says.

I glance over at her in the driver's seat with her cropped hair waving in the breeze and her face the picture of contentment. Over twenty hours in the car together and not only are we both still sane, but maybe even happy. And the funny thing is, I'm not really sure how we arrived to this point.

※　※　※　※

It's early afternoon by the time we make it to our final destination: Key West. The island hums with people, but no one seems to be in a hurry to get where they're going. Even inside the car, I can sense the unique energy all around me, like tropical paradise meets small town quaintness. It's definitely unlike any place I've ever been, that's for sure. As we drive down the main drag, I point out a Willie Nelson lookalike walking down the sidewalk with a parrot on his shoulder.

K. J. does a double take and laughs. "This place is amazing."

We find our hotel, a retro-looking two-story building called Senna's Place, and after driving around the same block three times, finally spot a place to park on a narrow side street. Lugging our suitcases to the front desk, we're greeted by an overly made-up receptionist with a beehive hairdo and fake nails so long they look uncomfortable. She checks us in and points the way to our room.

"I think Grandpa would have liked this place," I say, gazing around at the decor in the hotel hallway. It's a combination of tropical and flamboyant, the walls lined with paintings of golden pineapples and colorful fish, as well as neon abstract art. Hot pink and electric blue draperies adorn the windows. It's definitely eccentric.

"Probably so," K. J. says, pausing to look at a picture of a bright turquoise fish.

We stash our things in the room and decide to have a look around. After all, this isn't the kind of place where you hang out at your hotel.

"I heard that Ernest Hemingway lived here," I say as we pass back by the front desk. "I think his home is a museum now."

K. J. gives me a puzzled look. "Who's that?"

"You're kidding, right? You don't know who Ernest Hemingway is? *A Farewell to Arms* was probably my favorite novel from senior English."

K. J. finally cracks a smile. "I'm just jackin' with you. He had the six-toed cats, right?"

That's not exactly what he's best known for, but of course K. J. would know this piece of information. "I think so. Wanna go check it out?"

"Sure, I'm game."

We stop for a late lunch at a sidewalk café and soon learn that half the fun of being here is the people-watching. We see every kind of outfit imaginable—from leather pants to elegant floral sundresses. Several people wear full-fledged costumes, and there's even a demented-looking clown. Two guys Rollerblade past in nothing but skimpy Speedos, and a woman in a bikini top and purple tutu performs some kind of interpretive dance on the street corner.

"Are we even in America right now?" K. J. asks after finishing off her sandwich. "I've never seen anything like this place."

"Can you imagine living here?" I ask as two people in formal frilly dresses sashay past. "It would be so fun. Like a permanent vacation."

But K. J.'s attention has already been diverted. "Oh my god," she says. "Chickens!"

Sure enough, there they are, strutting along the sidewalk, right in front of us.

"What in the world? You think maybe they got loose from a farm or something?" Even as I say this, I can't imagine there being any farms around here—at least not like the ones in Arkansas. This island is way too small and crowded.

K. J. doesn't respond but instead jumps up from her seat to follow them. She attempts to reach down and catch one, but the chicken isn't having it. It darts across the street and into an alley between two buildings.

After leaving the café, we see more chickens in the strangest locations—some nesting in flower gardens, others pecking about small, grassy strips in front of restaurants or shops. A red rooster stands guard in someone's front yard and crows as we pass as if to warn us to stay out of his territory.

"This is freakin' hilarious," K. J. says. "I guess they just live around the island like pigeons do in the city."

"Apparently." All I can do is shake my head and smile at the oddity of it all. A few months ago, I didn't know Key West even existed. Now, I'm sure it's a place I'll never forget.

Using a map on a brochure we'd picked up along the way, we locate the Hemingway Home—a grand, two-story stucco place. Sure enough, dozens of cats wander the grounds as well as the house, and K. J. stops to pet each one that crosses our path. She examines their front paws, pointing out which ones have the extra toe. "Polydactyl, they're called," she says with a hint of authority.

Before, it would have gotten on my nerves, but now I know it's just her way of sharing one of those random facts she always seems so interested in.

"Come on," I say. "Let's look at the rest of the house."

"Okay, okay. I'm coming."

K. J. follows me into another room, this one featuring a large mahogany bed and matching nightstands with pineapple-shaped lamps. A collection of photos showing Hemingway with one of his wives—and there were several, it seems—hang on the wall.

I find a plaque that lists the names of his four wives, along with the dates they were married to Hemingway. "Ha! He's only got Mom beat by one."

K. J. looks at me, surprised. "Your mom's been married three times?"

"Yeah. You didn't know that?" I guess I thought it was common knowledge.

"Nope, my mom never talks about her." K. J. puckers her mouth up like she might say something else but seems to change her mind.

It strikes me how strange it is that we still know so little about each other. In a parallel universe—or in a normal family—we might be best friends or at least close, but in this universe we're neither.

In the hallway, another cat moseys our way, and, unsurprisingly, K. J. kneels down to stroke its back. "I used to have a cat," she tells me, now scratching beneath its chin. "Larry. Don't know what happened to him, though. He disappeared in the middle of a snowstorm one winter. I never saw him again."

"You named your cat Larry?"

"Yeah." She shrugs as if the name isn't strange at all. "Seemed to fit him."

I guess nothing should surprise me by now, but I offer what I hope looks like an expression of sympathy. "I'm sorry you lost him."

"It's okay. I'll get another one when I have my own place. My mom didn't care for the whole litter-box thing anyway."

My mom would be the very same way. Maybe they're more alike than I thought.

"I wonder why Grandpa never had any pets," K. J. says as we enter the study. "He didn't, did he?"

"No. Mom told me he didn't think anyone should keep pets—that animals should live in their natural environment."

"That kinda sounds like Grandpa, now that you mention it." She pauses, looking around the room, and then spots another cat in the hallway. "So what's a cat's natural environment, anyway?"

I think about that for a moment. "Good question."

We both laugh and spend the next ten minutes coming up with guesses as to where a cat should really live, and our answers only get more absurd as we go along.

After leaving Hemingway's house, we explore Duval Street, with all its unique shops, and watch the demented clown character we saw earlier ride a unicycle while juggling baseballs in some sort of street sideshow. It's interesting, to say the least.

Dinner is at another outdoor café, and then we finally head to the beach. Kicking off our shoes, K. J. and I wade into the ocean. It's what I've been looking forward to ever since we got here. The water is deliciously cool and a welcome relief from the humidity, but I stop when it reaches my knees, content to just admire the view. With the sun hanging low and the sky a beautiful shade of plum, it's like we've been painted right into a postcard. I've only been to the ocean one other time, after a soccer tournament in Southport, but the water is a completely different shade of blue here. Plus, it was March when we went to North Carolina, and the water was freezing.

K. J. stands nearby, gazing out into the depthless blue. I wonder what she's thinking about right now. I watch as she edges deeper into the water, and it climbs to the bottoms of her cutoff shorts. I think she might stop there, but she wades in farther, until just the very tops of her shoulders and her mass of short, unruly brown hair are visible.

The water feels so incredible that I consider joining her, but I really don't want to walk back to our hotel sopping wet. I'd also hate for my new shirt to get all stretched out, so I stay where I am. For the briefest moment, I'm envious of K. J. She doesn't seem to share any of my concerns about what people think or worry about any consequences, and I can't imagine what that kind of freedom must be like.

When she finally wades back my way, I could swear there are tears shining in her eyes. I pretend not to notice as I turn to walk back toward shore, my feet squishing in the soft sand. We walk up to the sidewalk and follow it back to the hotel in our usual silence, but this time, something feels different, like we're not really ignoring each other but maybe just needing a moment to ourselves.

I still don't know what to think about this change between us, but that's okay. For some reason, I feel like I've got plenty of time to figure that out.

CHAPTER 21

K. J.

"SO WHAT WAS GRANDPA LIKE?" I ASK, STARING AT the ceiling of our room. It's past midnight, but Becka and I are still awake on our separate beds.

"Strange, but you already knew that." She lets out a sigh and the bed springs creak as she moves to adjust her pillow. "He was so stuck in his ways. Never liked to do anything different."

"What'd you guys do when you went over there?" We used to go on walks in the woods near his house when I was little, but I don't remember doing much of anything the last time I went. Usually, he and Mom would get into an argument and then we'd jet.

"Most of the time, we watched his nature documentaries, and he'd tell me about his latest insect finds. He always made soup and sand-wiches for us."

I smile. "Chicken noodle, right?"

"Uh huh."

We're both quiet for a while. Voices carry through the door as people move past in the hallway outside our room, but I can't make out what they're saying. There's a loud "Oh shit!" followed by a peal of laughter. We're probably in bed early compared with some other people around here—it's a party town, apparently—but we've got to be at the dive center early tomorrow morning.

"Did he ever take you bird-watching?" Becka asks, interrupting my thoughts.

"Once, I think." Honestly, I don't remember much about it other than having to be really quiet for a long time and pressing binoculars to my eyeballs until they gave me a headache.

"That was my favorite thing," Becka says quietly. "The bird-watching. I didn't really care to search for bugs, but looking for birds was fun. There was this one bird called a Yellow Warbler that I loved. I told Grandpa all the other birds were boring colors, but that one was beautiful. It looked like it belonged in the rainforest—not Siloam Springs."

Listening to Becka talk about the bird makes me wish I had more memories of my own with Grandpa.

"He talked about you, you know," Becka continues.

"He did?"

"Mmm hmm. Used to annoy me so much."

My curiosity piqued, I turn her way, but in the dark I can only make out the outline of her face. "What'd he say?"

"Oh, just how you were so smart, and how he wished the two of us could be friends. He showed me a drawing you made for him once."

"What was it?"

"A bumblebee. It was really good, and I remember I was a little jealous, actually. I've always sucked at drawing."

Hearing her say this sparks a weird sensation inside me. Becka, jealous of me? How ridiculous. I'm the one who should be jealous—she's the one who's always had it all. "I think I remember drawing that," I say instead, trying to mask my surprise. "I was really into art when I was younger."

"You should have stuck with it. You were good."

I turn to stare at the ceiling again, thinking of the Grand Canyon sketch I started but never finished after our first trip. "That was about the only thing I've ever been good at," I mumble.

"Grandpa was a good artist," Becka continues. "Did you ever see his sketches?"

I search the recesses of my memory, vaguely recalling a sketchbook full of insects and birds. I must have been pretty young when he showed it to me. "I don't really remember."

"Grandma was, too. I'm sure you saw that painting she did in the living room."

"I don't think so, no," I admit. It's sad, but I can't remember anything specific from Grandpa's house. Other than the Bug Room, anyway. I close my eyes, trying to think of the last drawing I completed. A motorcycle or a car maybe? It would have been back in middle school or freshman year at the latest.

"We should probably try to get some sleep," Becka says, interrupting my thoughts again.

"Yeah, probably so." I roll away from her and over onto my side. "Night."

"Good night."

Sleep doesn't come easy because I'm still thinking about how fast things have changed between me and Becka. We might be getting along at the moment, but I know it isn't likely to last. When this is all over, we'll probably go our separate ways and never think twice about seeing the other again. We've made it eighteen years living completely separate lives, after all.

※　※　※　※

The sun hasn't been up for long when we set off on a big, white catamaran to our snuba diving destination, a coral reef a few miles off the island. I yawn and gaze out at the ocean while Becka sits beside me, sipping coffee from a to-go cup from our hotel. Everyone on the boat is pretty quiet because we're all still half asleep and it's super peaceful being on the water like this. Unfortunately, that peace can't last forever, though.

"Who's ready for some fun this morning?" a male voice calls over a loudspeaker. The crowd gives a weak cheer. "I said, who's ready for some fun?" he repeats.

Becka grimaces but I'm starting to liven up some. "Woot, woot!" I yell as the crowd cheers again, a little louder this time.

"All right," the guy continues, "everyone meet me up on the back deck in five. We've got some procedures to cover before we start having the time of our lives. You guys are in for an awesome experience today!"

An overly tanned guy in red swimming trunks and a white T-shirt hurries down the steps, giving several people fist bumps as he passes. The announcer, no doubt.

Everyone makes their way toward the back deck and gathers around our guide. Aside from being the tannest white guy I've ever seen, he also has gleaming white teeth, which he apparently loves to show off. He goes over our equipment and some instructions for snuba diving, grinning after every other sentence. "Everyone got it?" Mr. Smiles asks, giving a double thumbs-up.

"Got it," we answer in unison. Becka and I exchange a smile and an eye roll because he's cheesy as all get-out.

"How many Red Bulls do you think he's had this morning?" I ask her.

She eyes him again and smirks. "At least two."

We're fitted with masks and the rest of the equipment we'll need to snuba dive, and next comes breathing practice into the mouthpiece, which is a little freaky at first, but I finally get the hang of it.

Now wearing swim fins, Becka and I move clumsily toward the edge of the boat to peer into the water. I can see the reef in the distance—a big dark patch in the middle of all this sparkling blue— and I start to have a few second thoughts about this, because how do they know there aren't sharks around here?

"Now remember, everything you'll see in the reef is living, even if it doesn't look like it," Mr. Smiles says, and we turn back around. "So please don't touch anything. Let's leave things the way we find them."

He gives us a few more instructions, and then guides come around again to double-check our equipment as the boat comes to a stop. We separate into our assigned groups of two or four and head down a set of steps leading into the water, where a bunch of blue rafts with our air supply await. Once every group has claimed a raft, the crew swims around, connecting our breathing hoses.

As we all push our rafts away from the main boat, I want to ask Becka if she's nervous, too, but I've already got my mouthpiece in and I'm afraid to take it back out. Treading water nearby, Mr. Smiles reminds us how to check our air consumption and what we should do if we need help underwater.

"Everyone ready?" he finally asks, face splitting into his biggest grin yet.

People give him a thumbs-up.

I'm not really sure if I'm ready or not, but what the hell. I let go of the raft and sink into the lukewarm water. My breath comes in shaky gasps as I blow in and out of my mouthpiece, but I suppose everything is working like it should. I force my muscles to relax and swim toward the patch of darkness below. Becka is just a little ways ahead of me.

The view outside my mask is so unreal that my nerves quickly begin to fade. Light dapples the sandy floor and bright fish dart between chunks of coral. I swim closer to find the reef isn't dark and spooky like it appeared from the surface. Instead, it's a lighter tannish gray color with seaweed sticking out from between the rocks. A neon orange fish peeks out at me and I point to it before realizing no one else is around to see. I swim back to Becka and tap her arm.

Together, we make our way along the edge of the reef, checking out the creatures hiding in nearly every nook and cranny. Yellow, red, blue, green, and even purple—the colors of the fish are unbelievable. The ocean floor dips downward and we follow it, going as far as our twenty-foot hoses will allow. For a second, I'm frustrated that I can't go deeper but then I remember that this is still freaking amazing and way better than just snorkeling from the surface.

It feels like we've only been down here for a few minutes when one of the guides approaches in full scuba gear and points to his watch. *Crap.* We're almost out of time. I want to squeak out as much as I can from this experience, so I swim away from Becka, trying to get a closer look at a weird crustacean I've spotted on the ocean floor, but the next thing I know, she's tapping me on the shoulder and pointing toward the surface.

We kick our way back up to the raft, where even the fresh air doesn't keep my disappointment at bay. I was just getting comfortable down there.

"That didn't last nearly long enough," Becka says as we push our raft back toward the catamaran.

"No joke." For once, we're both in complete agreement.

❋ ❋ ❋ ❋

Back on land, we grab hot dogs and drinks from a beachside vendor and find plastic lounge chairs under a palm tree to sit and chill. If we can't be underwater, at least the view of the surface is a pretty good consolation.

"I could totally live here," I say, taking another sip of my lemonade. "I mean, what's not to love about Key West? Chickens. Snuba diving. The ocean. It sucks so much that we have to go home tomorrow."

"Agree." Becka heaves a sigh and fiddles with the hem of her cover-up. "Speaking of home, have you applied anywhere? For college?"

"Yeah, NorthWest actually."

"Community college?"

"Yep."

"You didn't want to shoot for any of the universities?"

"I figured it was too late for that at this point," I admit. And truth is, I had serious doubts any four-year colleges would accept my less-than-stellar transcript. "But maybe eventually."

Becka sweeps several crumbs from her lap and reaches up to tighten her ponytail. "You should do something with art or design. You'd probably be good at that."

"I haven't really thought that far ahead. Just want to get my basics out of the way first. But thanks." Once again, the compliment catches me off guard. I'm not sure if it's because I'm not used to them in general or just more shocked when they're coming from Becka.

I'm admiring the ocean view again when a tiny orange dragonfly lands on the end of my chair right next to my ankle. I study it for several seconds because it looks different than the ones I've seen back home. Grandpa probably would have known exactly which species it is. In fact, I can imagine him telling me all about it if he were sitting here right now. The dragonfly takes off toward the water and I watch until it disappears from sight.

"Oh my god," I say, turning to Becka. "I just got the best idea ever."

"What's that?" Her brow crinkles with that skeptical look I've learned to recognize by now.

"We should get bug tattoos. In honor of Grandpa."

"Tattoos?" She spits the word out like she's never heard it before.

"Yeah, what do you think?" I run my fingers through my hair, wondering if maybe it wasn't such a great idea after all. "I could design them . . . if you want," I suggest, like this might actually convince her.

Becka sips from her water bottle and appears to mull this over. "Like on our hip or something? My mom would never see that."

"Who cares if she sees it. We're eighteen. And plus, it's for Grandpa. I'm sure she'd be okay with that."

"Yeah, maybe." Becka grows quiet again, considering things.

"Let's go swim and you can think about it. How about that?"

This seems to appease her, so we strip back down to our swimsuits and head for the water.

Sometime later, after having our fill of swimming, we're back in the shade, this time with ice cream cones. Becka still hasn't given me an answer on the tattoos, and I haven't brought it up again, but I can't get the idea out of my brain. So while she's busy scrolling through her phone, I dig out the pen and stationery pad I'd swiped from our hotel room from the bottom of my bag and start sketching a dragonfly, similar to the one I'd seen earlier.

"Whatcha drawing?" she asks after a while.

"My tattoo design." I tilt the pad of paper her way.

Becka studies it for a second, taking another lick of her ice cream. "So . . . if we were both going to get a bug tattoo, what would mine be? Hypothetically speaking, of course."

I lower my sunglasses to peer at her. "You want my opinion?"

"Sure. Why not?"

I click my pen shut and tap it against the armrest of my chair absentmindedly. "I'd say something sophisticated. Maybe a butterfly?"

"I love butterflies, but isn't that kind of basic?"

"Okay, how about a ladybug, then?"

She licks her ice cream again and nods. "A ladybug. I could maybe live with that."

"Hold on," I say, clicking the pen back open and flipping to a fresh page in the notepad. I complete a new sketch and show it to Becka. "You'll have to imagine it with colors, but maybe something like this?"

She actually looks a little impressed. "Nice."

"So . . . do you wanna do it?"

"You're being completely serious?"

"Completely."

"And you think we could just walk into a tattoo parlor, show them those pictures, and get it done?"

"That's what I'm hoping."

Becka shakes her head and smiles. "You know, I never do things like this. Spontaneous, crazy things."

"If you want my opinion again, then I'd say you're in the perfect place to try something crazy and spontaneous."

Becka's lips pinch together and I prepare myself for a letdown. She's way too straitlaced for this kind of thing after all.

"You know what?" she finally says, straightening in her seat a little. "I'm down for it. Let's go get ourselves a bug tattoo."

"Really?" I can't contain my grin now. Or my surprise.

"Really," she says, eyes twinkling.

We find a tattoo place back on Duval Street, and, lucky for us, the guy is able to get us right in. He studies my sketches while Becka and I fill out the paperwork, and when he says he can make a copy of my designs and use them as stencils, I smile and give Becka a playful told-you-so look. How cool is it that *my* drawings are going to be a part of us both?

"You can go first," I tell Becka, mainly because I'm afraid she'll back out if she doesn't.

"I changed my mind," she says, and I inwardly groan. "I think I want it on my wrist instead."

Relief floods through me, though I'm not really sure why I'm making such a big deal about this. "Great idea," I tell her. "I'll do that, too," Honestly, I don't care where mine goes because I'll probably get more tattoos at some point anyway.

Becka only winces at the beginning and then stares out the front window while the guy works. The nice thing about tiny tattoos? They don't take all that long. The ladybug comes out just like my drawing, only in red and black, and it's pretty adorable.

My dragonfly takes a little longer, and I'd be lying if I said it didn't hurt. But I keep my mouth clamped shut, wondering how Becka made it through so calmly. Once it's finished, we hold our wrists side by side to compare.

"Mine's better," Becka taunts.

"No way. This dragonfly is sick."

"Okay, they're both pretty great," she admits. "My mom's gonna freak, but I think she'll love it. Once she gets used to it, at least."

After getting aftercare instructions and some ointment, we set off, still staring at our wrists. Mine's starting to sting a little more, but no way am I going to complain.

"I can't believe I have an honest-to-god tattoo," Becka says, pulling out her phone to snap another picture of it.

"Believe it," I say. "'Cause it ain't coming off!"

For dinner, we choose a French restaurant and sit outside at a table for two. Even though they have American food as well, I only order stuff I associate with France, like escargot, soufflé, and a strawberry creme-filled crepe, since this might be my only chance to eat at a place like this. No more fancy restaurants courtesy of Grandpa after this trip, especially since we used our cards to pay for the tattoos.

"You're brave, getting escargot," Becka says after the waiter brings out our meals. She'd ordered *coq au vin*—chicken cooked in wine.

"Want one?" I grab a shell and offer it to her.

She scrunches up her nose and I notice the slightest hint of freckles sprinkled across her face. The sun must have brought them out.

"No thanks," she says with a laugh.

I use the tiny fork to pry meat from the shell, examining the rubbery-looking substance before dipping it into the butter sauce and popping it into my mouth. Becka watches me with a look somewhere between disgust and anticipation.

"Well?" she asks.

I swallow and shrug. "It tastes like a chewy mushroom."

The look of disgust on Becka's face quickly wins out over her initial curiosity. "Ugh, gross." She takes another bite of her chicken. "Now *this* is good." We eat in comfortable silence for a while until she says, "Can I ask you a question?"

"Shoot."

"What does the *J* stand for? In your name? Is it Jackie?"

"No, my middle name is actually James." I don't know why, but I thought she already knew that, and maybe that's why I'm not embarrassed to admit it to her. But like everyone else who has ever asked me that question, her forehead wrinkles in confusion.

"Why James?"

I sigh. Usually I tell people it's a family name, but I figure that won't work with Becka, so I settle for the truth. "It's for James Marsden. He's an actor my mom was in love with at the time. Weird, I know."

But instead of making fun of me, she looks intrigued. "What was he in?"

"The only thing I've seen him in is *X-Men*, but he was in *Enchanted* and *The Notebook* and a bunch of other stuff, too." Mom told me all the movies once, but those are the only ones I remember.

The waiter reappears, interrupting our conversation. "And 'ow is everything?"

"*Très bien*," Becka says.

"Very good." I'm not sure if he's accidentally translating or just likes to speak English to customers.

"Actually," I say as he turns to leave, "could we get two glasses of your chardonnay *s'il vous plaît*?" I throw in a smile, realizing my one year of high school French wasn't a total waste.

He nods, all businesslike. "Of course."

Becka's eyes nearly pop out of her head as he walks away. "He's not going to ID us?" she whispers.

"Guess not." I figured it was a fifty-fifty shot and that it couldn't hurt to ask. "Just play it cool when he comes back, okay."

Only playing it cool isn't Becka's forte apparently. She sits ramrod straight as he places the glasses before us, her eyes growing as wide as our fancy dinner plates.

The waiter's expression changes as he looks at her. "May I see both of your IDs please?"

Shit. But maybe all isn't lost. "We just came from the beach," I explain. "We left them back at our hotel."

His lips purse and he shakes his head. That's probably an over-used excuse, now that I think about it. The waiter scoops up the two glasses. "I'm sorry. I can't serve you the wine, then."

Becka actually looks relieved as he carries them away. I shoot her an annoyed look. "That was not what I'd call *playing it cool*."

"I'm sorry! I didn't know what to do."

I let out a sigh. "It's fine."

Becka lifts her glass of iced tea, giving me an apologetic smile. "Cheers anyway?"

"Sure." I reluctantly return the smile and clink my glass with hers. "To Grandpa."

"And to bug tattoos," she says, eyes shifting to her ladybug again.

"And . . ." I add dramatically, "to the best damn vacation I've ever been on. Even if we didn't get our wine."

She laughs and we touch glasses again.

"This trip *has* been pretty awesome," Becka says.

Even sans alcohol, we're giggly as we head back to the hotel. Music drifts from open doorways of restaurants and bars, and I'm feeling all warm and fuzzy in a way that I haven't experienced in a long, long while. The island is giving me major good vibes.

"Hey," I say, "how about we clean up and go listen to a band or something? We could sit at one of the outdoor places."

"Yeah, that sounds like fun."

"I could even try to get us some alcohol again."

"Please don't. That was embarrassing."

I give her a playful nudge with my shoulder. "Okay, fine. I won't."

When we enter the hotel, the lady at the front desk calls us over, telling us we have mail. Becka and I look at each other, smiling again. Good timing, Grandpa.

CHAPTER 22

ELI

Greetings Dear Granddaughters,

I hope this letter finds you both well and having an incredible time in Key West. When I was a teenager, I worked for a man who had lived in the Keys for several years. By the way he described it, the place sounded like paradise. I've never been to the ocean, but I wanted my granddaughters to get the chance to not only see it, but experience some of the beauty beneath its surface. The reef off the coast of Florida is the only living reef in the United States. I hope your snuba diving experience was something you'll always remember.

As you know, there is still one more task for you both to complete, the rodeo event. You may be thinking your old grandpa was really off his rocker to want you to do such a thing, but when I was a kid, I had a pony (the only pet I've ever had, coincidentally) and I loved riding Penny every time I visited my granddad's ranch. It was another one of my crazy dreams back then to be a rodeo cowboy someday. Laughable, right?

I know you two don't have much (if any) experience with horses or livestock, but at the annual Decatur Dog Days of Summer Rodeo, held at the end of every July, they have several amateur events anyone can compete in—goat milking, mutton bustin' (I believe there's a weight limit, you'll have to check), and even a stick horse race—so rest easy. You won't have to ride a bull or a bucking horse! I attended the rodeo many moons ago and it was a lot of fun.

But as these trips draw to a close, I wanted to let you know there's another reason I've been writing these letters. A more important reason I specifically wanted you two to go all these places together. I guess you could say, I've been building up to this . . .

My greatest hope is that the two of you have become friends by now and that these magnificent destinations you've visited have made you realize how big and beautiful the world is. I also hope that all of these experiences have brought you closer together. Even if, by chance, they haven't, I still need to tell you both something because it's a secret I've held on to for far too long.

Seventeen years ago, someone showed up on my doorstep with some news to tell me. He wasn't a stranger. In fact, I'd known him since he was a teenager. He dated my eldest daughter for three years, and then he married her. He's the unfortunate source of all the contention between your mothers: Samuel Cowles.

Samuel told me something your mothers didn't want either of you to know. Something they never wanted me to know either. I won't go into the whole story—I'll leave that to my daughters—but I think it's time you two know the secret. You're not just cousins. You're half sisters.

Samuel is your father too, Katherine.

I'm so sorry to tell you this in a letter, but you both deserve to know the truth. I hope you can lean on each other for support from here on out. After all, that's exactly what sisters should do.

Love,

Grandpa

CHAPTER 23
BECKA

MY MOUTH REFUSES TO CLOSE, AND MY BRAIN IS racing a million miles an hour. I reluctantly hand the letter over to K. J., who's looking at me like I just sprouted antlers. It must be obvious from my expression that something's wrong. And, oh yes, something is very wrong, indeed.

I feel like someone has poured a bucket of ice water over me. Still, I watch K. J.'s face as she skims over the letter, blanching when she gets to the end. Those words still burning in my brain.

Half sisters.

It's impossible. My mom told me the affair happened after we'd both been born. Unless . . . did she lie to me about the timing of it all? My mind spins as I try to figure out why she would keep this from me—from us—and then my thoughts suddenly turn to Ricky.

We only shared a mother, but I never thought of him as anything other than my own flesh and blood. Now, if what Grandpa says is true, I'm supposed to accept that K. J. is the same thing? Sure, we might be getting along now, and maybe she's not as bad as I used to think, but sisters? It's too much to take in. I shake my head, as if that will be enough to rid myself of the idea. It's like my world has been flipped end over end, and I'm still hanging upside down.

"I don't know about this," I say, more to myself than to anyone, but what I mean is I don't know how it could be true. I glance at the hotel clerk behind the front desk, but she's too engrossed in her computer screen to notice the two of us still standing here.

K. J. slowly folds the letter and returns it to the envelope. Her eyes rise to meet mine. "Sisters?" she says, like she doesn't quite believe it herself.

I stare back at her, unspeaking. It hits me that maybe Grandpa is wrong. He *was* prone to wild ideas after all. This could all be a mistake, some strange theory of his. I study K. J.'s face for a moment. We don't look alike. Ricky and I at least had the same color eyes and the same fine, sandy-blond hair.

In a matter of moments, my disbelief morphs into anger toward our grandpa and his ridiculous letter, and my jaw locks tight. I want to snatch the envelope from K. J.'s hands and rip it to shreds.

"This is bullshit," I say, surprised to find I sound more like K. J. than myself. This only makes me angrier. I turn on my heel and stride down the hall, back toward our room. This may all be a lie, but I can tell K. J. is buying into it and I can't bear to look at her right now. There's no way our moms would keep something like this from us.

I fumble with my key card, dropping it twice before finally getting the door open. The room is warm and the faint smell of mildew hangs in the air. Funny how I hadn't noticed it until now. Sweat pools around my hairline, and I swipe at it with the back of my wrist. I feel like I've just played a soccer game in ninety-degree heat. I find the thermostat and turn the temperature down.

"Come on!" I mutter, willing the air conditioner to kick on. I fling myself onto the bed, head pulsing with each beat of my heart. The air clicks on and I think that maybe I should call Mom and put an end to this nonsense. But another part of me refuses to do that—not yet, anyway. I still need time to think.

I recall the Instagram photo of Mom and Tim at that restaurant. She was happy there—she's happier now—but that's the new Mom. The one only Tim has been able to bring out. I still remember the depressed and angry version, the one who spewed her hatred of my aunt and cousin at every possible opportunity.

Why does she hate Jackie so much? Is it just because of the affair? Or is it because K. J. was born—a child who would forever serve as a reminder of her sister's betrayal and my dad's infidelity? As much as I hate to admit it, the pieces of this puzzle are starting to fall into place.

If I decide to believe Grandpa, that is.

My mind continues to race as I think of what I'll say to K. J. when she comes in. No words seem appropriate after this bombshell.

Footsteps sound in the hallway outside and I brace myself, but they quickly fade away. This happens several more times before it dawns on me that she isn't coming back anytime soon. I don't know where she is, but I can't seem to gather the will to get up and go find her. I'd rather be alone.

The air conditioner is working too well now. I start to shiver as I climb under the covers and cocoon myself beneath them. Thoughts of Ricky flood in again, and before I know it, tears are sliding down my cheeks, soaking the pillow beneath my head. I flip it over, but soon I've soaked that side, too. Yanking the covers back, I throw the pillow to the floor and grab another one to place beneath my head.

I have no idea what time it is when the tears finally dry. I'm exhausted, but sleep still doesn't come. The air conditioner shuts off and silence fills the room. A dull throb pulses in my forehead. I roll onto my stomach, pressing my head into the pillow, allowing the pressure to soothe the ache. It's hard to breathe lying like this, but I don't move. More muffled footsteps sound outside the room, followed once again by silence.

Somehow, I manage to fall asleep.

✳ ✳ ✳ ✳

I wake to a scuffling noise outside the room the next morning. I sit up, wiping the sleep from my eyes as an envelope slides beneath the door. My first thought is that it's another one of Grandpa's letters, and my face tingles. Maybe this one will say "Just kidding, it was all a joke," but then again, I know that isn't likely.

"Hey, look . . ."

It's then that I notice K. J.'s bed is still perfectly made. I search the room for any signs that she's been here, but everything is just as we left it yesterday. Slowly, I push the covers away and climb out of bed. I pick up the envelope, discovering it's only a receipt and directions for checkout, and I'm not sure if I'm disappointed or relieved.

My stomach gurgles with uneasiness as I grab my phone on the nightstand, but when I pull up my contacts, I realize K. J. and I never exchanged numbers. I have no way to get ahold of her. I don't exactly rush getting dressed and brushing my hair, but I don't dally either. I splash water onto my face and pat it dry. After applying some loose powder and mascara and rubbing the ointment over my tattoo, I grab my key card and debit card and stuff them into the front pocket of my khaki shorts. The car is still parked in the alleyway, so K. J. couldn't have gone far, but I'm not sure where to start my search.

I walk down Duval Street, peeking in some of the windows of shops we'd been in before, though I know it's unlikely she would be in there now. My eyes scan everyone who passes by, but every face is unfamiliar. I'm not sure how I'll feel if I do find her. My anger has abated, but irritation mixes in with my uneasiness now. Why would she just disappear like this? I pass a shop displaying a colorful array of surfboards and suddenly it hits me. I make a left, heading toward the public beach where we spent much of yesterday afternoon.

It's there that I find her, standing knee-deep in the water with her hands shoved in the pockets of her shorts. She pulls one hand out and runs it through her wild-looking hair, and oddly enough, something tugs inside my heart. Has she really been out here all night? I move to the water's edge.

"K. J.," I call. She doesn't turn around, so I call her name again. A man and woman jog by, looking from her to me and back to her again. Is it obvious we received life-changing news last night? "We have to check out," I say, pulling out my phone to check the time. "In forty-five minutes."

God forbid I have to go in and drag her back to shore. I'm still deliberating about doing just that when she finally turns around. Her cheeks are flushed, and there's a glassy sheen to her eyes. "Where have you been all night?"

She nods toward a nearby row of lounge chairs before slowly making her way back to shore. Her eyes meet mine for a split second, and then she walks right past me.

"That's real smart." I shake my head and follow behind her. "So . . . what . . . are you mad at me now?" She doesn't answer and refuses to say a word as we walk back to the hotel. I let out a sigh of frustration after trying to question her for the third time. "Are you really going to act like a five-year-old and have a tantrum? Please talk to me."

Still nothing from her. I take a measured breath, trying to keep control of my temper. Back at the hotel, we pack up our belongings in silence and she trails behind me as we go to check out. After turning in our key cards, we head back outside to the car.

"What's your problem?" I demand as I start the engine. I leave the car in park, turning to face K. J. The glassiness from her eyes is gone, but she looks exhausted, like she's been awake for a week straight.

"All my life," she starts, her tone steely and her hands balled into fists at her sides. "My entire life, I wanted a sibling, but I pretty much gave up on Mom ever getting married or having any more children. She'd rather read those trashy romance novels than actually go on a fucking date." Her jawline grows rigid and she gives a slight shake of her head. "And now this? I'm eighteen, and I finally find out I have a sister. But oh, wait! She's also my cousin and we've hated each other for nearly all our lives." She pounds her seat with a fist, tears shimmering in her eyes. "This is so fucked up. Our family is so fucked up."

"I know it is." I draw my hands away from the steering wheel and into my lap, my anger cooling once more. "But maybe it's not even true. You know how Grandpa was."

"It's true, I know it is. Grandpa wouldn't make up something like this." K. J. takes a ragged breath and brushes her nose with the back of her hand before continuing. "And my fucking mom. She's lied to me my whole life, told me Robert was my dad. She went on and on about what a shitty father he was for taking off on us. Why would she do that?"

I'm clueless about how to answer that question.

"She told me the affair with Sam happened several years before I was born."

I shake my head, understanding finally sinking in. I turn to stare out the windshield, noticing the car parked in front of us has California tags. Somebody's a long way from home. "My mom told me we were both babies," I say quietly. "They changed the timeline so we wouldn't suspect anything. Guess they should have agreed on the same story, though." A strange sensation wells inside my chest as I realize this is all the proof I need. Grandpa *was* telling us the truth.

K. J. rams the heel of her hand into the dash, and the sound of it makes me flinch. "I'm done," she says. "This whole bucket list thing. I'm done. I don't give a shit about the money. My mom doesn't deserve her share, and who am I kidding to think I can get through college anyway? I barely made it through high school."

I forget my own jumble of emotions as my mouth drops open in surprise. "But we're almost done. All we have left is the rodeo, and Grandpa said we just have to do one of the easy events. We can't quit now."

"I'm done," she repeats, an evil smile forming on her lips. "I can't wait to see the look on my mom's face when I tell her it's over. *And* when I tell her I know who my real father is." She turns to face me, and even though the smile is gone, a wild look still blazes in her eyes. "And I'm moving out. I'm so done with my mom. She's a fucking liar."

I hold up my hands, unsure of what to make of this whole new side of K. J. I'm seeing. Everything feels so volatile and confusing right now. "Hey, we have a long drive ahead of us. Plenty of time to think, and maybe talk."

"It won't change anything," she snaps.

I hope she's wrong for both of our sakes. Looking in the rearview mirror, I pull out onto the street when the coast is clear, and Google Maps directs us toward U.S. Route 1, the highway that will take us back to the mainland. On the way here, K. J. informed me that it's the longest north-south highway in the United States, going all the way up to the tip of Maine—another one of those random facts she always seems to know. I glance at my ladybug, an unsettled feeling still circulating inside me. Getting our tattoos felt like we were making progress, like we were finally connecting on some level, but now I'm wondering if all of that is over for good.

I turn on the radio, using the auto-scan to find a station, and it stops on one playing "Girls Just Want To Have Fun," which feels kind of like the universe rubbing salt in our wounds. No one is having fun today. I press the scan button again, but it appears the only other option is a station playing classical music, so I go back to Cyndi Lauper.

K. J. stares out her window as we start across the bridge and officially leave Key West. The ocean stretches in every direction, beautiful and completely indifferent to our family drama.

"So where do you want to stop tonight?" I ask. "It's twelve hours to Atlanta. Probably don't want to go that far since we got a late start."

"I don't care. You can pick somewhere." There's an almost bored tone to her voice and I'm not sure if it's from exhaustion or something more.

K. J. digs through the bag at her feet, pulling out her earbuds and connecting them to her phone. I guess the eighties station isn't cutting it. I turn the radio off and roll my window partway down, hoping the wind and the ocean might have a soothing effect on me. The next four hours will probably be okay, but I dread reaching the mainland and the familiar views of cities and the empty farmland in between. The world we left behind, and now will never be the same again. Not after this. It's going to be a long drive no matter how we slice it.

Of course, there's something else I'm dreading aside from the nearly twenty-four-hour trip back home: confronting my mom and telling her I know all about her big secret. As my thoughts shift to that scenario, my hands tighten on the steering wheel, and a bubble of anger expands inside my chest once again. My aunt isn't the only one who's been lying to her daughter all this time. Maybe Mom thought she was protecting me from the truth, but I deserved to know. We both deserved to know, and Grandpa shouldn't have had to be the one to tell us.

CHAPTER 24

K. J.

I DON'T REMEMBER EXACTLY WHEN I QUIT GIVING A shit, but it was somewhere around the end of middle school. I used to have a few interests—art being one of them. I was also into Rollerblading and writing bad poetry, but somewhere along the way, I abandoned everything and took up smoking instead. Looking back now, maybe it was because I realized no one really had any expectations for me. Why did I need any for myself? Mom was too busy working or going to the casino, so I spent most of my time listening to music or hanging out with friends. Eventually, that narrowed down to one friend: Carter.

School was a pain in my ass, but it was more interesting than staying home, so that was the only reason I kept going. I enjoyed listening to some of my teachers, my social studies and history teachers in particular, because hearing about what people from the past lived through somehow made my life seem less shitty.

I especially loved my tenth-grade U.S. history teacher because he actually had a sense of humor and always told the best stories. Everyone paid attention in his class. Sometimes, I'd hang out after the bell to ask questions about the topic he lectured on that day. I think he was one of the few teachers who liked me, too.

Sometimes, I even wished he was my dad and wondered how different my life would be if he were. We wouldn't be rich, but maybe Mom wouldn't feel like she needed to work two jobs, and we wouldn't live in Maple Village, and maybe I'd have more friends than just the boy who lived next door. I begged my mom to go to parent-teacher conferences that spring, hoping, by some miracle, sparks would fly between the two of them. He didn't wear a wedding ring, so we all assumed he was single, but Mom had to work that night, and she'd never cared about my grades much anyway. Why would she suddenly start?

As Becka and I cross over the Tennessee-Arkansas border, that same empty feeling plagues me now. I don't care. Not about anything. Least of all my lying-ass mother.

Becka has been driving for most of the return trip. She probably doesn't trust me in this state, and I don't blame her. I'm not sure I would either. She's also been nicer about all of this than I would have guessed. I figured she'd only hate me more, but that doesn't seem like the case.

Pine trees line the two-lane highway, and I try to focus on the scenery instead of my reflection in the window. My hair is sticking up in places, and I look like hell. God knows, I could use a cigarette right now. My phone vibrates, and I check the screen. Another missed call from Mom. The third one today. I haven't talked to her since we were in the Keys. Since before we learned the news. She's probably pacing the living room right now. Or rearranging the dishes in the cupboard. I let the anger churn inside me. Let her think I'm dead in a ditch. Serves her right. If she really wanted to know if I was all right, she could pick up the phone and call her sister.

Becka texted RaeLynn not long ago to let her know where we were. I shoot Carter a quick text and ask if I can crash at his place tonight. I have no intention of staying at home, but I do plan to confront my mom because she *is* going to own up to this. She has to.

When I look out the window again, the forest has been replaced by farm fields of golden wheat. Funny how fast the landscape changes. Kind of like my life. One second, I think I know who I am, and the next, I realize I have absolutely no idea at all.

✳   ✳   ✳   ✳

It's dark and windy by the time I pull into the mobile home park that night, after having dropped Becka off at her own house. I don't bother getting my bags out of the car since I won't be staying long. The yellow glow of the living room lamp shines in the window. I know I'll find my mom sitting by it.

The front door is unlocked, and Mom looks up from her chair as I cross the threshold. She rises to her feet, her wringing hands a dead giveaway that she's been stressing the fuck out.

"K. J." She takes a tentative step toward me, looking half relieved, half ready to smack me into tomorrow.

I hold up a hand to stop her. "Stay away from me."

Her eyebrows shoot upward. "Excuse me? What makes you think you can talk to me like that? Especially after you haven't bothered to answer my calls or texts?"

For some reason this makes me laugh. The way I'm talking to her is about to be the least of her concerns.

She frowns, crossing her arms over her chest. "What's going on with you? Why are you laughing?"

"I didn't answer you because I was pissed, Mom. Still am. We've got something we need to talk about."

A shadow of something like fear darkens her features. "Okay." She clears her throat. "What is it?"

"Who's my father?" I ask point-blank.

Her eyes turn away from mine, like they usually do any time I mention my dad. "You know who your father is. Robert Huller."

"So why haven't I ever met him?"

"I don't know where he is. He wouldn't be a good father anyway. He left us, remember?" It's the same line I've heard time and time again.

I suck in my cheeks, chew on one for a second. "So Samuel Cowles isn't my father?"

Her face pales, but she recovers quickly and pretends to look offended. "What? No! Whatever gave you that idea?"

"Oh, just Grandpa. His last letter told us about a little secret you and RaeLynn have been keeping."

Her eyes widen, and I can't tell whether it's from anger or shock. Maybe both. She moves into the kitchen to get a glass from the cupboard. Filling it with water from the tap, she takes a long sip before turning to look at me from across the counter. "Your grandpa was sick, K. J. You know that. He was probably confused."

I shove my hands into my pockets and shake my head. "I don't think so. He seemed pretty on top of things to set up all these trips for me and Becka. And out of all his letters, why would he start to lie to us in this one?"

Mom sets the glass on the counter and comes back into the living room but keeps her distance from me. Her fingers drum against her legs, like she's not quite sure what to do with herself. She reaches up to push a strand of hair behind one ear, but it refuses to stay put.

"You did have an affair with him," I say. "So this isn't really all that far out there. Maybe you just forgot the year it actually happened."

I hold my breath, waiting to see how she'll respond, but if she's been lying, she's done a really good job of hiding it.

"I was already pregnant before the affair started. That's why Robert left me. He didn't want a child."

"Why does the story keep changing, Mom?"

She gives me a blank look and her mouth opens and shuts several times like a fish that's been pulled out of water.

I decide it's time to play my last card. "Guess I'll have to get a DNA test. Shouldn't be too difficult."

Her expression changes in a flash. "What? No!" Her eyes are pleading.

"Why not? If you're sure Robert is my father, then why are you worried about it?" My tone is so cold, I don't recognize my own voice, but I'm also getting some kind of weird enjoyment out of confronting her like this.

She bites her lip and her eyes flutter closed. Her arms cross her chest again, like she's hugging herself. She stays frozen like that for a long time. I'm about to turn around and leave when she moves toward the chair and falls into it again. Her hands cover her face, and her quiet sobbing pushes away the silence. Outside, the wind picks up, whistling and rattling in the windows. Seconds later, rain pings on the roof. A summer storm seems totally appropriate right now.

She finally looks up at me, her face splotched in red and shining with tears. "Yes," she croaks. "Samuel is your father." She breaks down again, letting out a mangled sob, but she manages to hold eye contact this time. "I'm sorry I never told you. I was . . . just . . . so ashamed. I wish the affair had never happened. I ruined everything between RaeLynn and me."

"So what about me? Does that mean you wish I'd never happened either?"

"No, not at all! I didn't mean it like that. I did love Samuel at the time, but . . ." She seems at a loss for how to dig herself back out of this hole.

"Yeah, Mom, you did ruin everything." I want to keep going, really make her pay for what she's done to me, but the adrenaline I'd felt just moments ago seems to drain right out of me. Now all I feel is numb. The raindrops pick up speed, hammering a steady pattern on the roof. In a few minutes, it will be pouring. A thin stream of water zigzags across the front window. "I gotta go."

Mom swipes at her face. "What? Where are you going?"

"Don't worry about it." With that, I turn and head for the door.

I'm on the verge of bawling myself as I speed toward Carter's place in the pounding rain. My clothes are nearly soaked as I knock on his front door. He lets me in with a worried expression that looks completely foreign on his face, but god it's good to see him again.

"You cut your hair," is all I can think to say. It's not super short, but more of a skater style, which hangs over his eye on one side.

"Yeah, last week." He pushes the strands aside and smiles.

In a totally uncharacteristic move, I step forward to hug him. His arms tighten around my back, and I can't believe how nice it feels. I don't even remember the last time I've hugged someone. He smells like Irish Spring and a little like spearmint, and I want to keep holding onto him, this one constant in my life, but I unlink my arms and take a step back, clearing my throat. "So, um . . . where's Dax?"

Carter runs a hand through his hair, and it falls over his eye again. "He's got the night shift. He works at the Shop N' Go on Eleventh."

"Oh, cool." I glance around the trailer. The living room is sparsely decorated, with only a worn couch and an old-style TV sitting on top of a metal cabinet. A framed poster of ZZ Top is the sole picture hanging on the wall—it's the same one that used to hang above his bed at his mom's house. The trailer is really clean, especially for Carter, and the greenish-tan carpet even looks freshly vacuumed. Did he do all of this for me? "I like your place."

"Thanks." An odd-looking smile crosses his face, like he's both embarrassed and pleased at the same time. "So how was your trip?"

"I don't really wanna talk about it right now."

"Oh." His brows pinch together as the look of concern returns. "So . . . are you okay?"

"Better now." I force the closest thing I can to a smile.

"That's good."

But the bad feelings are pressing back in, and all I know is that I just want them to go away. I can't help myself—I reach out to Carter again, and he pulls me toward him, back into a hug, but this time it's not enough. I tilt my face up toward his, and he seems to understand. Our lips press together, but before I can lose myself in this strange form of comfort, my brain catches up with my actions. *What the hell are we doing?*

I pull away again. "Shit, I'm sorry. I don't know why I did that."

Carter scratches at his neck, his gaze falling to the floor. "No, don't be. It's okay."

I shake my head and take another step back. "My head is all jacked up right now. I'm not thinking clearly." My cheeks flush as my heart starts to pound. Did I just completely ruin our friendship? Oh god, maybe I'm more like my mom than I thought.

Awkward silence descends and when our eyes meet again, Carter looks genuinely scared, too.

"Is there any way we can try to forget that happened?" I ask.

Carter gives a slight nod. "Yeah, sure. Don't worry about it."

"So . . ." I say, stepping around him to have another look at the trailer, because it's way better than looking him in the eye and trying to ignore all these weird feelings I'm suddenly having. "Thanks for letting me crash here tonight."

"Yeah, no problem. You want something to drink or anything?" He scratches at his neck again.

"Uh, sure. I'll take whatever you've got." I follow him to the kitchen and sit on one of the two mismatched barstools while Carter grabs two cans of pop from the fridge. I imagine he and Dax had to hit up a few garage sales to furnish this place, but I'm still a little in awe that they're actually living on their own. "Thanks," I say as he places a Mountain Dew in front of me.

Across the counter, Carter leans his elbows on the green-speckled laminate, which matches the carpet a little too well. "So, uh, you wanna tell me what's going on with you? No pressure, I just figured you might want to explain . . . you know . . ." He nods toward the entryway. A hint of teasing threads his tone, but I can tell he's also being serious. He's well aware that something major has happened. Otherwise, I wouldn't be here right now.

I take a slow sip of my pop, a mix of darker emotions rising over the embarrassment of the kiss. "Might as well."

After I tell Carter the whole story, he has the decency not to look completely appalled. "So, yeah," I say with a sigh, "that's the shit show that has now become my life."

A smirk slides across his face. "Oh, come on now. Your life has always been a shit show. It's what we have in common."

I can only smile at this. "You're probably right." I take another sip of my drink and then look him in the eye. "So are we still cool?"

Because I don't think I can stand it if I ruined the one good relationship I have left in my life.

Carter rubs at his chin, pretending to think about this for a moment. The smirk returns. "Yeah, we're still totally cool."

CHAPTER 25

BECKA

MOM'S ON HER SECOND CUP OF COFFEE, AND I'M picking the M&M's out of a bag of trail mix as we sit across from one another at the kitchen table. Tim went to bed a half hour ago. He knew this was something Mom and I needed to discuss alone. I wonder if he knows K. J. is my half sister or if Mom's kept him in the dark, too. Then again, I guess it doesn't really affect him one way or the other.

Mom didn't deny anything, surprisingly; she just said she never wanted to hurt me. It's strange, but in a way, I get it. My anger had faded quite a bit on the drive home, mainly because I was worried about K. J.

"Did you know Sam told Grandpa?" I ask, giving up on the M&M's and eating a peanut instead.

Mom's face puckers. "No. It surprises me that he did, actually. I didn't think he'd open his mouth to anyone."

I work my tongue over the inside of my top teeth trying to get at a piece of the candy stuck there. "Sam should have told me."

Mom gives a tired sigh and combs her fingers through her hair. "I asked him not to. I told him I would do it when the time was right. The only problem was, it never seemed like the right time."

"So if the affair between Sam and Jackie happened before I was born, you and dad must have gotten back together for a while, right?"

She gives a subtle nod. "Yes. We tried to make it work, for your sake, but we just couldn't."

I resume my search for one last M&M, and a red-coated piece of chocolate finally appears in the bag—a shining beacon amid the dull-colored nuts and raisins. I retrieve it and pop it into my mouth.

Mom frowns. "I wish you wouldn't do that. The rest of us like M&M's too, you know."

I shrug and say sorry even though I'm not. Chocolate is the least I'm owed after finding out my parents have been hiding a half sister from me my entire life.

"So why *would* Sam tell Grandpa? That's weird."

Mom takes another sip from her mug, and I notice it's the one she took from Grandpa's house that day. "I have no idea. Maybe he thought we would never tell Dad—and that he deserved to know the truth about his grandchildren."

I raise an eyebrow. The irony of this statement is not lost on me. "So he deserved to know, but K. J. and I didn't?"

Mom rolls her eyes. "Yes, you both deserved to know, but like I said, it was a difficult situation."

"That's not a very good excuse."

"I know it isn't. I'm sorry, Rebecka. Okay. I really am, and I'm glad you finally know the truth." She purses her lips, then opens them like she's about to say something else but takes a sip from the mug again instead. It's like her security blanket right now.

Her eyes trail to my wrist. "I still can't believe you got a tattoo." She didn't freak like I expected she might, but then again, she must have realized she had no right to get upset over something as insignificant as a little tattoo right now. "And you said K. J. got one, too?"

"Yeah. A dragonfly."

Mom seems confused, probably wondering why on earth we'd get tattoos together, but I don't feel like explaining that on this trip, things changed somewhere along the way, that K. J. and I became almost amicable. That evening at the French restaurant when we were laughing and talking, we could have actually passed as friends having a good time. Of course, everything changed after the letter, and truthfully, I have no idea where we stand now, especially since K. J. pretty much shut down on the drive home.

"Do you want me to call Sam and tell him that the two of you know?" Mom asks, though I can tell it's the last thing she'd rather do.

"I guess. Someone probably should."

Mom nods. "Okay, I'll do it tomorrow." She rises from her chair and takes her mug to the sink. She's been unexpectedly serene about all of this. I guess I'm still waiting for the crap to hit the fan. For her to get angry about the affair all over again.

I seal the bag of trail mix and push back from the table, stifling a yawn. "I'm going to bed."

After returning the bag to the pantry, I turn to find Mom standing behind me. She opens her arms and pulls me into a hug, holding me there for several moments. I pat her back but can't bring myself to fully return the gesture.

"I really am sorry," she whispers into my hair. "For everything."

It's not enough really. She can't expect me to forgive her for this right away. I clear my throat as she releases me. "Good night."

Her mouth twists into a sad-looking smile. "Good night, Becka."

An hour later and no closer to sleep, I switch on my lamp and grab my phone from the nightstand. Maybe I'll just go ahead and call Sam myself. I've never called him *Dad* to his face because, in my mind, he's never been deserving of that title. He can be all right sometimes, but for the most part, I still think of him as just a sperm donor. My two stepdads have been more involved in my life than he ever has.

He answers after four rings, sounding groggy. "Hey, Becka. Everything okay?"

"It's fine." Then I change my mind. "Actually, no. It's not."

"Oh? What's wrong?" His voice shifts, a bit of concern coming through.

"I know about K. J."

"Huh? Who's K. J.?"

I roll my eyes. "Your other daughter, you know, the one you had with my mom's sister."

Silence hangs in the air for several moments. "You mean Katherine?"

"She goes by K. J." Not that he would know that.

He clears his throat, pausing again. "I wanted to tell you, but your mom asked me—"

"I know," I say, cutting him off. "She told me."

Silence again. "I'm sorry."

I don't get why adults think those two little words are enough to excuse years of wrongdoing. I let out a quiet sigh. "Why didn't you ever contact her?"

"Jackie didn't want me to."

"Don't you think you should have at least paid child support?" My voice comes out angrier than I intended, but I don't apologize.

"She didn't want that either. I tried."

I rub my finger over an ink pen mark on my bedspread, wondering when that happened. "She's had nothing her whole life. They live in a trailer park. Did you know that?"

"Yes, I know."

"You should reach out to her. She deserves to hear from you."

"Yeah, okay. I can do that." He sounds terrified at the thought, though.

"Good." I yawn, fatigue suddenly making a reappearance. "Well, I'm gonna go. Talk to you later."

"Okay," he says again. He's beginning to sound like a broken record. Or a child who needs to be told what to do. It's funny how adults can be like that sometimes.

"Bye, Sam." I hang up before he can throw an awkward "Love you" in there. I touch the ink mark once more before switching off my lamp and laying my head back on the pillow. Just as I'm about to drift off to sleep, I realize I never told Mom about K. J. backing out of the rest of Grandpa's bucket list. There's no doubt she'll be upset. I don't need the money, but Mom obviously does. Maybe I can still talk K. J. back into it somehow, but I'll have to worry about that later. I close my eyes again, determined not to give any more thought to my cousin-slash-sister or my dad or mom.

I've had enough of them all for one night.

※ ※ ※ ※

I sleep until nearly ten o'clock the next morning but awaken with an uneasy feeling stirring inside my gut. I need to talk to K. J., and since I still don't have her number, I reluctantly decide to call the only person I know who would have it. Mr. Sisco seems surprised but also pleased that I'm asking. After saving K. J.'s contact information, I start a text to her:

Hey, it's Becka. How are you?

A few seconds later, a dot-dot-dot bubble pops up, but then disappears. The bubble appears twice more, vanishing seconds later each time, and finally, nothing. I frown at my phone and set it aside. Maybe she needs a few more days to adjust. I can respect that.

The house is quiet since both Tim and Mom are at work already. After scrubbing stain remover into the small line of ink on my bedspread, I place it in the washer to soak for a while. Then I pad to the kitchen to pour myself a glass of orange juice and grab a bagel from the fridge. As I nibble on my breakfast, I text Lexi and Maddie, asking when we can schedule our next coffee meetup. So much to tell them, and I don't want to do it via text message.

As I wait for my friends to respond, I check the weather, finding that it's supposed to be ninety-five today. Hopefully, it's not too hot yet. I should go do my morning run and maybe drop by the gym later today, too. My summer workouts have been sporadic with everything else going on, but I need to get back on top of my game for the upcoming soccer season.

Lexi responds, quickly followed by Maddie, and we plan for next Thursday morning. I'm about to get off my phone and grab my running shoes but decide to Google the rodeo from Grandpa's letter first. The Decatur Dog Days of Summer Rodeo is easy enough to find. The rodeo will be held July 22 and 23, along with some other festivities. I scan the events, finding goat milking, mutton bustin', and a stick-horse race in the list, just as Grandpa had said. At the bottom of the online flyer, it says contestants should show up early to the eight o'clock performance, as events fill up on a first-come, first-served basis.

We have a few weeks until the rodeo, so there's still time for K. J. to change her mind. Surely, she'll come around. At the beginning of the summer, Grandpa's tasks were the last thing I wanted to do. I was only going along with things so Mom would get her money, but now that we're down to the end, this whole thing has become about so much more than money to me. I want to finish it for Grandpa, and I want to finish it with K. J.

CHAPTER 26
K. J.

"COULD YOU HELP THIS LADY FIND THE RAIN-X wipers?" my manager, Doug, asks me.

"Uh, yeah. Sure thing."

I smile at the middle-aged woman, pretending like I know what the hell I'm doing here. It's my third day at Reynold's Auto Parts and I still feel like a duck out of water, but since I was desperate for a job and they had another spot open, this one sounded as good as any.

"What size did you need again?" I ask as she follows me down the aisle.

"Twenty-four inch."

"That's right." I stop before the array of windshield wipers—who knew there could be so many types?—and scan the names.

"Rain-X. Here it is." I grab the wiper and hand it to the lady. "Did you just need the one?"

"Yes, ma'am."

It's totally weird how people call me ma'am here, too. It makes me want to look around for the adult because they surely couldn't be talking to me. I return to my spot behind the counter to ring her up.

"Thanks for stopping in today," I say as she turns to leave. "Come back and see us!" I might be going a little overboard, but I really want to keep this job. It's the first one I've ever had.

"Go take your lunch, K. J.," Doug says as soon as the store clears out. The guy is big and burly and seems like the kind of boss you don't want to argue with, so I just nod and head to the back office to grab my keys from my cubby. Thirty minutes isn't much time to go anywhere, but I guess I can grab a sandwich and a pop from the Shop N' Go down the road. My gas tank is dangerously close to empty and I have no clue how much money is left on the prepaid card Grandpa gave me. I'm sort of regretting getting the tattoo because having an extra seventy-five dollars would be helpful right about now. Hopefully, there's still enough on there to fill up and buy lunch. I've been living off Carter and Dax's good graces for the past week, and payday isn't until next Thursday.

When I pull up to the pump, I'm not sure how to figure out how much money is left on my card, but after sitting in the car debating on what to do for a few minutes, I go ahead and put five dollars of gas in.

Lucky for me, there's enough for that, so inside the store, I choose a turkey and cheese sandwich, a bag of Doritos, and a small fountain drink before getting in line. Only this time, the card won't go through. "Can you take the chips off?" I ask the clerk, my stomach squirming with both hunger and anxiousness. I'm used to not having much money, but this really sucks.

"No problem," he says, ringing me up again.

I try the card, but it still won't work. "Um," I look at the drink, heat flushing in my cheeks. I don't think he'll let me put it back. "How about the chips and the drink?"

When I run the card again, the machine beeps and relief spills over me. Card accepted, thank God. I grab my things and turn around to find a man with crossed arms and a pissy look standing behind me.

"Sorry." I hurry to escape out the door. "Asshole," I mutter outside.

I've just made it to my car and ripped open the chip bag when my phone dings with a text:

Can I call u?

It's Becka again—but I don't feel like talking to her, so I toss the phone aside and take a sip of my drink instead. I finish off my lunch, if you can call it that, while driving back to work, but my stomach is still rumbling when everything's gone. I know there's food in the pantry at home, but I don't want to risk showing up and finding Mom there. Even if she's not home, she'd notice if I took food. I'll just have to tough it out for now.

It's also tempting to finish up Grandpa's bucket list and get my money. Maybe I could somehow finagle my way out of using it for college, but then Mom would get her share, too, and that's the last thing I want. This is the only thing I have complete control over, and even though I feel kind of bad about Becka and her mom not getting their share, it's not like Becka really needs it, and RaeLynn's husband probably makes plenty of money. They'll be okay.

Carter's truck is parked in the side lot when I arrive back at work, which makes my stomach flutter a little. Even though we agreed that things were cool between us, I'm always wondering if he's still thinking about that kiss, too. My phone rings as I'm getting out of the car, distracting me, and I frown when I see it's Becka yet again. I switch it to silent and stuff it back into my pocket.

✳ ✳ ✳ ✳

By the time my shift ends at four, my stomach feels like an empty crater. I drive straight to Walmart, grab two packages of ramen noodles, and pray there's at least seventy-five cents left on my card. If not, I plan to scour the store for dropped coins because that's how desperate I am. Success—my card goes through, and I can't get back to Carter's place fast enough in order to microwave those suckers.

The smell of the salty noodles floods the kitchen, and my stomach riots with impatience. I stir the steaming bowl with my fork, but just as I'm about to take a bite, my phone rings again. I snatch it up, finding it's none other than Becka. God, why can't she take a freaking hint? I press the green button.

"What?" I practically yell.

"K. J.?"

"Yeah? Hey." My voice softens because it's hard to feel angry when Becka sounds so calm.

"Don't you answer texts?"

"Sorry," I say, though I'm really not. I wasn't ready to talk then, and I'm still not ready to now.

She sighs into the phone. "Hey, I think Sam, you know, our dad, wants to contact you. Would that be okay? I didn't want to give him your number without permission."

My mouth opens, but nothing comes out.

"You still there?"

"Why?" I finally manage to ask.

"Don't you want to talk to him? I mean, surely you have questions for him."

"No, not really." He's obviously never given a shit about me.

"How about if I give you his number? I'll text it to you. In case you change your mind."

"Whatever." Neither one of us speaks for several seconds, and I can feel whatever comradery we managed to find back in the Keys slipping away like soapy water swirling down the drain. "I gotta go."

"Hey," she says before I can hang up. "Have you given any more thought to the rodeo?"

"Yep, and I'm not doing it." She doesn't respond, so I just say, "See ya later," even though I know I probably won't. I'm sure she doesn't really want to see me again, and sister or not, I don't really care if I see her. I hang up and toss my phone on the table, picking up my fork again.

The ramen noodles are the perfect temperature now, so I slurp them down in a rush. The weird thing is, even after I've had my fill, I still feel somewhat empty inside. I'm not sure if that has to do with the phone call from Becka or something else.

Maybe it's a whole lot of things.

CHAPTER 27

BECKA

"SO WHICH NIGHT ARE YOU GOING THIS WEEKEND?"
Mom asks as I'm sitting at the kitchen table, filling out a four-page information packet the university sent me. "Tim and I want to come watch."

I haven't found the courage to tell her K. J. won't be attending the rodeo and that no money will come even though I've decided to finish the last of the tasks. I twirl the pen in my hand, stalling for time. "I'm not sure yet."

Mom raises an eyebrow, like she's on to me, but says, "Okay, well let me know when you decide." She grabs her purse and thermos of coffee before scurrying out the door. "See you tonight," she calls over her shoulder.

I finish up the paperwork and then consider trying to call K. J. again. Surely, she's gotten over some of her hard feelings by now.

If I were in her shoes, would I have gotten over all this yet? I think about that question for a minute, tapping my pen against the papers in front of me, but I can't settle on an answer. I'd be pissed for sure, but I don't think I'd waste the opportunity to get a free ride to college. Then again, we're two completely different people. Maybe college doesn't mean the same thing to her, or maybe she just wants something different for her life.

I try her number but get the automated answering message right away. Her phone must be dead or turned off. I fold the paperwork and place it inside the self-addressed envelope that was included. Guess I'll run this to the post office. Mom's always had a thing about not putting mail with personal information in the mailbox for pickup. "That's how people get their identities stolen," she's told me. I have a feeling that happens more from online stuff, but whatever; the post office isn't that far away.

But after dropping my mail off, impulse strikes and I turn left instead of right. I need to talk to K. J., and I'd much rather do it in person. I know they live somewhere between West Siloam Springs and Colcord, but I Google their address as I drive. It's not hard to find. Mom wouldn't be happy knowing that it's possible to find practically anyone's address online.

I arrive at Maple Village Mobile Home Park twenty minutes later, but locating the right trailer proves somewhat more difficult. Unlike my neighborhood, where the house numbers are prominently displayed on both the houses and mailboxes, the numbers are much more discreet here. Plus, the trailers all sit sideways, making it nearly impossible to see anything from the road. I search for K. J.'s car, but it's nowhere to be seen. On my third time around the loop, I spot a car that I think might be Jackie's. It's worth a shot, anyway.

I park and get out, slowly making my way to the house. The number 4792 is engraved on a wooden sign hanging from the front porch rail, just above a frog planter full of what looks like dead grass. I double-check the number with the address on my phone. This should be it.

Drawing in a deep breath, I knock on the door.

I'm not sure who's more shocked to see the other, Jackie or me. Her face is pale and thinner than I remember, like she's been ill, but she opens the glass door and invites me inside. I glance around the place before taking a seat on a faded tan couch. It's surprisingly tidy, but the smell of stale cigarettes cancels out any nice first impression I might have had. Jackie sits in a chair opposite me.

"Is K. J. around?" I ask, filling in the long silence.

She shakes her head, eyeing me with a look of apprehension. "I was hoping maybe you knew where she was."

"No, I have no idea. I'm sorry."

Jackie wrings her hands together and frowns. "She was so angry with me. I don't blame her, but I'm worried. She won't answer any of my texts or calls."

Hmm, that sounds familiar. "How long has she been gone?" I ask.

Jackie's frame seems to wilt before me. "Since that night you two came back from the Keys."

Her appearance makes more sense now.

"I've talked to her," I say, hoping to put her at ease. "It was about a week and a half ago, but she's okay." At least I hope that's the case. I honestly don't have any better idea of where she is than her mom does.

"I have a feeling she might be with her friend Carter," Jackie says. "I've tried his phone, but he doesn't answer either. I can give you his number if you want. Maybe you'll have better luck."

"Okay, sure." I remember K. J. talking about Carter.

Jackie rises and heads toward the kitchen where she writes something down on a blue sticky note. She also grabs a white envelope from the counter and hands them both to me. The letter is addressed to both K. J. and me, written in Grandpa's familiar cursive.

"This came in the mail the other day," she tells me. One corner of her mouth turns upward, like she wants to smile, but can't quite find the energy to do so.

"Thanks."

Jackie sees me out, and it strikes me as I get back into my car that this is the first time I've felt pity instead of hatred toward my aunt. She's made some big mistakes in her life, more than I probably know about, but unlike my mom, she's never been able to get away from them. She's still knee-deep in the muck.

After K. J.'s phone goes straight to voicemail again, I give Carter's number a try. To my surprise, he answers on the second ring. I explain who I am, not at all shocked when his voice suddenly turns cold. Still, after some semi-pleading on my part, he gives the phone to K. J.

"Hey. Can we talk? Please?"

"Yeah," she says, sounding completely unenthused. "What's up?"

"In person maybe? Plus, I have something for you."

She hesitates before responding. "I guess so."

Then she gives me an address, which I scrawl down beneath the number on the sticky note. After tapping End Call, I read the address to Siri, and she directs me to another mobile home park a few miles away. K. J.'s silver Honda sits outside the fifth trailer on the left. I park between it and a beat-up pickup truck—the one I'd seen her get into that day at Pour Jons.

K. J. answers the door. "Hey," she says, looking less than thrilled to see me. Even so, I'm relieved to see that she's okay.

She lets me inside and I try not to gawk. I didn't know trailer houses were all that different, but this one is much older and dumpier than her mom's. The same stale cigarette aroma hangs in the air, only here it's mixed with the scent of something else, like mildew. I try to ignore it as I hand over the envelope.

"Your mom gave me this."

She cocks an eyebrow. "So that's how you got Carter's number. I was wondering."

A blond boy wearing a red Reynold's Auto Parts shirt and jeans appears from the hallway. Carter, I can only assume. He has one of those skater hairstyles and a sort of hardened look about him, but he's not bad-looking.

"This is Becka," K. J. says by way of introduction. "Becka, Carter."

He eyes me somewhat warily before looking back at K. J., who has settled onto the couch now, her feet tucked up under her. A folded blanket and pillow sit on the other end, and I'm guessing this must be her bed for now. "See you after while," Carter says to K. J. before heading out the front door.

"Anyway," I continue, "I came to talk to you about the rodeo. It would be stupid not to do it."

Her eyes narrow, and her whole demeanor changes. She crosses her arms, leaning back into the couch. "I told you. I'm not doing it."

"But don't you want to go to school? And get your inheritance?"

She shakes her head. "You know as well as I do that I'm not cut out for that shit. Besides, I've got a decent job now. Pays nine bucks an hour."

"Where at?"

"Reynold's Auto Parts."

I want to tell her she's too smart to spend her life working at an auto parts store or living in some dump like this, but I don't. Sometimes the truth only makes people angrier. I nod toward the letter sitting beside her on the couch. "You can read it first if you want."

K. J. glances down at the envelope before giving a one-shoulder shrug. "Fine."

At first, her face is unreadable as her eyes move over the words, but at some point, her expression darkens, the corners of her mouth shifting downward. Her forehead creases, like she's become lost in thought. A few seconds later, her eyes shift from the letter to the floor.

"Well?" I ask.

K. J. doesn't say anything, just hands the letter to me.

I sink into the couch beside her to read it.

CHAPTER 28
#

Dear Katherine and Rebecka,

I hope you don't hate me for sharing the news you both deserved to hear long ago. I hope you don't hate your mothers, either. They've both made some mistakes in their lives and, in my opinion, not telling you two the truth earlier on was one of them. At the same time, I understand why they chose not to tell you—it was out of love and the belief that they were protecting you—but you are both adults now and I believe you can handle the truth.

I'm going to be completely honest: I have no idea where I'll go after I die. But I'd like to think that, as you're reading this, I'm still with you in some small way. People say you carry your loved ones with you in your heart, even after they're gone. I think of it a little differently, though.

I miss both of my parents dearly, and even all these years later, I can still hear certain sayings my father had or the sound of my mother's soft laughter. I like to think they now occupy a small, but very real, space in my brain. They're a part of me and will remain so even after I die.

It's the same with you and me. Maybe you get annoyed when you think about my insect collecting or all of my issues that prevented me from going to the places I've asked you both to go. However, I'm sure there are a few things you recall fondly, too. At least, I hope so. Even with as little time as we spent together, I believe I'll always occupy a small part of your brain as well.

Please know that I'll be cheering you both on at that rodeo. I'd say break a leg, but that's the wrong sentiment in this type of sport. So go get 'em, cowgirls!

This will be the last letter you receive from me. I'm afraid my hand is growing too tired to write much more. I'm just tired in general these days.

The trips you've now gone on were intended to both create and solidify what I hope will be a lasting bond between you two. I also hope your relationship will continue to grow from this point forward, but that, of course, is up to the two of you.

So goodbye, my dearest granddaughters. Go live the life you've always dreamed of. I hope the money I'm leaving will help you get a good start.

Love always,

Grandpa

CHAPTER 29
K. J.

FOR A SECOND OR TWO, I CONSIDER CHANGING MY
mind and doing the rodeo after all, but then I remember the look on
my mom's face when I confronted her. She wasn't sorry for lying to me
all these years; she was only sorry she got caught.

Becka finishes the letter and hands it back to me. "Don't you want
to do it for Grandpa?" she asks.

"He's dead. What does it matter?"

Her eyes widen, like she can't believe I just said that. She still
doesn't know me, apparently, the way I can turn my emotions off like
a switch whenever I want to. I pull my phone from my back pocket
and check the time.

"I've gotta get ready for work," I say, even though I still have a
few hours before my shift.

"You're being completely selfish, K. J." Becka's mouth forms a thin, tight line.

I hold her gaze. "You know what? I don't really give a rat's ass what you think. You and your mom don't need the money, you said so yourself, and my mom doesn't deserve anyone's last dime." I push up from the couch and glower down at her. "Now get out of here. I don't remember inviting you over anyway."

We stand within an arm's length of each other, and even though it shouldn't, my three inches over Becka makes me bold. I know I'm being shitty right now, but I can't seem to stop. We hold eye contact for several silent seconds before she finally looks away.

"Fine," she says, "be like that." She turns to leave but stops at the door, looking back over her shoulder. "You know what the sad thing is? You're only screwing yourself by doing this. That seems to be your biggest talent."

I roll my eyes. "Fuck off, Becka."

✳ ✳ ✳ ✳

Becka's visit leaves me in a foul mood for the rest of the week, and the stormy weather pattern isn't helping things. Friday evening, Dax and I have the six o'clock news on to make sure no tornadoes are heading this way. Even though it's July, you just never know in Oklahoma.

"This is some freaky weather we've been having, huh?" Dax says. He's perched on a kitchen barstool drinking a Red Bull while I sit on the carpet, experimenting with painting my toenails black. I've never painted my fingernails or toenails any color, but I'm feeling a little more adventurous these days. And black totally fits my mood right now.

"Guess it's all part of global warming." I glance back at the television, taking a small amount of comfort in the fact that we're only in a yellow "watch" area.

"Could be." Dax takes a long sip before tossing his can across the room and into the kitchen sink.

I don't know why he always does that, but it's not my house, so I can't really complain. The news anchor lady comes on blabbing about all the cancellations in the area, and I focus in on painting my big toe nail. "Crap," I say, accidentally smearing polish on my skin. I use my fingernail to scrape it off. This is way harder than it looks. When I hear something about the "Dog Days of Summer," I look back up at the TV.

". . . one of the most anticipated festivals in our area each July, but it looks like both the festival and the rodeo will be rained out this evening. This is also the case with the 49th Annual Dickinson Outdoor Car Show that was supposed to be held tonight. Hopefully, tomorrow will be drier and both events will be back on. What do you think, John?"

The gangly-looking weatherman laughs. "Oh, I believe so, Randi. Tomorrow's looking to be a typical sunny July day. In fact, we'll get up to ninety-six degrees, and it's gonna be a steamy one, folks!"

"That guy is such a doofus," Dax says, getting up from the barstool. Like he's one to talk. Dax is six foot something and skinny as they come. He nods toward the television. "All right if I play *Mass Effect*? Looks like we're safe for now."

"Sure." To be honest, I'm sick of watching him and Carter play video games, but once again I have to be nice about it.

"You making dinner tonight?" Dax asks, and I fight the urge to roll my eyes. We recently decided to take turns cooking, but when it's one of the guys' turns we either have sandwiches or frozen pizza. I'm the only one who knows how to make an actual meal around here.

"Yeah," I say with a huff and stand to hobble on my heels into the kitchen.

Frozen chicken breasts are in the oven and sliced potatoes are frying in a pan when Carter arrives home at half past seven. He tromps across the carpet in his wet tennis shoes, and once again, I bite my tongue. Mom would have such a fit.

"Smells good," he says. "Whatcha making?"

"Stuff," I say, because they'll find out soon enough. But then I feel guilty for being rude when I'm getting to stay here for free and all. "So how was your shift?" I ask, working hard to make my tone more friendly.

"Good. Busy." Carter gives my arm a playful pinch and grabs a Mountain Dew from the fridge before going to plop down on the couch and watch Dax play the video game. I sigh. This is how our evenings seem to go anymore. Though it's about as exciting as watching a fly buzz around the room, I watch for a while until the timer for the chicken goes off.

"Food's ready," I say, but the guys aren't paying attention. They're totally wrapped up in their game. I shake my head and make myself a plate, sitting at the counter to eat by my lonesome. Lately,

I can't shake this growing, unsettled feeling about living here. It's like, aside from work, this old mildewy trailer and violent video games have become my life. I don't want to go home, but I wish I had another option. Maybe even a place of my own.

Grandpa's money sure would be nice. That little voice keeps piping up, but it's completely pointless. I'd have to use it on college, and that defeats the whole purpose because I'm not going to freaking college.

✳ ✳ ✳ ✳

Saturday, Carter and I both have the afternoon shift at Reynold's. When I step out for a smoke break around three, I realize that dorky weatherman was right. It's suffocating out here. But the blazing summer sun has at least dried up all the puddles that were here when we came in at noon. I'm sucking in one last drag when my phone dings in my pocket. I pull it out to have a look. Becka again.

I'm going tonight

I type *good for u* and then delete it, stuffing the phone back into my pocket instead. I stub out my cigarette and head back inside, where I can get some relief from this hellhole, otherwise known as summer in Siloam Springs.

The afternoon drags on, and though I'm still grateful to have this job, I find myself thinking about all the other things I could be doing instead of organizing car batteries on the back shelf.

I could work at the vape shop on Aspen, I think. No that's dumb. What about a job at the art studio where people come with their friends to paint a Christmas tree or a giant purple heart with pink polka dots inside? I'd seen those two pictures outside the window one time anyway. Or what about a restaurant? Waiters probably make decent money, especially at the nice places. If I waited tables, maybe I'd make enough to get my own apartment or something. Some place that doesn't have to be brought in on wheels.

I sigh and hoist yet another battery onto the shelf. I just don't see how it's possible. How will I ever make enough to live on my own? So far, most of my money has gone for groceries and gas. And cigarettes, although I recently decided I should quit for good because the habit is just too dang expensive.

When eight o'clock finally rolls around, I follow Carter out to his truck since we rode together today. It's cooled off by maybe half a degree or so. "So you wanna do something fun tonight?" I ask as I slide into the passenger side. "We could go see a movie or something. My treat."

"I think Dax was wanting to play *Call of Duty*, actually." He gives me a sheepish smile as he starts the engine.

I take a deep breath of semi-cooled air. "Really? You know, we never do anything like we used to, even if it was driving around or shit like that." Maybe neither one of us wants to admit that we might have messed things up with that kiss.

Carter's smile disappears, replaced by a look of irritation. "I don't have much extra money to go out and do stuff, K. J. You know that."

"Um, hello? I just offered to pay for the movie, and you still don't wanna go."

"How about tomorrow? We're both off work. I just wanna chill at the house tonight." He backs out of his space, and we bump through a series of potholes before exiting the parking lot.

I stare straight ahead. "Forget it."

Carter sighs but doesn't say anything else. We make the rest of the drive in silence.

Dax already has the PS4 fired up at home, and Carter immediately settles onto the couch beside him, ready for their dude-date or whatever.

"I'm leaving," I announce after grabbing a Dr Pepper and a granola bar.

"Where ya going?" Carter asks without looking up.

"Dunno yet." I grab my keys and leave before he can say anything else. Not that he was going to anyway. I definitely need some time to rethink this whole living here thing.

I start driving with no destination in mind, but the farther I head east, the more I realize I do know where I want to go.

I pull into the Decatur Round-Up Club at eight forty-seven and hand five bucks to a man at the gate. Luckily, I had some cash on me since I totally forgot about having to pay. Trucks and trailers and horses and hillbillies litter the rodeo grounds. I find a parking spot near the back and start toward the arena with my Dr Pepper can still in hand. Country music blares from speakers near the announcer's box and several girls ride past me on horses. They wear fancy western shirts covered with fringe and straw cowboy hats, making me wonder if they're barrel racers or rodeo queens or something like that.

The stands are spilling over with spectators, and I'm lucky to find a seat on the bottom row on one end. Someone will probably be returning from the bathroom to find I took their seat. Oh well, their loss.

I've only been to one rodeo before, but it looks like they're doing the calf roping right now. A guy swings a lasso over his head while riding his horse down the arena, chasing a black and white calf. He misses, and the crowd lets out a collective groan. I turn and scan the bleachers for Becka, but she could be anywhere in this sea of faces.

"Alrighty, folks," the announcer says with even more twang than normal for this area. "The calf ropin' is wrapping up, but we're ready for some more amateur fun: goat milkin's up next."

Cheers erupt from the crowd, and I swipe at the beads of sweat that have formed along my brow line. Wish I'd thought to change out of my work shirt and jeans before I left.

Several goats are led into the arena and tied to a row of stakes about halfway down. Some are bigger than others, but it's obvious by the way they waddle around at the end of their lines that they all have overly full udders just begging to be milked.

"I like the black one!" a little girl exclaims a few seats down from me. She runs to the fence, grasping the railing with both hands in order to watch. She's skinny with short, curly brown hair, and I wonder if that's what I looked like at that age.

"Are the contestants ready?" the announcer asks. I peek around the girl to see a line of people holding metal pails near the arena entrance. I recognize Becka's blond ponytail bobbing among them.

"Now wait for my cue," the announcer continues.

A murmur of excitement rises from the crowd.

"Ready. Set. Go!"

Everyone takes off running full throttle toward the goats, who jump around at the end of their lines. This should be interesting, I think, as I lean forward, keeping my eyes trained on Becka. She's the only one wearing shorts and tennis shoes, which was probably a smart move. It's no surprise she's one of the first ones to get to a goat—the black one the little girl declared as her favorite. She immediately falls to her knees and grabs the lead rope, and though it takes a little while for her to persuade the goat to come near her, it finally stops protesting and stands still. She stuffs the bucket beneath it and starts milking. How does she even know how to do that? She was scared of riding a mule, but she somehow knows how to milk a goat?

Most of the contestants are still trying to get ahold of their rowdy goats, but a few have begun filling their own pails. People around me laugh after a goat tries to head-butt one guy. He jumps backward, splashing the pail of milk all over his shirt. I let out a snort of laughter. This definitely beats watching Carter and Dax play *Call of Duty*.

"Sixty seconds left," the announcer says, which only increases the frantic activity in the arena. Three contestants still haven't even touched their goats, much less milked them. Becka's got her serious face on—maybe it's her game face, I don't know—but she's definitely in it to win it.

"Thirty seconds."

One contestant scrambles around to the other side of his goat, tripping over the lead line in the process, and falling face-first into the dirt. The crowd howls with laughter as the announcer begins the final countdown. A buzzer sounds.

"Time's up!"

A judge makes his way down the line, inspecting the pails. He pauses at Becka's and compares the contents of her pail with someone else's. He then jogs toward the announcer's box and shouts something up to the people inside.

"We have a winner, folks! Becka Cowles!"

From somewhere behind me, someone gives a squeal of excitement. I turn and notice Aunt RaeLynn and the man who must be her husband cheering about five rows above me. But unlike the last time I saw her, I'm not stricken with the same surge of bitterness. Instead, I feel nothing except a small pang of jealousy. She's here supporting her daughter. My mom would never do that.

"All right, let's clear out to get ready for the team ropers," the announcer says, drawing my attention back to the arena.

I need to pee, so I head toward the row of porta-potties I'd seen coming in. On the way there, I spot Becka. She smiles and waves at me before seeming to remember our last conversation. Her face becomes blank, but I wave back. My cheeks warm as I think about how nice she's been lately and what a jerk I've been. Becka was right, I *was* being a pain in the ass just to spite my mom.

"Nice job," I say, approaching her. "I figured you had it in the bag from the beginning."

She stares at me for a moment before giving a reluctant smile. Dirt is smudged across one of her cheeks and the tip of her nose.

"Thanks. It was actually pretty fun." She peeks back over her shoulder at the small herd of goats being led to a pen set up near a stock trailer. "I may have cheated a little, actually. I made friends with the little black goat ahead of time, but no one said I couldn't." Her smile grows broader, and I play-punch her in the shoulder.

"Doesn't sound like cheating to me."

"So what are you doing here? Did you decide to go through with this after all?"

"I dunno," I say with a shrug. "It was kinda a spur-of-the moment decision." I don't feel like elaborating any further. "Do you think it's too late to enter one of the events?"

"I'm not sure. We can check, I guess." Her face is hopeful with the possibility. I should never have backed out on this. It was stupid— *I* was being stupid.

"My mom doesn't know you weren't planning to come," she says. "I couldn't bring myself to tell her. She still thinks we're getting the money. I guess I was hoping you'd show after all."

I frown. "I'm sorry. I was being a total bitch about things." I glance toward the line of blue porta-potties a few yards away. "Could you go check for me? I need to use the bathroom. I'll meet you right back here."

"No problem."

Five minutes later, she's back at our meeting spot, but one look at her face tells me it must be too late. Crap, I should have known.

"There's only one event still open," she says.

"What is it? I'll do it. I don't care."

"Money the Hard Way."

My forehead scrunches. "What the hell is that?"

"It involves bulls."

A jolt of fear pierces straight through me. "Riding them?"

She shakes her head. "No, not riding them, but you have to be in the arena with one. I think you're supposed to get a ribbon off its horn or something like that."

I consider this for a moment. "So, all I have to do is go in there right? I don't need to win."

"I guess so, as long as we have a record of you competing."

I reach for some cash in my front pocket. "How much is it to enter?"

"You don't have to pay for the amateur events—just sign up."

My heart begins to thud, but I gotta do what I gotta do, I guess. "Okay, let's get me signed up, then."

Becka bites at her lip. "Wait, maybe we should see if there's something else. Maybe you could borrow a horse or something. You know how to ride."

I wave her suggestion away. "It'll be fine. I'll be careful."

Becka gives me a skeptical look, but then leads the way to a van with a card table set up out front. A heavy-set woman sits behind it, writing on a notepad. A large box fan teeters on a plastic bucket beside her, blowing her curly hair to one side.

"Um, hi there," I say. "I need to enter Money the Hard Way." My voice sounds slightly off.

"You eighteen?"

"Yep."

She smiles and pushes a clipboard with a consent form toward me. "Sign here, then."

My stomach turns queasy as I sign on the line, and my knees suddenly feel like they might be made of Jell-O. I'm not sure which is more idiotic: me trying to back out of getting my eighty-seven thousand dollars or willingly signing up to play hide-and-seek with a bull.

CHAPTER 30

BECKA

MY PALMS ARE SWEATING, AND IT'S NOT FROM THE heat. The barrel racing event just wrapped up, and a crew in a big white truck circles the arena, picking up the three barrels. I'm back in the stands, squeezed in next to Mom and Tim.

The loudspeaker crackles. "Okay, folks. It's time for the part everyone's been waiting for." The announcer gives a dramatic pause. "The bulls!"

My heart beats extra hard against my chest.

"First up," he continues, "Money the Hard Way. Then our cowboys will brave the backs of those beasts in our final event of the night—the bull riding."

The crowd cheers again, but I wipe my hands on my jeans, feeling slightly nauseous.

Mom bumps me with her shoulder. "So what is it K. J. will be doing exactly?"

"I'm not sure." All I know is that it involves a bull, and since it's called Money the Hard Way, it's not too hard to guess that it also involves a fair amount of danger.

Moments later, "Eye of the Tiger" starts blasting from the speakers as eight contestants make their way into the arena. K. J. is the only girl. The contestants are directed to the center of the arena, right where the goats had been tied for my event, and we listen as the announcer explains the game and what may or may not happen with a bull named Psycho. Then, after that lengthy buildup, several loud bangs reverberate from the chutes beneath the announcer's stand. A gate swings open and a bull comes trotting out. With menacing eyes, it stares around the arena for several seconds before stalking toward the contestants. I suck in a breath between my teeth as the crowd cheers again.

"Did I mention two hundred and fifty dollars is up for grabs here?" the announcer says.

The cheering grows louder.

"Get it, Justin!" someone yells from a few rows below us.

The bull paws the dirt, and Mom gasps, bringing a hand to her mouth. "Oh my god! This is awful!"

All I can do is watch, helpless. *Get out of there*, I silently plead with K. J.

She's entered the event and made an appearance. That should be enough. She doesn't need to stay out there; we're technically done now. Then I think back to the mule ride into the canyon and how she wasn't scared of the bear at Yellowstone. The Bull Sluice was just another adventure in her eyes, not something to be frightened of. As I watch her now, I know, without a doubt, that she is not going to just walk out of the arena and quit.

With their feet apart in a semi-crouch stance, the contestants start an awkward dance with the bull. A red ribbon dangles from one of its big white horns, and it waves in the air every time he turns his head. It looks easy enough to get ahold of, but the trouble will be getting close enough to do it. The music changes to a heavy metal song I've never heard before. I keep my eyes glued on K. J., who stays near the back of the group. She wipes sweat from her brow and crouches lower, like she's ready to dart in either direction should the bull come her way.

Please, God, let her be fast.

The bull stops pawing and finally makes a move, taking off toward a pudgy guy in black jeans and an oversized belt buckle. The man tries to dodge left, but he doesn't stand a chance. The bull flings him through the air like an oversized rag doll. Mom screams, but the sound is drowned out by more cheering. I don't know how, but my heart is pounding even harder, and I'm really starting to sweat. Are these people freaking nuts? The guy jumps to his feet, pumping a fist into the air like he's just scored a touchdown.

The bull goes after another man, but he's quicker than the pudgy guy and darts out of the way in plenty of time. No one has even tried to get the ribbon yet, and I can't really blame them. The bull pauses, seeming to survey his opponents, and K. J. moves in closer.

The music changes again. "We Will Rock You" is blaring through the speakers now and people start stomping their boots on the wooden floorboards of the bleachers in time to the beat. The sound grows until it becomes almost deafening. Psycho turns a circle, eyeing the crowd and looking more agitated by the second. He aims at another human target, paws at the dirt, and takes off.

Mom covers her eyes. "I can't watch this!"

A guy trips over his own feet and goes down, but Psycho is already focused elsewhere.

"He's okay, Mom." At least he's back on his feet. I want to tell K. J. to get out of there, but she just inches closer to the bull.

"One minute remaining," the announcer says. "Who's it gonna be this year? Psycho or one of you brave souls?"

K. J. tenses and then makes her move.

"No!" I shout, but my voice is lost in all the excitement.

She steadily creeps toward the bull, who's temporarily distracted by the crowd and, with one arm outstretched, she leaps toward his head. Psycho ducks and moves away, recovering with lightning speed. In the next instant, he rams smack into K. J., knocking her to the ground and trampling her before he turns his attention to another contestant.

"No!" I scream again, jumping to my feet. My pulse throbs in my temples as I push my way down the bleachers, running to the arena fence. K. J. lies in a crumpled heap in the dirt.

The announcer's voice has replaced the cheering, but his words are just background noise. They don't seem to register in my brain. Other people are in the arena now: a rodeo clown, who steals the bull's attention away from the other contestants, and two men, who run to kneel by K. J.'s side. I start to climb over the pipe fence when someone grabs my leg, pulling me back down.

"Not yet," the man says. "Wait until they get the bull out of the arena."

Guilt burns inside me. Why didn't I talk her out of this? I should have put up a bigger fight. It seems to take an eternity, but as soon as Psycho is lured back into the pens behind the arena, I clamber over the fence. I nearly trip on a clump of dirt as I run to where K. J. lies. Two medics tend to her, while several other people form a circle around her. I stand on my tiptoes to peer over their shoulders, terrified of what I might see. She's covered in dirt, but there's no blood. That's got to be a good sign, but I also notice she isn't moving. My breath catches in my chest as I push my way in closer, praying that this is just unconsciousness.

"Is she okay?" I ask in a breathless whisper, but the medics don't answer.

"Your friend?" a man standing next to me asks.

I shake my head, tears pooling in my eyes. "My sister."

He puts a gentle hand on my shoulder. "I'm sure she'll be fine. Probably just knocked out is all."

I desperately hope he's right, but my stomach twists into knots of doubt because what if she's not all right? What if she dies like Ricky did?

The seconds drag on and I'm only aware of K. J.'s motionless body and the medics moving about in front of me. Her face is so pale.

"Is she going to be okay?" I ask, louder this time, because I can't seem to stand here in silence.

Again, no one answers.

The announcer is still trying to smooth things over and assure the crowd that everything is under control, but he seems to be running out of things to say. It's not until they finally have K. J. on a backboard and I'm following them out that I realize the crowd is still watching intently. Several wide-eyed young kids stand next to the fence, their fingers curled around the pipe. As they're putting her into the ambulance, someone taps me on the shoulder. It's the same man who'd spoken to me earlier.

"I'm sorry," he says and hands me a phone. It must have fallen out of K. J.'s pocket back in the arena. "Hope she'll be okay."

I nod as a tear escapes down my cheek. They shut the doors, and the ambulance drives forward, lights flashing, but no sirens. Mom and Tim appear by my side.

"What's going on?" Mom asks, worry lines creasing her forehead. "Is she hurt bad?"

I shake my head. "I don't know. Can you take me to the hospital?"

"Sure," she says, handing me my backpack, which I'd left on the bleachers. Tim places a hand on my back as we walk toward the Jeep. Mom digs in her purse and pulls out her own phone. "Damn it," she mumbles, "I don't have her number. Give me K. J.'s phone."

She must have seen the man giving it to me. I hand it over, knowing Mom's going to make the difficult call to Jackie. I'm filled with gratitude that I don't have to do it, but I'm also in awe. She's finally acting like an adult and doing what needs to be done.

* * * *

Fifteen minutes later, we arrive at Siloam Springs Regional and park near the emergency room at the back. An ambulance sits by the entrance, and medics are unloading a patient. I feel sick at the thought of seeing K. J.'s unconscious body again, but once I'm closer I realize it's not her. They must have already taken her inside.

A sense of overwhelming dread fills me as I enter the building. I haven't been here since Ricky was sick. I know lots of people get better at the hospital, but it only reminds me of death. Tears well in my eyes once more.

The trauma of being here again is written all over Mom's face, too. I don't think either of us will ever be able to come to a hospital without the bad memories flooding back in. I wipe away my tears and breathe in deep before going to check with the receptionist. She confirms that K. J. has been admitted and is being attended to right now.

"Is she conscious?" I ask, my voice wavering.

"I don't have any information on her, dear," she tells me, "but I'll let you know when you can go back. I assume you're family."

"Yes."

She smiles sympathetically. "What's your name?"

I tell her and she writes it down.

"I'll let you know, Becka," she reiterates.

Returning to the waiting area, I take a seat next to Mom, who's rummaging through her purse again. She finds some lipstick, applies it, and then checks her makeup in a compact mirror. The heel of her boot taps a fast rhythm on the tile floor as my stomach endures sporadic waves of nausea.

I'm trying to distract myself by watching the muted late-night news program on the TV on the opposite wall when Jackie hurries through the doors. Her eyes dart wildly around the room. She's pale and thin and her black Dollar General uniform shirt nearly swallows her whole. She freezes when she spots the three of us, and I wave her over. She's been through hell, and it shows not only on her face, but in her whole demeanor. Her shoulders slump forward as she approaches.

"Hey, Jackie," I say.

She avoids looking at my mom, instead focusing only on me. "How is she? Can we go back to see her?"

"Not yet. They said they'd let us know when we can."

She bites her lip, like she's trying to fight off tears, but then straightens. "Okay."

Her eyes search for a chair to sit in. There are at least a dozen people scattered around the waiting area and plenty of open seats, but I can tell she's trying to decide if she should sit next to us or somewhere else. Tim is watching this whole scenario without a word. Meanwhile, my mom has busied herself flipping through a magazine and hasn't so much as said hi to her sister yet. So much for being an adult . . .

"Sit next to me," I tell Jackie. "Please."

She gives an imperceptible nod and pushes her hair behind one ear.

Once Jackie is seated, Mom finally lowers the magazine to her lap. She clears her throat as she turns to look her sister's way. "I'm sorry," she says, so quiet I'm not sure if Jackie even heard, but then my aunt looks at my mom. I'm just sitting here in between them, hoping to God I'm strong enough to be Switzerland.

Jackie swallows and pushes her hair back again. "Thank you for calling me."

"Sure," my mom says before clearing her throat again. "It's not a problem."

"Becka," the receptionist calls.

My heart gives a lurch, and I hurry up to the desk.

"They tell me she's awake. You can go see her now. Room fourteen."

Oh, thank God, I think as my whole body goes limp with relief. I go back to tell Jackie.

She frowns and draws in a wavering breath. "She may not want to see me. Maybe you should go first."

"Okay. I'll be back soon to let you know how she is."

Another wave of relief washes over me when I find K. J. looking alert and sitting up on the cot. So the man was right—she just got knocked out—but her face is tight with pain as the nurse straps a blood pressure cuff around her arm.

"You're looking much better," I say.

She starts to smile but then grimaces, her free hand going to her side. "But how does the bull look?"

I smirk. "Completely fine."

She tries to shift her position on the bed. "Oh God, that hurts."

"She cracked a rib," the nurse says.

"It hurts like hell," K. J. mutters.

The nurse pats her shoulder. "She has a concussion, too."

I'm not surprised. "You were completely out," I say. "Back at the rodeo."

"I don't remember anything really—just the bull coming at me," K. J. says. "The next thing I knew, I was waking up in an ambulance."

I step to the side of the small room to allow the nurse to pass. She's moved over to the counter to jot something down on a clipboard. "Your mom's here. She wants to see you."

K. J. rolls her eyes. "Tell her I'm fine. She can go home."

"Come on, K. J. She's worried. At least let her see that you're okay."

She doesn't say anything for several moments. "Fine. She can come take a look." K. J. tugs at the sleeve of her hospital gown. "But I'm not talking to her."

"Real mature." I glance at the nurse who has busied herself with more paperwork. She probably deals with family drama in here all the time. I'm sure this is nothing new. "I'll go get her."

Jackie's lips tremble as we enter the room, but relief softens her features once she sees her daughter alive with four limbs intact. There's no telling what possibilities had been running through her mind. The nurse is gone and K. J. is leaning back on the reclined bed, eyeing us both with a look of annoyance. Like we only came here to bother her.

"How are you feeling?" Jackie asks, taking a tentative step closer to the bed.

K. J. looks from me to her mom and back to me again, but her lips stay sealed. I proceed to explain the injuries to Jackie: a concussion, broken rib, and a bruised ego. K. J. works hard to refrain from smiling at that last one.

Jackie steps back and leans against the wall, clasping her hands together in front of her. "Thank God it's nothing worse." Her gaze drops to the floor, and she shakes her head. "Damn you, Dad, for making my baby girl get in an arena with a bull."

I start to explain but K. J. cuts in.

"It was my fault. I got there late and that was the only event I could still enter."

Jackie's expression changes from worried to angry, and she looks like she wants to go off on K. J. for doing something so dumb, but instead she mumbles, "That figures."

The door opens and a young doctor and the nurse from before come striding in. The doctor turns to Jackie. "Are you Mom?"

"Yes, sir."

He introduces himself as Dr. Yin, shaking her hand. "We'd like to keep Katherine here overnight just for observation. To make sure she doesn't develop any other symptoms from the head trauma. She took a pretty hard hit."

Jackie opens her mouth like she might protest, but then promptly closes it again. "Okay, whatever my baby girl needs."

I don't miss K. J.'s exaggerated eye roll.

Dr. Yin shines a small light into each of K. J.'s eyes.

"Pupils still dilated some," he notes. He examines her head, asking where it hurts. K. J. touches the back—probably where her head hit the ground. The doctor stands upright, depositing the flashlight into his lab coat pocket. "Okay, Athena's going to help get you moved to a room."

The nurse bustles out of the room, reappearing a few seconds later with a wheelchair in tow. Dr. Yin examines the paperwork on the counter and then turns to pat K. J.'s knee. "No more playing with bulls, young lady."

"Don't worry," she says, "I won't be doing that ever again."

"That's good. I hear kittens are much safer," he says with a wink. "Take care."

Nurse Athena helps K. J. into the wheelchair. I can tell she'd like to say a few choice words as she settles into the oversized seat, but just like Jackie, she holds her tongue. We follow them out of the room, but Athena directs us to use the public elevators back near the waiting area. Jackie hangs back while I explain what's going on to Mom and Tim.

"Are you ready to go, then?" Mom asks. She's obviously tired. It's been a long night for everyone.

"Actually, I think I'll stay here with K. J. tonight. I'll call you in the morning."

Mom frowns. "But you don't have your car."

"I can bring her home," Jackie offers. "I'll stay, too."

Mom catches my eye, and I know she's wondering if I'm okay with that.

"Thanks, Aunt Jackie." It sounds strange to be calling her that to her face after all these years.

Mom gives me a semi-smile. "Okay. Call me if you need something."

"I will." I turn to Jackie. "Ready?"

She gives a nod, and we start for the elevators.

"I'll stay out in the waiting area," Jackie says once we've arrived on the second floor. "I just want to be here in case anything goes wrong."

She goes to pour herself a cup of coffee from a nearby pot while I head for K. J.'s room. The door is partway open, but I knock before going in.

"Come in," K. J. responds in a bored tone I've heard before. She's sounding more like herself every second, thank goodness. Another nurse attends to her now, trying to help her get comfortable on the bed. K. J. winces with every little movement but finally settles back onto the pillow, which has been placed behind her head. The nurse pulls a blanket up over her.

The room is cold and bare, with only a small television and a blank whiteboard on one wall. There's a padded maroon recliner near the bed—my sleeping spot for the night, I guess.

K. J. catches me eyeing it. "You crashing here?"

I yawn and make my way around her bed. "I don't have anything better to do."

"Did my mom go home?"

"No, she's out there."

K. J.'s lips tighten, but she doesn't say anything. She's pissed at her mom, but deep down, I'm sure she still loves her and is glad she's here.

I set my backpack in the windowsill and grab a folded blanket from a corner table before sinking into the chair. It's not super comfortable, but it will do. "Let me know if you need anything," I tell her.

"'Kay," she says sleepily. They probably gave her some good pain meds. "Oh, crap," she says a moment later, sounding startled. "Someone should call Carter. Let him know where I am and all."

"I have your phone." I reach for my backpack to retrieve it. "Want me to do it?"

"Do you mind? I'm so tired."

"Yeah. No problem." I scroll through her contacts and find his name. It rings five times, but then goes to voicemail. I hang up. "He didn't answer."

K. J. is already snoring softly.

I smile, switch both our phones to silent, and put them away.

CHAPTER 31

K. J.

"GOOD MORNING, SUNSHINE!"

I open my eyes and blink, trying to take in my dim surroundings.
For a split second, I'm completely lost and then a sharp pain shoots
through my chest, and I remember everything at once. Shit, my ribs
hurt. Or rib, I should say. It's hard to believe one little bone can cause
a person so much pain.

A blond, smiling nurse leans over my bed, smelling like cinna-
mon and coffee. She adjusts my pillow and I blink several more times,
keeping my mouth closed tight. I highly doubt she wants to smell my
morning breath.

"I've got some more pain meds for you, Miss Katherine," she says,
handing me two white pills and a small cup of water.

I take them without saying a word and the nurse backs away, moving toward the whiteboard across from my bed. She writes "Joy" next to where it says "Nurse" in bold black marker before returning to take the empty cup from me.

"Okay, Miss Katherine," she says loudly, as if the bull might have damaged my hearing, too. "We've got you scheduled for another CT scan this morning, and if everything looks good, you'll be headed home later."

"Okay," I mumble, since I don't think I really have much say or a choice in the matter. Nurse Joy fiddles with one of the machines near my bed as I attempt a stretch, but any big movement hurts way too much, so I tuck my hands back beneath the covers instead. "What time is it?"

"Seven fifteen," she says with a smile.

Way too early to be awake right now.

The chair to the right of my bed creaks, and Becka pulls the covers down from her face to peek over at me. Her ponytail is lopsided and she has mascara smeared beneath her eyes, but she spent the entire night here. I'm impressed. She moves the recliner up to a sitting position and rubs at her face.

"Hey," I say quietly. Unlike some people, I don't feel the need to be all loud and chirpy this early in the morning.

"Hey," Becka says. "How ya feeling?"

"Sore," I admit.

Joy bustles over and straps a blood pressure cuff on my arm. While that's going, she swipes a thermometer across my forehead. "Everything looks great," she says. She unstraps the cuff and goes to write my numbers on a clipboard. Apparently, she's both efficient *and* cheerful. "Okay, I'll be back in a little bit to take you for your CT scan. Buzz if you need anything." She flashes another pageant-winning smile before leaving.

Once she's gone, Becka stands and stretches with a loud yawn.

The yawn is contagious, and I'm rewarded with another stab of pain. "Ouch! Shit."

Becka laughs. "I'm proud of how you've held your tongue here."

I pretend to look affronted. "Hey. I can use self-control . . . when I want to."

"Apparently so." She walks around the bed, entering the bathroom. I need to go, too, but I'm scared of having to get out of bed. Maybe I should wait on the meds to kick in again. The toilet flushes and she's out a few seconds later.

"Did you talk to Carter last night? I must have fallen asleep."

"I tried. He didn't answer."

I guess I shouldn't be surprised. He sleeps like the dead. Becka hands me my phone, and sure enough, there are three missed texts, all from Carter. I respond, telling him I'm in the hospital, but fine. I tell him I'll call him later.

"Is my mom still here?" I ask Becka.

"I'm sure she is. Want me to go check?"

"Nah."

"Think I'm going to go grab a Starbucks. There's one on the first floor."

"No fair," I whine.

"I'll get you one, too."

I hit my buzzer, and when Joy pops back in, I ask her if I can have a cappuccino.

She smiles like it's a funny question. "I don't see why not, and you can order breakfast whenever you're ready. I set a menu there." She points to my side table. "I recommend the Belgian waffles," she adds with a wink.

"Awesome, thanks." I'm liking Joy more and more, and Belgian waffles sound pretty amazing right now.

Ten minutes later, Becka reappears with two coffee cups in hand. "Your mom asked how you were." She hands me my cappuccino, but I can tell from the steam billowing from the opening that it's still too hot to drink. I carefully set it on the table next to the menu.

Maybe I should at least be civil to my mom, but it's too hard to forget our last big conversation. She can just stay out in the waiting room. I don't want her in here, not after betraying me like she did. "What'd you tell her," I finally ask.

"That you seem better this morning, and about the CT scan."

"Tell her she can go now. I'm fine."

Becka's lips pucker as she seems to consider something. "I would, but she's my ride. Probably yours, too."

"Damn. I forgot, my car's still at the rodeo grounds."

"Hopefully Psycho hasn't gotten to it."

"If he did, I'm gonna have to hurt him."

Becka laughs. "I'm sure he's shaking in his big bull boots."

I've just finished with lunch when a doctor enters my room to tell me everything on the CT scan looked good.

"You're all set to check out," she says.

"Yes! I mean, no offense to you all. I'm just ready to ditch this joint."

"Totally understandable," she says, and I can tell she's not offended in the least.

After signing some papers, Joy helps me back into a wheelchair and pushes me out of the room. My mom is still there in the waiting area and she looks like shit, no makeup and her hair a tangled mess, but she stands and gives me a tired smile. I do my best to ignore her.

"I'll go get the car," she says to Joy.

"I can walk you know," I grunt.

"Yes, you can," Joy says. "And I'll let you as soon as we get to the front door."

I can't see her right now, but I know she's smiling.

Once the three of us are in Mom's car, an awkward silence seems to fill every corner of it.

Mom clears her throat as she pulls out onto the street. "Should we go get your car? Maybe Becka could drive it home, and then I could take her back to her house." She stops, realizing the error of her words. "Or she could drive it to wherever you're staying."

"I'm staying at Carter's," I say, staring straight ahead, but I'm not one hundred percent sure I want to go back there.

"Oh," Mom says, though she doesn't sound completely surprised.

I look at the time on the dash. "Crap, I'm supposed to be at work in thirty minutes."

"Work?" Mom glances my way, definitely surprised this time.

"I work at Reynold's Auto Parts now."

Her gaze shifts to the dirty shirt I'd had to put back on in order to leave the hospital. "Oh, so that's why you're wearing that."

I quickly Google their number and call the store, telling Doug about my situation. He asks when I think I'll be able to come back in.

"Um, I'm not sure . . ." I tell him. "I'll let you know as soon as I can, though." When I hang up, I have a feeling that I've lost my job already, but maybe it's for the best.

We arrive at the rodeo grounds to find my car safe and sound in the middle of the empty field. Psycho, as well as all the other livestock, are all gone now, much to my relief. I did *not* want to see him again. In fact, I don't want to see another bull as long as I live. I hand Becka my keys and she hops out.

Mom takes it slow as we leave, but I still wince as we drive over a series of ruts. The rough ground is hell on my cracked rib. Becka follows behind us in my car. Mom pushes her hair behind one ear, giving me a nervous glance. "So . . . where to?"

I'm still not sure where I want to go, but somehow the idea of being laid up on Carter and Dax's couch watching talk shows or video games all day sounds less than appealing. "Home, I guess . . . for now."

Out of the corner of my eye, I can see a slight smile pulling at Mom's lips. "Alrighty."

We don't talk for the rest of the drive home, but I can feel a small shift in things between us. Like maybe I'm slightly less pissed at her now. Or maybe I'm just too tired and uncomfortable to care. I lay my head back on the headrest and close my eyes, not opening them again until we pull into the mobile home park. Becka parks my car next to Mom's.

"You staying here?" she asks as I open my door and try to find the least painful way of getting out.

I nod. "Yeah, think I need to go lie down."

I finally manage to get out, and we both stand there for a moment, like we're not sure if a hug is in order or not. Then Becka just waves and takes my place in the front seat. "Take care, K. J. I'll check on you later."

I creep up the porch stairs, trying my best not to jar my broken rib. Only after Mom and Becka back out of the drive does the strangeness of this whole situation strike me. For the first time in my life, there's not a humongous freaking wall dividing my family, and I'm not sure how to feel about that.

The house smells mildly of lemon disinfectant and that floral carpet freshener Mom likes to use. She's probably been cleaning like crazy since I've been gone. I'm not sure what will happen now that I'm back, but I'll dwell on that later. Right now, I'm beat. I grab a Dr Pepper and a bag of potato chips from the kitchen and settle onto the couch. I'm about to turn on the TV when my phone rings on the end table beside me. I don't know the number but answer just in case it's someone from the hospital with lab results or something like that.

"Katherine?" an unfamiliar male voice asks.

"Yes?"

"Um, hi. It's Sam. Your, uh, father."

Well, that's definitely not who I was expecting. My eyes go wide and my voice catches in my throat as I try to mumble any word in the English language.

"I heard you were in the hospital, and I just wanted to call and check on you."

A million questions are running through my mind, like, "Why now?" or "Why do you even care?" But instead I clear my throat and just say, "Uh huh," like a dummy.

"Are you okay?"

"Fine." At least I can manage words now.

We're both quiet for several seconds. I have no clue what to say to the man who has been missing for my entire life.

"So—" he gives a nervous chuckle "—I don't know where to begin really, but I'd love to meet you. You have no idea how often I've thought of you over the years."

"Oh yeah?" I wish I could think of something better or more profound to say.

"Could I maybe take you to lunch one day? After you're feeling up to it, that is?"

I rack my brain for excuses but can't seem to think of any. I could just say "No, I don't want to," but my vocal cords defy me again. "I guess." I run a palm down the side of my face.

"Oh. Oh, good." He actually sounds excited and nervous, like he didn't expect me to agree to this, but hell, I didn't expect to give in so easily either. "That would be great. Maybe next weekend? Or if that's too soon, we can plan another time."

"What about Becka?" I blurt out. "Can she come, too?"

"Oh, yeah. Of course. I just . . ." He doesn't have to say it. I already know what he's thinking.

"We get along now. It's fine. I'd like her to be there with me." As I say this, I realize Becka must have gone ahead and given Sam my number, but I'm not really mad about it.

"Yeah, that'd be great. Both my daughters." He seems to choke on that last word—like he's still trying to get a handle on all of this, too.

"All right." I lean back on my pillows and cringe from the movement.

"I'll let you get some rest. I'm sure you're tired, but I'll be in touch later this week . . . if that's okay."

"Yeah. Sure. That's fine."

"I'm glad you're okay," he says. "Talk to you later."

"Later." I hang up and stare at the phone. Did I actually just have a conversation with my dad? I'm not sure this month could get any weirder.

I turn on the TV and take a sip of my Dr Pepper, but it doesn't take long for exhaustion to take over. Ever so carefully, I scoot down so that I'm nearly flat on my back. The TV drones quietly in the background, and in a matter of minutes, I'm out.

✳ ✳ ✳ ✳

I'm still in a sleepy haze when I hear two voices softly floating across the room. I turn my head to see Mom and Carter in the kitchen. There's a vase full of yellow daisies on the counter, and Mom's telling Carter about my accident. They don't know I'm awake, so I just lie here, listening for a minute.

"Christ," Carter says, "she's lucky it wasn't worse."

"I know," Mom says. "I can't believe she entered that event. I mean, they shouldn't even let people do things like that. It's so stupid."

"I can hear you, you know," I say.

Both their heads snap in my direction.

"Oh, sorry," Mom says, "but it is a stupid event."

I have to agree with her there, but I don't feel like saying so out loud and giving her that satisfaction.

I scooch back up to a sitting position, my jaw tightening as I do so.

Mom's expression quickly mirrors my own. "Do you need another one of your pain pills? I got your prescription filled while I was out."

Wow, look at her being all responsible and motherly now. "Yeah, please." Carter comes to sit on the other end of the couch, concern evident in his sea-green eyes. "Sorry, I forgot to call you," I tell him. "I fell asleep."

"It's okay." He jiggles one knee while staring at the floor. "Sorry about last night," he says. "I should have gone with you."

"Don't blame yourself. Even if you had gone, I doubt you could have stopped me from doing the event."

He smiles. "True. You do what you want usually."

"Yep, but at least I finished Grandpa's list. I might have to spend all my inheritance on hospital bills, but it's done."

"I hope not. Aren't you supposed to spend it on college?"

"You don't need to worry about the bills," Mom butts in as she hands me a pill. I wash it down with a sip of lukewarm Dr Pepper. "I'm taking care of everything."

Carter and I both turn to look at her. She's changed clothes since we left the hospital and now wears a sleeveless denim shirt and jeans, but still no makeup. She looks like she could crash at any moment.

"Okay," I say. She's trying to redeem herself, and I'm going to let her. After all, she has inheritance money coming, too. "You should really go take a nap, Mom."

"Yeah, I probably should. I took the day off, so I guess I've got time."

"Oh," Carter says, pushing to his feet. "I brought you flowers." He grabs the vase and brings it over, setting it on the end table next to my Dr Pepper. "I wasn't sure what color you'd like, but yellow seemed good. It's a happy color, you know."

I snort, but my hand flies to my mouth as I realize I'm coming off as rude. I'd only done it because I'm wondering who this person is inhabiting my best friend's body. "Thanks," I say. "I like them, and yellow's good."

Little splotches of pink have begun to color his cheeks. "Glad you like them. I mean, I figured that's just something you're supposed to do when someone's in the hospital . . . or just got home from one anyway."

I can feel my own cheeks starting to color as I search my brain for something else to say. It's like we're back at that awkward moment right after the kiss again.

Mom busies herself in the kitchen, wiping down an already-clean counter and putting a few dishes away. Then she gives a yawn, which seems totally forced. "Boy, I *am* tired. Think I'll go lie down now."

Once her bedroom door closes, Carter sits down again, turning to watch the television, where some infomercial on microwavable Tupperware is playing. "So are you staying here?" he asks. It's subtle but I think there's a hint of something like sadness in his voice.

I shift in my seat, then grimace again. I've got to quit moving around so much. "I think so. For now, anyway. Don't know what my long-term plans are yet."

He nods as if maybe he suspected that might be the case. "I'm gonna miss having you around."

"I know, but it's probably better this way."

"Sorry. I guess I've been a pretty sucky friend lately."

"It's okay."

"No, it's not. I promise to do better." He turns to look at me. "If you still want to hang out, that is."

"Of course I still want to hang out."

Carter looks more than a little relieved at my response. Did he really think I was going to ditch him just because we had a little spat?

"Well, I guess I should let you get some rest," he says, getting to his feet again. "Glad you're okay and not brain damaged or anything."

"Ha ha."

He smiles and sweeps his hair behind one ear. "I'll text you later, 'kay?"

"Yeah, sounds good."

After the front door closes, my gaze travels back to the daisies beside me, and I can't help but smile. No one has ever brought me flowers before.

CHAPTER 32
BECKA

THE SCENT OF SPEARMINT FILLS MY CAR AS K. J. chomps on what must be her third piece of gum, her jaw moving about a hundred miles an hour. I've never seen her like this before, but I'm guessing it's just a major case of nerves.

"How's your rib?" I ask, peering her way. She's wearing a black Nirvana T-shirt and cutoff jean shorts, but she's done something different with her hair—maybe put some gel in it. It brings out the curliness, which is surprisingly cute on her.

"Still hurts, but it's getting better." She rolls down the window and spits the gum out, only to start bouncing a knee instead. "Do you think he'll like me?"

I offer a reassuring smile. "I'm sure he will. But honestly, who cares? It's not like he's an outstanding dad or anything."

K. J. drops a hand onto her leg, stilling it, as if annoyed by her own nervousness.

"Hey, listen," I say, "I need to apologize for something. It's been bothering me for a while now, actually."

"What's that?"

"I'm sorry for punching you in the face. Back at Yellowstone."

"No worries," K. J. says, one side of her mouth lifting in a smirk. "I deserved it."

Despite my guilt, I have to smile, too. "Yeah, you kind of did, but I still feel bad. It left a bruise."

"Johan was probably impressed with your upper arm strength."

A laugh bubbles out before I can stop it. "I don't know about that. He was probably just shocked I hit you. Everyone was—even me."

K. J. scratches at her arm. "Guess I should apologize, too. Sorry I ruined things between you two. I mean it was probably a lost cause anyway, because of the whole long-distance thing. And maybe the age. But I was a shit, I know that."

"You didn't ruin things. We've been texting. He'll be coming through Siloam Springs this winter on a road trip, and we're going to meet up."

K. J. peers at me, incredulous. "You sneaky son of a . . ."

"I doubt anything will come of it, but . . . I guess stranger things *have* happened."

"That's for sure."

We give each other a small smile before I turn my attention back to the road. There's no need to mention what those things are. We both know all too well.

"I actually kinda liked Johan," she says. "I hope you two end up getting married or something."

I hold up a hand. "Whoa, no one said anything about getting married. It's just a date." At least I'm hoping that's what he'll see it as. "I don't plan on getting married for a long time." If at all, considering our family's track record when it comes to committed relationships.

We pass through another stoplight, and Cathy's Corner, with its giant red and white sign, appears ahead on our right. It was Sam's suggestion.

"You ready for this?" I ask K. J.

She draws in a deep breath. "Ready as I can be, I guess."

Inside, the restaurant smells like greasy hamburgers and fried chicken, and even though I had a big breakfast with Mom and Tim just a few hours ago, my stomach still rumbles in response. We're a few minutes late, so I scan the tables for Sam. He waves from a booth near the middle of the restaurant. Beside me, K. J. freezes.

"Come on," I say, tugging at her elbow. "He won't bite."

Sam stands and runs a hand through his dark, wavy hair before offering a smile. He looks nice, though he's wearing his usual car salesman attire—tan slacks and a white polo.

"Hey," I say, mustering the nonchalance I always use around my father.

"Hi, girls." His eyes keep moving to K. J. as if he can't believe she's really here.

"K. J., this is Sam," I say, motioning between the two of them. "Sam, K. J."

He extends a hand and K. J. shakes it. "Nice to meet you, sir," she says.

I raise an eyebrow at K. J. as Sam gives a nervous laugh.

"You don't need to call me 'sir.'" He gestures to the seat across from him, urging us to sit. I let K. J. scoot into the booth first.

Sam's eyes ping-pong between us, and then he shakes his head. "Wow . . . Just wow. I can't believe I have both my daughters here. Together."

I refrain from rolling my eyes. "Yeah, well it's happening."

He focuses on K. J. again, who seems to be at a loss for words. "So, Katherine. Tell me about yourself."

"It's K. J.," I correct him.

"It's fine. He can call me Katherine."

I squint at her. Who is this person sitting next to me?

She clears her throat. "Um. I'm eighteen. I'm sure you know that, though. I graduated from Colcord High School in May, and I'm starting at NorthWest Arkansas in a couple weeks."

"You are?" I ask. We hadn't gotten around to talking about college on the car ride over.

"Yep, I got my acceptance letter and enrolled . . . and stuff."

I grin. "Good for you!"

"That's really great," Sam says. "What are you planning to major in?"

"I've been thinking about art and design. Or graphic design. But those are just some ideas. Need to get through my basics first." She clears her throat again.

Sam looks at me. "And you're still planning to major in sports medicine?"

"Probably." I've always had a straightforward plan for my life, but after all that's changed in the last few months, I want to at least keep my options open.

A waitress appears, placing a menu in front of each of us. "Sorry about the wait," she says, sounding out of breath. "Can I go ahead and get your drinks?

We each order a drink and then read over our menus. I already know what I want—the chicken tender basket. But K. J. seems indecisive and is still reading over the options. I think back to the last time we ate together, how confident she was trying to order wine for the both of us. That was back when we were just cousins—not sisters. She seems like a different person today, and I wish she wasn't so nervous.

Sam's eyes flick between the tattoos on our wrists, but he doesn't ask about them. "Order anything you like," he reassures K. J. "My treat."

Damn right, it's your treat, I think, and then smile because it's something K. J. would say.

The waitress returns, and Sam and I order first, giving K. J. a little more time to make up her mind. She finally opts for the Philly cheesesteak sandwich. The waitress takes our menus, leaving us with nothing to look at but each other again.

Sam shifts in his seat, still appearing uncomfortable. His phone buzzes, but he ignores it. "So Becka told me you girls did some traveling this summer?"

K. J. nods but doesn't offer any information.

He takes a sip of his iced tea and smiles again, revealing the dimple on his left cheek. The one he passed on to me. I suddenly find myself wondering if K. J. has it, too. "I'd like to hear all about it," Sam says. "Where'd you go first?"

"The Grand Canyon," K. J. answers. "We rode mules down to the bottom."

His eyes widen in surprise. "Wow, that musta been something."

"I loved it," she says as she nudges me with her elbow, "but Becka about peed her pants she was so scared."

I roll my eyes. "Whatever."

K. J. laughs. "Don't lie. You know you were terrified."

I give a small shrug. "Okay, maybe a little." Then I can't help but smile. "It was soooo pretty, though. I'd do it again, but definitely not on a mule."

K. J.'s eyes light up with excitement. "Yeah, we could hike it. I'd have to get in better shape, but I think I might be able to do it. And we could stay at Phantom Ranch again."

"Maybe after we graduate from college," I suggest. "It could be a reunion trip."

She nods her head. "If we're doing a reunion trip, I wanna go back to the Keys, too. That place was so awesome."

"Yeah," I agree. "We need a do-over at the Keys, but maybe we can fly instead of drive next time."

"That *was* a long-ass trip." K. J.'s hand flies to her mouth, and she quickly looks at Sam. It's like we'd both forgotten he was here for a moment.

He laughs. "I'll bet. Sounds like you two really got to know each other this summer. And it sounds like it was a great experience."

K. J. and I turn to look at one another, and she smiles again. Sure enough, the dimple is there, though not nearly as pronounced as mine or Sam's. Still, the fact that it's there makes me so unexplainably happy.

"It's been pretty incredible," I say. In more ways than one.

Sam's face grows more serious as he studies K. J. for several seconds. She notices and squirms uncomfortably in her seat.

"I just want to say I'm sorry," he says. His eyes shift to me. "To both of you, really, but especially to you, K. J. I've really let you down. I wish I would have spoken up, but your mom . . . well, I just didn't know what to do." His gaze drops to the table. "I'm sorry."

Several responses come to my mind, but I can't seem to choose which one is most appropriate. It seems everyone is apologizing today, but this is one I didn't see coming.

"You *should* be sorry," K. J. says, surprising Sam and me both.

His head snaps up. His brow furrows and then falls, and he looks sadder than I've ever seen him. It's almost enough to make me feel sorry for him. Almost. K. J. straightens in her seat and levels him with a hard gaze.

"You and my mom both have a lot to be sorry about, but I've decided to be the bigger person in all this. I'm an adult now, too, after all. So I'm going to do the adult thing and forgive you. I forgive both of you." It's like she's just waved an invisible magic wand because a weight seems to lift from her entire frame as she says this. She draws in a shuddering breath, the only hint telling me that what she just did, no matter how it looked or sounded, wasn't easy for her.

Sam's face softens. "Thank—"

"I'm not doing it for your sake," K. J. cuts in, her snarky tone returning in full force.

Sam nods. "I understand." He seems to consider his next words before speaking. "I can't make up for what I've done . . . or haven't done. I know that, but I'd like to be at least a small part of your life now. If you'll let me."

K. J. scrutinizes his face, maybe trying to get a read on his sincerity. "We'll see."

I bite my lip to keep a straight face. "Maybe you can have us over around Thanksgiving," I say before K. J. and I exchange a momentary look of unspoken solidarity.

She shrugs and looks back at Sam. "Yeah, maybe so."

"I'd love to," he says. "That would be great."

The waitress reappears with a large tray, which she manages to balance on one hand while placing each of our plates in front of us with the other. My chicken tenders smell incredible, and despite everything, my stomach rumbles again. "Can I get you anything else?" she asks.

K. J. and I both shake our heads. I'm already snatching up a chicken finger.

Sam gives the waitress a thumbs-up. "I think we're all good."

We start eating, setting the former conversation aside. For now, at least. Over the past few months, K. J. and I became masters at sitting together in silence. So what if our dad happens to be here this time?

As the clinking of silverware and murmur of other people's quiet conversations carry across the restaurant, Sam's words to the waitress play on repeat in my head.

He'll never be a bigger part of my life than he has been for the past eighteen years, and I think I've accepted that. There's no way he's going to suddenly become K. J.'s favorite person either, but that doesn't matter. K. J. and I don't need Sam. We have each other now and a whole lifetime ahead of us. We won't make the same mistakes our mothers did, I'm sure of it.

I'm also getting a second chance to be a sister myself, and that's something I'll never take for granted again. I take another sip of my Coke, stealing a glance at K. J. My sister—it's finally starting to sink in. A warm, contented feeling floods through me—the kind I used to get on Christmas morning or after winning a big soccer game. It has nothing to do with our dad, but everything to do with his words just now.

You got it right for once, Sam.

We *are* all good.

CHAPTER 33

ELI

Hello girls,

I know I said the last letter was my final one, but I just couldn't help myself. Believe it or not, I've grown rather fond of writing these letters to you. It's been cathartic for me. My days are drawing to a close and, as I write these words, none of you have any idea of what's going on with me. That's okay. That's how I want things. I've accepted that this is how my life will end.

In Brazil, there's a species of ant where it is common practice for a few members of the colony to sacrifice themselves in order to ensure the rest are safe. At sunset, these ants will stay outside in order to seal up the nest, pushing sand over the entrance hole until it becomes invisible to the outside world. Of course, then the problem is that there's no way for them to get back in. After dusk, the ants are blown away by the wind or die from exposure to the cold.

Researchers aren't sure why these ants choose to do this job, but some think that they might be older workers who are approaching death anyway—that they're more dispensable than their younger nest mates.

I'm no hero for sure, but I feel like this final act before my death may just help to seal up our own nest, so to speak. Someone needs to patch the hole in our family and, since I haven't done anything to help in the past, it's only fitting that I should make an attempt now.

I also told you the story about the ants because it shows that insects are far more complex than most people believe them to be. They're capable of love for the greater good, in a sense. Certainly, a sense of honor and duty. Perhaps they're more like us than we think.

RaeLynn, Jackie, Rebecka, and Katherine: It's been my greatest honor to call you my daughters and granddaughters. I truly mean that.

Be well my dears. Enjoy each day as if it were your last, because you just never know if it is.

Love always,

Elijah

ACKNOWLEDGMENTS

As any writer will tell you, getting a book from first draft to publishing-ready form is far from a solitary achievement. Yes, we, writers, give birth to the book idea and get it on paper, but it often takes a whole team of people to help bring the story to life.

So with that in mind, I owe much thanks to my critique partners and beta readers who were the first to offer invaluable feedback for this story: Summer Nicholson, Justine Manzano, Maddie Dorminy, Jelsa Mepsey, Melissa Poettcker, Wendy Cross, Anne Stubert, and Jude Bayton.

Many thanks to PitchWars mentor Carrie Allen, who, along with her co-mentor, Sabrina Lotfi, requested this book in 2019. Even though they ultimately didn't pick me, Carrie read my entire manuscript and her incredibly thoughtful feedback helped me to make this book better.

Every writer needs a tribe, and I'm so thankful for mine: the writers I've met through local critique groups who have given constructive feedback on each of the books I've written, including this one. So thank you to Shirley Hall, Jeff South, Deniece Adsit, Layton Isaacs, Dan Gamble, Jude Bayton, Steve Moore, and Mary Miller (who told me, "This is the one!").

Thank you to the Pitch2Pub ladies for their continual support and encouragement. It is truly an honor to be a part of such a talented group.

In my former life, I was a middle school teacher, and I'm grateful for the students who shared my enthusiasm for reading and books (most notably *The Giver* and the *Twilight* series). These kids helped to plant a seed which would lead me to start writing books for young adults, and even though they're all grown now, I hope at least a few of them will read this one.

I must also thank the all-around-amazing Brenda Drake, founder of PitchWars and #pitmad, whom I first met at a writing conference in Oklahoma City. I religiously participated in these contests for five years until I finally found my match, and now I will be forever grateful to my editor, Britny Brooks-Perilli at Running Press Kids, for favoriting my pitch and proving that yes, Twitter pitch contest dreams can come true.

Thank you to my wonderful and wise agent, Janna Bonikowski, whose advice has helped me successfully navigate this thing called publishing. And thank you to the rest of my awesome team at Running Press Kids: my book designer, Marissa Raybuck; my production editor, Amber Morris; and my cover illustrator, Monica Garwood.

Thank you to my husband, Mike, and my two lovely kids for supporting my writing journey, and to my long-time best friend, Summer, who helped me work through plot problems on numerous occasions and always referred to K. J. and Becka as if they were real people and not just characters in my head.

Last but certainly not least, thanks to YOU, dear reader, for reading this book. You're the one I wrote it for, after all.